THE FIRST MOUNTAIN MAN

PREACHER'S PURSUIT

THE FIRST MOUNTAIN MAN

PREACHER'S PURSUIT

William W. Johnstone
with J. A. Johnstone

PINNACLE BOOKS
Kensington Publishing Corp.
www.kensingtonbooks.com

PINNACLE BOOKS are published by

Kensington Publishing Corp.
850 Third Avenue
New York, NY 10022

PUBLISHER'S NOTE
Following the death of William W. Johnstone, the Johnstone family is working with a carefully selected writer to organize and complete Mr. Johnstone's outlines and many unfinished manuscripts to create additional novels in all of his series like The Last Gunfighter, Mountain Man, and Eagles, among others. This novel was inspired by Mr. Johnstone's superb storytelling.

ISBN-13: 978-0-7860-2004-1
ISBN-10: 0-7860-2004-0

First printing: January 2009

10 9 8 7 6 5 4 3

Printed in the United States of America

Chapter 1

Preacher pressed his back against the gully's rock wall and tightened his hands on the flintlock rifle he carried slantwise across his chest. He listened intently, ignoring the thudding of his heart and trying instead to pick up the stealthy sounds of the man creeping up the gully after him.

His side stung a little where a rifle ball had ripped his buckskin shirt and burned across his flesh. He put that pain out of his head, too. 'Tweren't nothin', he told himself. He'd been hurt lots worse plenty of times.

A tall man in his thirties, dark-haired and bearded, lean-bodied but still powerfully built, Preacher knew these mountains as well as most men knew their own faces . . . or the bodies of their wives. The two varmints who'd tried to ambush him had made a bad mistake in doing so.

One of them had already paid the ultimate price. He lay dead or dying on one of the slopes higher up, his guts torn open by a shot from Preacher's rifle.

His companion was still alive, though. He was the

one trying to sneak up on Preacher now. Normally, Preacher would have just waited for the man to come along and then blown a hole through him, but that was hard to do without any powder.

A lucky shot aimed at him had clipped the rawhide thong by which the powder horn was slung over Preacher's shoulder. It had skittered over the edge of a long drop, gone before he could even try to grab it. He had already emptied his rifle and both pistols while trading lead with the two would-be killers, so he couldn't reload.

But that didn't mean the man called Preacher was helpless. Far from it.

He'd been toiling up a long, steep slope to check on some traps. His horse and dog were down at the base of the slope, left behind because there was no real reason for them to have to make the tiring climb. He was halfway to the top when he heard the shrill neigh from Horse and the half-snarl, half-bark from Dog and recognized them as warning signals. Somebody was close-by who shouldn't be.

The first shot had rung out as Preacher started to turn. The heavy lead ball struck a small rock near his feet and blew it to smithereens. He saw the puff of powder smoke from a clump of fir trees and was bringing his rifle to his shoulder to return fire when another rifle cracked from above him and he felt the fiery lance slice across his side.

They had him between 'em, drat the luck.

He let loose with a round aimed at the fir trees anyway, then turned and dashed along the face of the slope, figuring to work his way around a rocky shoulder that jutted out ahead of him. More shots came after him, but his long legs carried him too fast for the lead to find him.

He reached the shoulder, ducked around it. Behind him, a couple of men yelled at each other. White men, Preacher noted. They were speaking English, peppered with a lot of cussin'.

"I got him, I tell you!"

"The hell you did! Did you see the way that bastard was runnin'? No son of a bitch who was wounded could move that damned fast!"

He could tell from the sound of their voices that they were angling toward him from above and below. He set the rifle down and drew the pistols from behind his belt. Both were double-shotted, with powder charges heavy enough that the recoil from them might break the wrist of a normal man.

Preacher was anything but normal.

He heard rocks clatter close by, kicked loose by the man who was closing in from above. Preacher swung around the rugged knob and saw the man trying to skid to a stop about fifteen feet away and bring his rifle to bear. Preacher squeezed the trigger of his right-hand pistol before the muzzle of the rifle could line up on him.

One of the balls missed, but the other one plunked itself in the man's belly. He screamed as he doubled over and pitched forward, rolling a couple of times before he came to a stop. He kept writhing and wailing.

"You son of a bitch!"

The cry came from the other man, who fired a pistol at Preacher even though he was still a good forty feet away. The ball missed, but it came close enough that Preacher heard the hum of its passage through the air. He darted around the rocky shoulder, stuck the empty pistol behind his belt, grabbed up his rifle, and started running again.

He had gotten a good look at the man he'd shot, and knew that he had never seen the son of a buck before. The fella was squat and bearded, with a big felt hat that had fallen off when he collapsed. Preacher hadn't taken the time to study the other fella's face, but he had a feeling he had never seen that one either.

Now, why would two men he had never met before want to kill him? He had a decent mess of plews back at his camp, but nothing worth killing—or dying—over.

Preacher didn't spend a lot of time pondering the question. It was enough to know that they'd tried to ventilate him, which, according to his way of thinking, meant it was perfectly all right for him to blow their lights out.

He kind of wanted to talk to that second man, though, and maybe find out what was going on here. That meant he had to take the rapscallion alive.

For that reason alone, Preacher hurried along the side of the mountain, looking for a spot where he could turn the tables on his pursuer and get the drop on the man. Otherwise, he never would have run.

Fleeing from trouble stuck in his craw. He had always been one to face up to it head-on. That was the way he had lived his life ever since he came West some twenty years earlier.

Of course, he hadn't come straight to these mountains. There'd been a little matter of fighting the British first at New Orleans, under ol' Andy Jackson . . .

Preacher put those thoughts out of his mind, too. Bein' chased across a mountain by some son of a gun who wanted to kill him was no time for reminiscing.

Preacher threw on the brakes as he leaped over a rocky hump and found himself teetering on the brink of a hundred-foot drop. Footsteps pounded behind him. He still had one loaded pistol, so he whirled around and brought the gun up. He and the man chasing him fired at the same time.

That was when the ball clipped Preacher's powder horn loose, just as neat as you please, and over the edge it went without even bouncing once. The two balls from his pistol powdered rock at the man's feet and made him skip backward with a yelp of alarm.

Left now with empty weapons and no way to reload, Preacher turned and stepped off the edge of the cliff, vanishing into empty air. The fella chasing him let out a startled yell.

Preacher hadn't done away with himself, though. He had spotted a narrow ledge about a dozen feet below the rim with some hardy bushes growing on it. He landed with a lithe agility and grabbed hold of some branches to steady himself and keep from plunging the rest of the way to the bottom.

Once he had his balance, he began working his way quickly along the ledge. The cliff face jutted out above him, cutting him off from the other man's view. More importantly, the varmint couldn't get a shot at him from up there.

But the man could hear the pebbles that Preacher kicked off the ledge clattering all the way down the drop-off, so he could track his quarry by the sound of Preacher's passage. Likewise, Preacher heard the fella scurrying along up above.

The ledge angled down, and eventually Preacher found himself at the bottom where a narrow creek twisted its way along the base of the cliff. He followed it and came to the gully. During snowmelt season a stream probably ran through it, but it was dry now, so Preacher followed it, deliberately making enough of a racket so that the man behind him would be able to tell where he had gone.

So that was where he found himself now, wounded slightly, a little winded, and with empty guns.

But he still had a hunting knife with a long, heavy, razor-sharp blade, and there was a Crow tomahawk tucked behind his belt as well. He wasn't defenseless, not by a long shot.

He hadn't moved for several minutes. The fella chasing him had to be wondering by now if Preacher had given him the slip. Preacher heard him drawing closer, hurrying along now and muttering frustrated obscenities to himself.

"Sumbitch couldn't've got away. Maybe Jonah was right. Maybe he *was* wounded. I know he came along here, damn his hide."

The words came clearly to Preacher's ears, along with the panting breaths that the man took. He was right around the bend in the gully where Preacher had waited . . .

The man stepped around the bend and yelled in alarm as Preacher lunged at him, swinging the empty rifle. He jerked his own rifle up, not trying to fire the weapon, just making a desperate effort to fend off Preacher's rifle.

The flintlocks came together with a loud clash of wood and metal, knocking the rifle out of the man's hands, and the blow Preacher aimed at his head bounced off his shoulder instead.

That still had to hurt. The man yelled again and lowered his head, driving forward with powerful thrusts of his legs while Preacher was slightly off balance. He was almost as tall as Preacher and weighed more, and when his head slammed into Preacher's chest, Preacher was knocked backward.

The collision sent both men sprawling to the ground. When Preacher slammed into the earth, it jolted the rifle out of his hands.

No great loss, he thought. The rifle was empty, and it wasn't very good for fighting at close quarters anyway. A long-barreled flintlock only made a good club when you had room to swing it.

He snatched his tomahawk from behind his belt and swung it instead. The other man rolled out of the way, his desperation giving him the speed to barely avoid the tomahawk's slashing head.

He kicked out at Preacher as he moved. The heel of his boot caught Preacher on the elbow, making Preacher's entire right arm go numb. The tomahawk slipped out of his fingers, but he caught it with his left hand before it hit the ground.

The man grabbed Preacher's arm and twisted it. Preacher aimed a knee at the man's groin and sank it deep. The man screamed in Preacher's face but didn't let go.

They rolled over and over, grappling with each

other. The man's hat came off. Long, fair hair flopped over his face. A mustache of the same shade drooped over his mouth. Preacher was more certain than ever now that he had never seen this varmint before.

That was mighty curious, too. Usually when folks tried to kill him, they had a good reason, or what they *thought* was a good reason anyway.

The man drove his face at the side of Preacher's head. His mouth was open, and Preacher knew what was coming next. The son of a bitch wanted to bite his ear off!

Preacher jerked his head to the side, avoiding the snapping teeth. He whipped it back the other way so that their skulls banged together. Preacher would match the hardness of his noggin against anybody else's, but he had to admit that he saw stars dancing around behind his eyes. Both men groaned and seemed a little addlepated.

The feeling was coming back into Preacher's right arm and hand. He reached for his knife and closed his fingers around the leather-wrapped handle. He pulled the weapon free of his belt and slashed at the man's legs with it.

The blade cut through buckskin and flesh. The man howled, let go of Preacher's other arm, and drove the ball of his hand hard against Preacher's jaw. Preacher's head was forced back until it felt like his neckbone would crack.

Whoever this fella was, he could fight! He was almost as adept at rough-and-tumble as Preacher.

But there was only one Preacher, and he had come by his reputation as the toughest he-coon in the mountains honestlike. Preacher kneed the man again, in the belly this time instead of the balls. He walloped him across the face with the brass ball that was at the end of the knife's grip. The man's struggles were growing weaker now.

Sensing maybe that he was losing the fight, the blond man made a last-ditch effort. He heaved himself up off the ground, arching his back so that Preacher was thrown off to the side. Then he rolled over and scrambled frantically for the rifle he had dropped when the fight began.

He was closer to the weapon and got there before Preacher could stop him. Grabbing the rifle, he lunged to his feet and swung around, earing the hammer back to full cock. Preacher scrambled up, too, and saw the barrel swinging relentlessly toward him.

The survival instinct took over then. Preacher still gripped the tomahawk in his left hand, but he was almost as deadly with his left hand as he was with his right. His arm swept up and back and then flashed forward.

The 'hawk spun across the space between the two men with blinding speed and landed with a meaty *thunk!* just as the man pulled the trigger. The flintlock roared, but its owner was already going over backward, his skull split open by the tomahawk that had landed with terrific force in the middle of his forehead. He fell on his back and lay there twitching as blood and brains oozed out around the blade.

"Well, *hell*!" Preacher said with heartfelt disgust. The man wouldn't be answering any questions now.

And Preacher still had no earthly idea why the two varmints wanted him dead.

Chapter 2

The settlement had no name. It wasn't even much of a settlement, at least so far. And it would be just fine with Preacher if it stayed that way.

First had come the trading post established by a pair of cousins, Corliss and Jerome Hart, who had been brought here to this beautiful valley in the shadow of the Rocky Mountains by Preacher. They'd had some mishaps and adventures along the way, but things had finally settled down once they got here. Corliss and his wife Deborah had even unofficially adopted the boy Jake, who had run away from his brute of a father in St. Louis and come along on the wagon train journey that had ended here.

Another wagon train had followed close behind, bringing with it a handful of settlers—and customers for the trading post, which was doing a brisk business even before the building that housed it was completed.

Word of the trading post and tiny settlement had spread among the fur trappers and traders who made their living from the beavers and other animals in the mountains. There had been other trading posts out here far beyond the normal reach of civilization—one in almost the same spot as the Hart cousins' venture, in fact, some twenty years earlier, not long after Meriwether Lewis and William Clark returned from their epic journey to explore the Louisiana Purchase.

None of those posts had lasted for more than a few years, though. Savage Indians, brutal weather, disease . . . something had always happened to either wipe out the businesses or send their owners fleeing back to civilization.

Corliss and Jerome Hart swore that their trading post would be different. They would stick it out, they said, come hell or high water. The fact that Preacher had befriended them during their journey West gave their claims some credence. Everybody west of the Mississippi and north of the Rio Grande knew Preacher, knew the sort of man he was.

So the trappers came to the post, and so did the traders. Some of them had Indian wives, and they built a handful of cabins near the post, sturdy log cabins that reminded them of the homes they had left behind back East.

Of course, not all the men *wanted* to be reminded of such things. Some of them had come West to get away from unpleasantness back East. But the little no-name settlement grew anyway. A few of the trappers even went back to St. Louis and brought out their *real* wives, the ones they had married in a church or a judge's chambers instead of the ones they just shared buffalo robes with in lodges made of hides.

There had been a minister with that first wagon train, and as time went by more missionaries showed up. Not black-robed Jesuits like the ones who had been some of the first white men to penetrate the vast Canadian wilderness and on across the border into the northern reaches of the United States. No, these missionaries were Baptists, and they brought their wives and even their children with them. Within a year, nigh on to a hundred people lived within rifle shot of the Harts' trading post.

It made Preacher's skin crawl to think about it. Having so many people around in St. Louis was bad enough, but he could handle it because he made the trip down the Missouri River only once or twice a year. But he visited the trading post more often than that, and whenever he did he felt cramped, like he didn't have any elbow room, and it seemed like there were too many folks breathing the mountain air. They might use it up, he worried, although that seemed unlikely when he looked at the vast blue arch of the sky above the mountains.

He could see the trading post and the settlement far below him as he rode through South Pass. The big, sure-footed horse he had named Horse—Preacher was nothing if not a practical man—picked its way down the trail with ease. The shaggy, wolflike cur Preacher had dubbed Dog bounded ahead.

Preacher was leading three horses: his own packhorse, which carried his supplies and the load of pelts he had taken since his last visit to the trading post, and the two that belonged to the pair of dead bushwhackers. He had found the animals tied to a tree not far from the spot where the men had ambushed him, but there had been nothing in their belongings to tell him who they were or why they had tried to kill him.

The would-be killers were lashed facedown over their saddles. Preacher had thought seriously about leaving their carcasses for the wolves. He had even considered burying them. But in the end, he had decided to bring them with him since he was less than a day's ride from the trading post and the dry, cool, high country air helped keep dead varmints from rottin' too fast.

He wanted to see if anybody at the settlement recognized them.

It took him almost an hour to make his way down from the pass to the broad, grassy park where the trading post was located. Folks had seen him coming. Dogs barked and kids ran out to meet him. Most of the youngsters were 'breeds, the children of trappers and their Indian mates, but some belonged to families that had come out here from St. Louis and other places in the East, looking for a place to call their own.

A stocky, round-faced boy of eleven or twelve grinned at him and called, "Hey, Preacher! What you got there?"

"Couple o' skunks in human form, Jake," Preacher answered the boy as he reined to a stop. "Ever seen either one of 'em before?"

Some folks would've tried to keep the boy away and not expose him to the sight of the dead bodies, but Preacher figured anybody who was going to live in these mountains had to be tough enough to handle such things. Death was a fact of life, and it didn't do any good to coddle young'uns and try to hide that fact from them.

Jake wasn't bothered by it. He'd been through hard

times already despite his young age. He grasped the hair on one of the dangling heads and lifted it so he could see the man's face. After a moment, Jake let go and the head flopped down again.

"Nope," Jake said. "He's a plumb stranger to me, Preacher. Lemme look at the other one."

Jake studied the face of the second corpse with the same result. Other kids crowded around him while he was holding the man's head up, and Preacher asked the same question of them, only to have all of them shake their heads in the negative. It was beginning to appear that the two bushwhackers hadn't visited the settlement before coming after Preacher.

He hadn't asked any of the grown-ups yet, though, so he hitched Horse into motion again and rode toward the big log building that was the center of the community.

Corliss and Jerome Hart's trading post was solidly built, with thick walls that had been notched out here and there to create plenty of rifle slots. In addition, a stockade fence made of vertical logs with sharpened tops had been erected around the place, with watch-towers at the corners and a parapet that ran inside it where defenders could stand and fire. The cousins had run into enough Indian trouble on the way out here that they had built the post with fighting off attacks in mind.

So far, the Indians in the area had left them alone. But a man who was prepared for trouble, whether it came or not, usually lived a lot longer on the frontier.

The double gates in the stockade fence stood open right now. Preacher glanced up and saw that all of the watchtowers were manned. If the sentries saw any sign of hostiles approaching, they would sound the alarm and the gates would be closed and barred before the Indians could get there. Everyone in the settlement knew to listen, and if they heard the bell mounted on top of the trading post tolling, they knew it meant to get inside the wall as quickly as they could. All the settlers would gather there in case of trouble.

Today, though, peace reigned in the valley, and folks strolled in and out through the gates, visiting the trading post for supplies or just some conversation, then heading back to the log cabins that dotted the grassy park. With a procession of youngsters trailing him, Preacher rode through the gates as well, and brought Horse to a stop before the trading post just as Corliss Hart stepped out onto the shaded porch.

Corliss smiled and lifted a hand in greeting. He was a muscular man in his thirties with a friendly face and a shook of dark hair.

"Howdy, Preacher," he called. "Didn't expect to see you back here quite this soon."

"I was lucky and already got a good load o' plews," Preacher drawled. He shifted Horse to the side so that Corliss could see the other two saddle mounts and their grisly burden. "Got a load o' something else, too."

Corliss's smile disappeared and his eyes widened. "Good Lord!" he said. "Who's that?"

"You tell me," Preacher said. "They tried to kill me this mornin'."

"Well, that was a foolish mistake," Corliss muttered as he came down the steps from the porch and moved forward to get a closer look at the bodies.

Grimacing a little in distaste, he did what Jake had done: lifted the heads by the hair and studied the faces of the dead men.

He was shaking his head when he turned away from the horses. "I'm sorry, Preacher, but I never saw them before. They look like pretty unsavory sorts, though."

"They ain't any sort anymore 'cept dead."

Corliss looked at the youngsters crowding around and said, "You children run along. You don't need to see this." He added to his adopted son in particular, "Jake, go inside and give Deborah a hand."

"Aw, Corliss," the boy complained. "I seen dead folks before, you know."

"You've seen too much in your life. Run along."

Grumbling and dragging his feet, Jake went inside. The other kids went back to whatever they had been doing. Dead bodies started to lose their novelty pretty quickly. They didn't *do* anything.

As Preacher swung down from the saddle, Corliss asked, "Is that blood on your shirt? You're hurt, Preacher!"

The rangy mountain man shook his head. "Naw, not to speak of. Just got a little hide scraped off where a rifle ball come too close for comfort. I already slapped a poultice on it. It'll be fine."

"Deborah could take a look at it if you'd like."

The idea of Corliss's pretty, dark-haired wife poking around at his bare torso made Preacher a mite uncomfortable, so he shook his head. "No, thanks. It's all right."

"Suit yourself. Anyway, you probably know as much about treating bullet wounds as anybody else in this part of the country."

"I've patched up a fair number of 'em," Preacher admitted. "On me and on other folks, too."

A short, slender, sandy-haired man wearing a thick canvas apron over his clothes bustled out onto the porch. "Preacher!" he said. "What's this about dead men?"

"They tell no tales," Preacher said. He inclined his head toward the corpses. "Wish they would, though. I'd kinda like to know why they wanted to kill me."

Corliss's cousin Jerome came down the steps. Unlike the easygoing Corliss, who sometimes seemed to be on the verge of dozing off even when he was wide awake, Jerome Hart was nervous most of the time, whether there was really anything to be nervous *about* or not.

During the journey out here, there had been a rivalry between Corliss and Jerome for Deborah's affections, a rivalry in which Corliss had emerged victorious. For a while, it had looked as if the resulting bitterness would divide the cousins permanently. But they had made their peace and as far as Preacher knew, there had been no more problems between them.

"I've never seen them before," Corliss said, referring to the two dead bushwhackers. "Take a look, Jerome, and see if you recognize them."

Jerome frowned and hesitated. "I, uh, I'm sure that if you don't know them, Corliss, then I wouldn't—"

"Oh, for goodness' sake," Corliss snapped. "They're dead, they can't hurt you." He lifted the corpses' heads one after the other.

Jerome paled and swallowed hard as he looked at

them. "I'm sorry, Preacher," he said. "I don't know them. I don't think they've ever been here."

"That's what I figured when Jake didn't recognize 'em. That younker keeps his eyes open."

"Jake?" Jerome repeated. "You let Jake look at these . . . these cadavers?"

Preacher nodded. "And the other kids from the settlement, too."

Jerome looked horrified, but he didn't say anything. Preacher knew that the ways of the frontier were different than anything Jerome was accustomed to. Jerome was trying to get used to them, but it might take him a while.

News of what Preacher had brought in was already spreading through the settlement. People began to show up to have a look at the bodies. Anything different, even something like this, was a welcome break from the hardships of everyday life. Deborah Hart, her gently rounded belly starting to display that she was expecting, came outside and took her turn checking to see if she recognized the bushwhackers. It came as no surprise to Preacher that she didn't. Neither did Pete Carey, the stocky jack-of-all-trades who helped the Hart cousins run the trading post.

"Well, Preacher," Corliss said after a while, "you seem to have drawn a blank. What are you going to do now?"

Preacher spat. "Only one thing to do. Reckon I'll need to borrow a shovel."

"You're going to bury them?"

"I killed 'em. I'll plant 'em."

Jerome said, "Surely we can give you a hand with that at the very least. And Reverend Porter can say a prayer for their souls . . . although I'm not sure they deserve it if they tried to murder you, my friend."

"That's for somebody else to sort out, not me," Preacher said. "Once they're in the ground, I figure on sellin' that load o' pelts to you fellas and the two extra horses, and then I might buy me a jug o' whiskey."

Corliss frowned. "But they tried to kill you, and you don't know why! Doesn't that bother you?"

"I'm a mite puzzled," Preacher admitted, "but I'll let you in on a little secret . . . This ain't the first time somebody's tried to kill me. And I got a real strong feelin' it won't be the last . . ."

Chapter 3

By nightfall, the two men were buried, Reverend Thomas Porter had said the proper words over the graves, and Preacher had gotten a good meal cooked on a stove in the trading post rather than over a campfire. Now he sat in a barrel chair in a corner, his long, buckskin-clad legs stretched out in front of him as he took an occasional nip from the earthenware jug he held. Several other trappers of his acquaintance sat with him, swapping windies. Preacher was mostly silent, though, a frown on his face as he pondered what had happened.

Despite the nonchalant answer he had given Corliss Hart, the attempt on his life *did* bother him. Life on the frontier was fraught with enough dangers already. Even though the two strangers had been unsuccessful in their efforts to kill him, the very fact that they had tried told Preacher that somebody else could show up out of the blue and do likewise.

"What do you think, Preacher?" a red-bearded trapper named Bouchard asked.

The direct question shook Preacher out of his brooding. "What do I think about what?"

"Jock thinks there'll be real towns out here someday."

"Aye," another trapper said. "Jus' like Glasgow or Edinburgh, wi' factories and shops and row after row o' houses."

Preacher shuddered at the thought. "Lord, I hope not. If things ever start to get like that, just take me out and shoot me 'cause I don't wanna see it."

"Maybe that's why those fellows ambushed you," Bouchard suggested with a grin. "They were just trying to spare you from having to witness the ravages of civilization, *mon ami*."

Preacher downed a snort of hooch. "Yeah, I reckon," he said caustically.

The Scottish trapper, Jock, leaned forward and said, "Ye dinna kin why those scuts came after ye, Preacher?"

Preacher shook his head. "I don't have any idea. Maybe I had trouble with a friend o' theirs in the past, and they were tryin' to settle the score."

He didn't have to explain what he meant. The other men knew that whenever somebody had trouble with Preacher, that somebody usually ended up dead, or at least hurt mighty bad.

Corliss Hart came over and said, "Why don't you stay here at the trading post tonight, Preacher?"

A frown creased Preacher's forehead. "Sleep with a roof over my head? I ain't in the habit o' doin' that very often. Hell, it ain't even been a year since I was last in St. Louis."

Jock said, "Next thing ye kin, he'll be wantin' ye

t' take a bath, Preacher!" The Scotsman slapped his thigh and laughed uproariously at the very idea. The other trappers joined in the laughter.

"No, I'm serious," Corliss said. "Surely, it would be safer staying here than camping somewhere in the area. Maybe those two men were the only ones who are after you, but you can't be sure of that."

"Fella can't be sure of much of anything in this life," Preacher said. "He gets up in the mornin' not knowin' if he'll see the sun go down that evenin'. But worryin' about that too much will drive him plumb out of his head if he ain't careful."

"Well, the offer stands, if you're so inclined. Deborah and Jerome and I would be glad to have you as our guest."

Preacher took another drink from the jug and wiped the back of his other hand across his mouth. "I'm obliged, Corliss. I truly am. But I reckon I'd have a hard time goin' to sleep without the stars up yonder lookin' down at me." He pulled in his legs and stood up, moving with the easy grace of a big cat. "Fact is, I'm a mite tired, so I think I'll go on and find a place to lay my head."

He said his good nights and walked out of the trading post, dangling the jug from his left hand. The thumb of his right hand was hooked behind his belt, not far from the butt of one of his pistols. The weapon was in easy reach if he needed it, and it was loaded and charged again. He had taken the powder horns and shot pouches off the two men he had killed that morning. They wouldn't be needing 'em again.

Torches burned at the watchtowers and at intervals along the walls, casting their glow over the area outside the stockade. The gates were still open, but a couple of armed guards stood just outside them keeping watch. Preacher paused on the porch to look out at the night. Dog lay on the porch a few feet away. He raised his head and pricked his ears forward as Preacher stood there.

The valley was peaceful. Lights burned in the windows of some of the cabins in the settlement, and silvery moon glow washed over the grass. At moments such as this, it was hard to believe so many dangers lurked in the darkness.

But hostile Indians could be watching the settlement at this very moment. So could lawless white men, for that matter. Bandits weren't common on the frontier, but they weren't unheard of either. Storms could be brewing . . . natural or man-made. A fella never knew.

Preacher gave a little shake of his head. It wasn't like him to mope around like this. He had left his belongings on the porch, wrapped up in his bedroll. He picked them up now, growled, "Come on, Dog," and stepped down from the porch. The big cur rose and padded after him.

He had already put Horse away in the paddock adjacent to the stockade after dickering with Jerome over the load of pelts and the two horses. They had come to an agreement without much trouble. Preacher knew he could have gotten more for the furs in St. Louis . . . but that would have meant going to St. Louis. The Harts paid him enough to take care of his simple needs.

He planned to walk out into the trees that came right up to the edge of the settlement in places and find a good spot to spend the night. As he left the stockade, he nodded to the guards and said, "Might as well close 'em up for the night, boys. I don't think anybody else is leavin'."

"All right, Preacher," one of the men said. They knew his reputation. If he offered an opinion about anything, nine times out of ten it could be taken as the gospel. The guard went on. "I'm sort of surprised that you're not staying inside the walls tonight."

"Why's that?"

The man shuffled his feet a little uncomfortably. "Well, I mean, since those fellas tried to kill you and all . . . not that I think you'd worry about that even for a second, Preacher . . . !"

The mountain man chuckled. "Forget it, son. I ain't offended. But I ain't worried neither."

To tell the truth, if there was somebody else out there in the night looking to kill him, he almost hoped they'd go ahead and do their damnedest. That beat waiting around. He'd take his chances against almost anybody, especially with Dog around to warn him and pitch in if need be.

And if somebody *did* come after him, maybe this time he'd be able to grab them and make them tell him what in blazes was going on. He had learned a few tricks from the Blackfoot about the best ways to make a fella talk . . .

Despite the fact that Preacher was halfway hoping his enemies would come after him again, the night passed quietly and peacefully. He slept lightly, as always, resting but ready to come fully awake at an instant's notice. His soogans protected him against the nighttime chill, which was year-round at these elevations.

The next morning, he returned to the trading post to pick up Horse, and as he led the stallion out of the paddock, Jake came up to him and asked, "Are you gonna take me with you this time, Preacher?" The youngster asked him that same question almost every time he paid a visit to the trading post. "I could be a big help to you."

"Well, I dunno, Jake. You're a mighty big help to your ma and pa, I expect."

"Corliss and Deborah ain't really my ma and pa. But I reckon you'd know that."

Preacher nodded. "'Deed I do. But they been takin' care of you like you're their own young'un, and I reckon you sort of owe them for that. And with Deborah bein' in a family way, they're gonna need even more help around here."

"Yeah, but Preacher . . ." An anguished expression appeared on the boy's round face. "They say there's gonna be a *teacher* on the next wagon train headin' this way. There's gonna be a *school* here. You just can't leave me to face that!"

Preacher sympathized; he truly did. He had never had much education himself before he left the family farm and headed West when he was about Jake's age. He had learned to read, some on his own, some with the help of other mountain men who'd had some book learning. He could cipher some, too. A fella had to be able to do that if he wasn't going to be taken advantage of by the fur traders.

But the thought of sitting in a building and letting

some soft-handed gent try to pound facts into his head while *life* was going on outside . . . well, that was just horrifying.

There was nothing he could do, though, except slowly shake his head. "I'm sorry, Jake," he said. "Maybe one o' these days, but not yet."

"Damn it, I was afraid that was what you were gonna say! Am I gonna have to run off again?"

Preacher knew how badly that would upset Corliss, Deborah, and Jerome, who looked on the youngster as a member of the family. He gave Jake a hard stare and said, "If you do, I'll have to find you and tan your hide good, boy. That what you want?"

Jake swallowed. He knew that there was nowhere he could go in the mountains where Preacher couldn't find him. "All right," he said, not bothering to hide the reluctance in his voice. "I guess I can give it a try, Preacher. But only if you promise me that one o' these days I'll be your partner."

Preacher hesitated. He wasn't the sort of man who gave his word lightly. At the same time, he couldn't really see himself taking some green kid under his wing and trying to teach the sprout how to take care of himself. Jake had him over a damn barrel, he thought.

"All right," he finally said. "But I decide when you're ready to go with me. Deal?"

Jake held up a pudgy hand. "Deal."

Preacher shook with the boy and then handed him the packhorse's reins. "Here, hold these while I mount up." He swung up onto Horse's back and took the reins from Jake. He had already said his good-byes to the Harts, and to Pete Carey and Bouchard and Jock as well. He lifted a hand in farewell as he said, "Be seein' you," and nudged Horse into a trot that carried him through the open gates of the stockade.

He looked back once and saw Jake standing there just outside the walls, watching him ride away.

Preacher left the settlement behind him and worked his way up toward the pass. He was going back to the same area where he had been when the attempt on his life was made. He had traps there that still needed tending to, and he sure wasn't going to let what happened scare him off.

When he reached the pass, he paused to look down into the valley at the settlement. Even though he didn't like the idea of civilization encroaching on the mountains, he had to admit to himself that he had grown fond of some of those folks down there. Corliss was a bit of a wastrel at times, Deborah could be a mite bossy, and Jerome was just downright annoying more often than not. But they were good people and had demonstrated that on more than one occasion. Jake was . . . well, Jake was Jake. For good or bad, there was no other kid quite like him. Preacher liked quite a few of the other folks, too. Maybe, in the long run, civilization wouldn't be such a bad thing . . .

Lost in those thoughts as he rode through the pass leading the packhorse, at first Preacher almost didn't notice the low-pitched rumble that sounded somewhere above him.

But he heard it, and his instincts warned him that something was wrong. He jerked his head up to peer toward the direction of the noise, and his eagle-sharp eyes saw instantly what was happening.

High above him in the pass, rocks had begun

to fall, taking other rocks with them, and in little more than the blink of an eye, thousands of tons of stone had gathered steam and were sliding down the slope right toward Preacher, crushing everything in their path.

Chapter 4

Dust billowed up from the avalanche, but the thick gray cloud didn't obscure the vanguard of the slide. Preacher could see the massive boulders bounding down the slope like they were no more than pebbles. Any one of those giant rocks would be enough to smash him into something that didn't even resemble a human being.

That is, if he waited around and let one of the stony bastards land on him.

He dug his heels into Horse's flanks and leaned forward over the stallion's neck, yelling encouragement to the animal as Horse lunged ahead in a gallop. Dog ran alongside, stretching his legs to keep up with the stallion. Preacher hung on tightly to the packhorse's reins and dragged it along with them.

He had known instantly that their only hope was to charge straight ahead. The angle of the slide made it impossible for them to turn around and get clear in time, going that way.

There was a slim chance, though, that they might

be able to get ahead of it. Horse was an ugly, hammer-headed brute, but he had speed and strength and stamina to spare.

The same could not be said of the packhorse, however. Preacher realized that after only a few strides by Horse. The other animal was holding them back. If Preacher hung on to the reins, they were all doomed.

Hating to do it, both for the sake of the packhorse and for the supplies that the horse carried, Preacher let go of the reins and called to his own mount, "Let 'er rip, you son of a gun!"

The roar of the falling rocks was deafening now. Preacher watched the inexorable advance of the slide from the corner of his eye as Horse raced along the winding trail that led through the pass. Those twists and turns slowed them down; a flat, straight run would have given them a better chance.

But a fella had to play the cards he was dealt . . . and Preacher would always stay in the hand until the end. He'd be damned if he would fold.

He glanced around, saw that Dog was falling behind. "Come on!" he yelled, not knowing if the big cur could hear him over the unholy racket or not. "Come on, you shaggy varmint!"

Dog lunged ahead harder, digging for all the speed he could muster. The two animals were Preacher's best friends in the world, and he wasn't going to leave either of them behind. He slowed Horse slightly, and Dog drew closer.

"We'll make it together, or we won't make it!" Preacher said through gritted teeth.

On they raced, until it seemed that the roar of the avalanche would be enough to crush them by itself, until the dust reached them and clogged Preacher's mouth and nose and stung his eyes, until it seemed that the whole world was about to come crashing down on top of them.

Then suddenly, they were in the clear as they broke out of the great swirling cloud. The earth shook under them as countless tons of rock came smashing down a mere matter of yards behind them. Smaller rocks pelted them, and Preacher lifted an arm to protect his head. Even a fist-sized chunk of stone might catch him in the head and knock him out of the saddle, and then the edges of the slide could still engulf him.

Gradually, the punishment eased and the rumbling began to die away. Preacher slowed his mount. Horse's sleek hide was covered with foamy sweat and his sides heaved from the exertion. Dog's head hung low and his tongue lolled from his mouth as he padded along. Preacher was a mite weary from the strain himself, but at least he hadn't had to do any of the running. His gallant companions had handled that.

He reined Horse to a stop and leaned forward to pat the stallion on the shoulder. "You're the damned finest horse any man ever rode," he said. He looked behind him regretfully. Dust still obscured the pass. The packhorse was back there somewhere, trapped under the avalanche. Poor son of a gun had never had a chance, Preacher thought.

Then he lifted his head and looked up toward the rimrock. It was possible that the rock slide had started on its own and that it had been just a coincidence that he was traveling through the pass at that moment.

Yeah, it was possible . . . but he didn't believe it.

Not for a damned second.

Somebody had been up there watching him, waiting for just the right moment to shove one of the precariously balanced boulders that littered the rimrock and launch that avalance into deadly motion. Luckily for Preacher, Horse, and Dog, whoever it was had misjudged things a mite. Just enough to give them the narrow hope of escape that they had seized so fiercely.

Preacher wanted to hitch Horse into motion again and start circling through the rugged terrain, heading upward toward the rimrock to find out exactly what had happened. But after the valiant dash that had saved Preacher's life, Horse was too played out for any more effort right now. The stallion had to rest for a while.

That was all right, Preacher told himself. He would get up there before the day was over, and when he did, he would find the sign that the man who started the avalanche had left behind. There was always sign of some sort, if a man knew how to look for it.

Preacher knew, and once he had the trail, he wouldn't lose it.

That fella didn't know it yet, but he had bought himself a world of trouble when he rolled that stone.

Horse was strong enough that he recovered quickly, but Preacher gave him a little extra time anyway, waiting until midday before starting the climb to the rimrock. Preacher had some jerky and a biscuit in his saddlebags, so he and Dog made a skimpy lunch on that.

Then he rode the rest of the way through the pass and began the arduous task of circling back and climbing, following faint game trails that most men barely would have been able to see. Horse was almost as sure-footed as a mountain goat, so Preacher didn't hesitate to trust his life to the stallion's balance, even though at times hundreds of feet of empty air yawned right at his elbow.

By the middle of the afternoon, they reached the rimrock where the avalanche had started. Dog ran forward and sniffed the ground. Preacher dismounted and left the reins dangling as he hunkered down and studied the place that interested Dog. He saw some pebbles that had been disturbed recently, so that their undersides now lay upward, and he knew the man who'd tried to kill him had walked along here.

"Trail, Dog," he said.

Nose to the ground, Dog followed the command, leading Preacher away from the rimrock's edge. A few minutes later, they came to a place where fairly fresh droppings and the marks of steel-shod hooves on the rock told Preacher that three horses had waited here for a while.

Three men, Preacher reflected. One to hold the horses, two to push a boulder over the edge and start the avalanche. And the dumb bastards hadn't even tried to hide the evidence that they'd been here.

Of course, they had assumed that they were going to kill him and that no one would ever follow them.

They would find out just how wrong they were about that.

Even now, they probably thought he was dead. After escaping from the avalanche, he had stayed close to the side of the pass so that anyone looking down from above might not be able to see him. The dust had been too thick for anybody to see anything for a while, and once it cleared away, there would have been no sign of him from the rimrock. The natural thing would be to think that the huge rock slide had caught him and crushed the life from him.

Preacher whistled Horse over to him and swung up into the saddle. He followed the scratches on the rocks left by the horseshoes, and Dog stayed on the scent for good measure. The men hadn't made any effort to hide their trail, more evidence that they thought Preacher was dead.

The tracks led northwest through rugged but beautiful country. The men had dropped down quickly from the heights of the pass to a long, grassy valley watered by a stream that sparkled in the sunlight as it flowed over a rocky bed.

Preacher had been through here many times in his wanderings. He knew the country well. To the north was the area known as Colter's Hell, named after the legendary mountain man John Colter. At first, folks had thought he was crazy when he came back and reported that there was an area where geysers of steaming water shot hundreds of feet in the air and bubbling mud pits stank of brimstone, like they were entrances to Hades. Of course, as it turned out, the place really existed and Colter hadn't been exaggerating. Preacher had seen it more than once with his own eyes.

The would-be killers might be headed there, or

their destination might be closer. Preacher didn't know and didn't care. He would stay on their trail wherever it led.

Since he had given Horse that extra rest, he kept the stallion moving at a fast pace now. The men who were his quarry had been dawdling along, yet another indication they didn't think anybody could be following them. The sign Preacher saw told him that he was closing in on them. He might even catch up to them before nightfall.

He wasn't sure he wanted that. Might be easier to deal with them once they had camped for the night. Let them fill their bellies, maybe pass around a jug . . .

Then see how they liked it when the man they thought they had killed rose right up out of that grave under hundreds of tons of rock.

When he was no more than an hour behind them, Preacher slowed down and maintained that distance. Dog whined a little in eagerness, but Preacher just smiled and said, "Just be patient, old fella. We'll settle up with those varmints before much longer."

The sun dipped behind the mountains to the west, and night settled down quickly. Preacher waited until he spotted the tiny orange eye of a campfire and then steered for it, still taking his time. It didn't surprise him that the men had built a fire. He'd been able to tell from the trail they left that they were greenhorns. Still potentially dangerous, of course, but not as experienced in the ways of the frontier as some.

When he was close enough to smell the wood smoke, he dismounted and tied Horse's reins loosely to a sapling. The stallion would be able to pull free if he needed to.

"Stay here, fella," Preacher said quietly as he patted Horse on the shoulder. "Come on, Dog."

Horse threw his head up and down as if he didn't appreciate being left behind, but he didn't try to pull loose. Preacher and Dog padded off into the darkness.

The Indians knew Preacher by many names, most of them having to do with his expertise at killing. They frightened their children with tales of this white man who came in the night like a phantom and left death behind him, silent and lethal. Preacher knew this and did nothing to discourage it. A reputation as a dangerous man could be an annoyance at times, but mostly it came in handy.

Dog at his side, he moved through the night with an uncanny stealth practiced over many perilous years on the frontier. The glow of the campfire was visible through the trees from time to time, but Preacher didn't really need to see it or smell the smoke. Now that he knew where he was going, his uncanny sense of direction would have taken him right to his destination without anything else.

He and Dog didn't make a sound as they closed in on the camp. When Preacher was close enough to hear the men talking, he went to the ground and tugged Dog down beside him. They lay there listening. Preacher hoped that the men would drop some hints into their conversation about why they had tried to kill him.

The tone of their voices told him he'd been right about them having a jug. It sounded like they'd been passing it around for a while. Most of their comments were profane observations about the talents of various whores who plied their trade in the waterfront taverns of St. Louis. That confirmed another of Preacher's suppositions, that they weren't frontiersmen. They had come out here from back East, probably recently.

Had they come all this way just to kill him? That was crazy, he told himself, and yet he couldn't rule it out.

They finally got around to talking about their attempt on his life. One of the men said in a slightly whiskey-slurred voice, "Wish I could'a seen that damn Preacher's face when all those rocks started comin' at him."

"Prob'ly shit right in his pants," another man said with a giggle that put Preacher's teeth on edge.

The third man said, "Important thing is that he's dead. Thass all that matters. Now gimme that damn jug!"

"Get your hands off it! You been hoggin' it all night!"

"The hell you say! I'll learn you to talk to me like that!"

"Dadgum it, Parker!" That was the first man, trying to make peace between the other two. "You can't just— Oh, shit! No!"

The roar of a gunshot drowned out his voice, then another shot blasted and somebody screamed.

Preacher bit back a curse of his own.

So much for that plan, he thought bitterly.

Chapter 5

He lunged to his feet and burst out of the brush surrounding the clearing where the camp was located. His keen eyes took in the scene instantly, noting the rocks and the logs scattered around that the men had been using for seats by the fire in the center of the clearing.

One man lay on his back, kicking and thrashing as he screamed. His hands pawed at his chest, where blood bubbled and spurted between his fingers from a wound. Preacher figured the first shot had downed that gent.

He couldn't tell who had fired the second shot or what the result of it had been, because the other two men were rolling around on the ground on the other side of the fire. The red light from the flames glittered on the knives they held. Each man was trying to bury his blade in the other's body, and as Preacher entered the clearing, one of them succeeded. He managed to get on top and drive his knife down into the chest of the other man, who howled in pain as the steel penetrated his body. He jerked and shuddered and then went limp. Preacher could tell from the knife's location that it had pierced the man's heart.

Just then the man on the other side of the fire gave a gurgling gasp and fell silent. Preacher figured that one was dead, too.

That left only the one fella, who left his knife in the body of the man he had just killed and staggered to his feet. He didn't seem to realize at first that Preacher was there, but then Dog let out a low, rumbling growl and the man stiffened. He turned slowly, his eyes widening in horror as he realized who was standing there.

"You didn't figure I'd let you get away with it, did you?" Preacher asked.

The man started to back up. He was tall and slender, but had a potbelly. His hat had come off during the struggle, revealing a mostly bald head. His mouth worked, but no sound came out for a moment. Then he managed to say, "You . . . you can't be here. You're dead. You're dead!"

"Not hardly," Preacher said.

The man had blood on his shirt. Preacher figured he'd been nicked by that second shot, which must have been fired by the man who now had the knife in his chest. Even though Preacher hadn't seen it, he had a pretty idea how the fight had played out. This fella and the one on the other side of the fire had argued over the jug, which lay broken near the flames. The survivor had whipped out a pistol and shot the man he was arguing with. Then the third varmint had shot this one, who wasn't wounded badly enough to stop him from pulling a knife and going after that third man . . .

Preacher had seen men kill each other in equally senseless arguments during rendezvous. The apparently limitless capacity of human beings to do stupid things had long since ceased to surprise him.

He stalked forward as the man began to back away. The man raised a trembling hand and held it out in front of him as if to ward off Preacher's inexorable advance.

"Go away!" he cried. "You're supposed to be dead!"

Preacher had never seen the man before. The two who had already died here were strangers to him as well, just like the day before.

"Why'd you try to kill me?" Preacher demanded. Beside him, the big cur growled, and Preacher added, "Talk or I'll turn Dog loose on you."

He had seen the primitive fear in the man's eyes, and knew that the bastard was probably more afraid of Dog than he was of him. That was all right with Preacher. He just wanted to know why it was suddenly open season on him and didn't care what loosened the man's tongue.

"I . . . I swear, Preacher," the man stammered. "I got nothin' against you. I just wanted—"

What he wanted would remain a mystery forever, because at that moment a crimson flood welled from his mouth and washed down over his chest. He swayed back and forth for a second, made a strangling noise, and then pitched forward on his face. Blood began to pool around his head.

"Well, son of a bitch," Preacher said. The man had been hit worse than he'd thought. The pistol ball must have done a lot of damage inside him, but the man's anger had allowed him to ignore it long enough for him to kill the fella who had shot him. It had caught up to him in the end, though.

And Preacher was still no closer to finding out who wanted him dead, and why, than he had been when he took up the trail earlier in the day.

About five miles to the north, an even larger campfire burned. Twenty men were gathered around it. Four more were posted around the camp, standing guard.

The man who led this group had just enough experience on the frontier to know that such a fire might attract the attention of hostile Indians. He didn't believe that redskins would attack such a large, well-armed group, but you couldn't ever tell with those savages. It was better to take precautions than to lose your hair . . . not that he had very much hair to lose.

Colin Fairfax sat by the fire, a beaver hat perched on his mostly bald head. He had regained some of the weight he'd lost during his long, harrowing trek back to St. Louis the year before, so his face was no longer as gaunt and haggard as it had been when he returned.

But his eyes were still haunted by the fear and torment he had gone through.

He had almost been killed by Indians. He had almost been caught by grizzly bears and wolves on more than one occasion. He had almost starved, going without food for so long at times that the empty pain in his belly made him cry as he stumbled along. The sun had burned his skin, turned his nose and his lips raw. And terror had been his constant companion. Simply put, he had gone through Hell.

And it was all Preacher's fault.

Fairfax would never forget that awful trek back to St. Louis after Preacher killed his partner Schuyler Mims and ruined their plans to steal the wagon train full of supplies that belonged to Corliss and Jerome Hart. Fairfax and Mims had been working for Shad Beaumont, the most powerful figure in St. Louis's criminal circles, and it was to Beaumont's mansion on the outskirts of the city that Fairfax had gone when he finally made it back, the only survivor from the group Beaumont had sent west.

Everything Fairfax had gone through had left him filled with hatred for Preacher, so when Beaumont suggested that he return to the mountains and settle the score with the bastard, Fairfax had agreed . . . but not without a little hesitation. Part of him didn't want to face Preacher again, not after what had happened the first time.

But an even larger part wanted revenge, and so Fairfax had said yes. Beaumont had agreed to supply more than two dozen men to come along with him. Brutal, dangerous men who didn't mind killing.

Fairfax was smart enough to know that Beaumont had some other reason for wanting Preacher dead. Beaumont didn't really care about what had happened to Schuyler. Fairfax figured that Beaumont had some other criminal enterprise in mind involving the area Preacher called home and didn't want the mountain man interfering with his plans. It didn't matter either way to Fairfax. All he cared about was Preacher dying.

Accordingly, when the group of men he'd led out here arrived in the vicinity of South Pass and the Hart trading post, Fairfax had sent out several groups of scouts to search for Preacher. They weren't supposed to try to kill him, just determine his location and send someone to fetch Fairfax and the rest of the gang.

Fairfax didn't want to take any chances on Preacher getting away again. He worried, though, that Beaumont might have put a bounty on Preacher's head without telling him about it, and he didn't know if the men with him could resist a temptation like that.

A burly man named Sherwood came over to Fairfax and held out the jug he carried. "Want a snort, Boss?" he asked.

Fairfax detected a faintly mocking tone in Sherwood's voice. Sherwood was his second in command, and even though he referred to Fairfax as "Boss," Fairfax knew the man didn't really respect him. Sherwood's real boss was Shad Beaumont. Fairfax had been put in charge of the expedition because he knew the country and knew Preacher, but he was also smaller and weaker than the men who accompanied him. The only thing that really mattered to such men was power, either personal strength or the power that wealth and influence gave a man, as in the case of Shad Beaumont.

Fairfax shook his head in answer to Sherwood's question. "No, and I don't want the men getting drunk either," he snapped. "A man whose brain is muddled by whiskey stands a good chance of getting killed out here."

"Nobody's gonna mess with us, Boss," Sherwood

insisted. "There are too many of us, and we got too many guns."

Fairfax had been thinking just about the same thing, but he didn't like hearing the arrogance in Sherwood's voice as it was put into words. Arrogance led to overconfidence, and overconfidence led to death. Fairfax wasn't going to make that same mistake again.

"Just tell them what I said," he told Sherwood.

The man shrugged. "You're the boss."

Fairfax waved Sherwood away, then looked into the fire again and grimaced. He knew that staring into the flames ruined a man's night vision, but he didn't care about that. With so many hardened, well-armed men around him, he didn't think he was in any danger right now.

And as he looked into the fire, he seemed to see a lean, bearded face there, a face that he despised.

"You're going to burn in Hell, Preacher," he whispered. "You have my word on that."

With three dead men who couldn't tell him what he wanted to know, no trail to follow, and no supplies other than what he had in his saddlebags, Preacher decided to ride back to the trading post. Everybody there would be surprised to see him again so soon, but he needed to pick up more provisions. Luckily, he had some money left over from what Corliss Hart had paid him for his pelts.

Preacher didn't bother taking the bodies with him this time. He was sure that it would be like before. Nobody at the trading post would recognize the dead men. And since the drunken idiots had killed each other, he didn't feel any responsibility for burying them. He left them for the scavengers. That was one thing about the mountains. When a few months had passed, nobody would even know that the murderous bastards had ever been here.

He started back to the trading post in the morning leading the three dead men's horses. It was around the middle of the day when he reached the pass. The avalanche had blocked part of the trail, but not all of it, so Preacher was able to ride through it without any trouble. He didn't see any sign of the unlucky packhorse. The animal was completely buried under the rocks.

When he reached the other side, he was able to look down into the valley far below and see the buildings of the settlement. To his surprise, he saw a row of white dots lined up outside the stockade wall. After a moment, he realized that they were actually the canvas covers over the backs of the wagons in a wagon train. He hadn't heard anything about a train coming in, but there it was. He counted fourteen wagons.

Preacher's lips tightened under the drooping mustache. That many more people crowdin' in, takin' up space, breathin' the air . . .

"Take it easy, old son," he told himself. He might not like the influx of new settlers, but there wasn't a blasted thing he could do about it. He lifted the reins and heeled Horse into motion.

From the top of the pass it took him a little over an hour to make his way down to the valley floor. As he rode across the grassy plain toward the settlement, the covered wagons grew larger. He began to be able to make out details, like the people moving around the vehicles.

He wondered if they planned to stay here or if they were bound for someplace farther west. So far as Preacher knew, the Harts' trading post was the last outpost of civilization, but he was sure it wouldn't stay that way. There was always somebody who wanted to go farther, to extend the boundaries. There would never be any progress without folks like that. Somebody always had to be the first . . .

"Now I'm *really* surprised to see you again so soon," Corliss Hart greeted him from the front porch of the trading post as Preacher reined in a short time later. "You just left yesterday, Preacher." Corliss's eyes narrowed as he realized something. "Where's your packhorse and where did those other horses come from?"

"Lost the packhorse," Preacher said as he swung down from the saddle. "You hear a rumblin' noise yesterday mornin' a while after I left?"

"Now that you mention it, I think I did. What happened?"

Preacher looped Horse's reins around the hitch rail, tied the other horses leads, and told Dog, "Stay." He stepped up onto the porch, into the shade of the awning, and pointed toward South Pass. "Avalanche."

"In the pass? My God, are you all right?"

"The three o' us managed to stay out of its way. The packhorse wasn't so lucky. Lost him and all my supplies."

"That's terrible. No wonder you came back." Corliss shook his head. "You've had so much bad luck, it almost seems like someone is out to get you, Preacher."

Preacher nodded. "They are."

Corliss stared at him and asked, "What do you mean?"

"Three men started that avalanche on purpose. They were tryin' to kill me, just like the two the day before."

"But . . . but . . ." Corliss struggled to understand. "Did you know any of them?"

Preacher shook his head. "Also like the day before. The varmints were strangers to me. I didn't bring their bodies back with me this time. Didn't seem like there was any point to it."

"You, uh, killed them? Not that I blame you—"

"Matter of fact," Preacher said, "they got in an argument and killed each other. I was just about to step into their camp and start askin' them some questions, too."

"Like why they were after you?"

"Yep." Preacher nodded toward the door of the trading post. "Reckon I need to buy some more supplies. Hope you'd trade some more provisions for two of the horses. I'll need one to replace the packhorse."

"I'll be happy to trade with you, Preacher, you know that. I'd give you the supplies even without the trade. You've done so much to help us . . ."

Preacher said dryly, "Jerome might not take kindly to you givin' away the tradin' post's stock. Anyway, let's see how much the two horses will buy me."

Before he could go on, someone stepped out of the store and said, "Excuse me, Mr. Hart, I was wondering— Oh, I'm sorry! I didn't mean to interrupt."

Preacher turned his head to look at the newcomer, and for a moment his breath seemed to stick in his throat. Even though he liked pretty girls as much as the next fella, normally the sight of one didn't affect him so strongly.

However, this wasn't just any pretty girl standing in the door of the Harts' trading post.

This was the most beautiful woman Preacher had seen in a long, long time . . . maybe ever.

Chapter 6

When she smiled and looked vaguely embarrassed, Preacher became aware that he was staring. He forced his eyes away from her and looked at Corliss Hart again, saying gruffly, "You go ahead and help the lady, Corliss. You and me can talk later."

"No, that's all right," the woman said. "Help this gentleman, Mr. Hart. I'm in no hurry. After all, I'm not going anywhere, am I?"

Preacher took that to mean she was one of the new settlers who had arrived with the wagon train and meant to stay there. That was hard to believe. A woman like her would be as out of place in this tiny frontier settlement as a boar hog in a fancy drawing room.

She was tall . . . not just tall for a woman, but enough so that she didn't have to tip her head back very far to look Preacher in the eye. She wore a dark green traveling outfit and had a hat of a matching shade on her short blond curls, not a hair of which looked out of place in an elaborate arrangement that framed a lovely face with rich brown eyes and full lips. He wasn't sure how she had managed to come all the way out here and not even have a hair out of place, but she had. Like most blondes, she was fair-skinned, but she had begun to acquire a honey-golden tan from the time she'd spent in the sun on the journey out here. With the rude chivalry of the frontier, Preacher believed in respecting women, but he couldn't help but notice the way her breasts thrust proudly against the bosom of her outfit.

"Preacher knows what he needs, Miss Mallory," Corliss said, "and he knows he can go ahead and help himself. What can I do for you?"

"Well, in that case . . . I was wondering if you have any tea? I brought a supply with me, of course, but the journey took longer than I expected and I'm afraid that I may run out."

She was so pretty that Preacher hadn't noticed her accent at first, but he heard it now. That and her asking for tea told him that she was British. He'd run into more than a few Englishers out here, and they all loved their tea. He could take it or leave it himself.

"Yes, I have some," Corliss told her. "Not a whole lot, but enough that I can sell you some."

"Splendid," she said with a radiant smile. She surprised Preacher by turning to him again and extending her hand. "By the way, I'm Laura Mallory."

Preacher wasn't accustomed to shaking hands with women, but since she'd made the offer, he took her hand and tried not to squeeze it too hard. "They call me Preacher," he said.

"Surely, that's not the name your parents gave you," she prodded, still smiling.

"It's, uh, Art. Arthur."

Corliss said, "I didn't know that."

Preacher sent a quick glare in his direction. "It ain't what I go by." He became aware that he still had hold of Laura Mallory's hand, so he let go of it right quick and went on. "I'm mighty pleased and honored to make your acquaintance, ma'am."

"The pleasure is all mine, Mr. Preacher."

"Just, uh, Preacher. That'll do fine."

"All right . . . Preacher. I must admit, the name does seem to suit you. Are you a minister of the Gospel as well as a fur trapper?"

Preacher shook his head. "No, ma'am, not hardly. It's a long story involvin' a fella I saw once back in St. Louis and some Blackfeet who had it in their heads to torture me to death."

A little shudder went through her. "Good heavens. You'll have to tell it to me sometime . . . if it's not too horrifying, that is."

"It might be, for a lady."

"In that case," and she chuckled, "you'll have to tell it to me when I'm not feeling very ladylike."

Good Lord, Preacher thought. Was this beautiful creature flirtin' with him?

Corliss said, "I'll get you that tea, Miss Mallory." He went back into the store, leaving Preacher alone with Laura. Suddenly, Preacher was more nervous than if he'd been facing a horde of Blackfoot warriors after his scalp.

He wasn't sure why he felt that way. It wasn't like he was a boy anymore. He'd been with a number of women, including the beautiful young prostitute Jennie, who had taught him just about everything there was to know about what men and women could do together under the blankets, or the buffalo robe, as the case might be.

Of course, he wasn't thinking about that sort of frolicking with Laura Mallory. He'd just met her, for goodness' sake!

But since they were both still standing there on the trading post's front porch, and she was smiling expectantly as if she were waiting for him to say something else, he figured he'd better come up with something. With the sort of life he led, alone most of the time with Dog and Horse, conversation wasn't his strong suit.

"You, uh, come out here to settle, Miss Mallory?"

"That's right," she replied. "I came along with my brother Clyde."

"Oh? Where's he?"

"Over there with the wagons." Laura pointed with a slender, graceful finger.

Preacher turned to look, and saw a man in a buckskin jacket and broad-brimmed hat bustling around, apparently supervising the unloading of goods from the wagons. Clyde Mallory also wore whipcord trousers and high-topped boots, and he packed a pistol on one hip and a sheathed knife on the other. In that outfit, and with his lean, weathered face, he looked more like a frontiersman than an expatriate Englishman.

"Appears he brought a whole passel of supplies with him," Preacher commented.

Laura laughed, and to Preacher it sounded like the clear, cold water of a mountain stream flowing over a rocky bed. "Indeed he did," she said. "Everything in the wagon train, in fact."

Preacher frowned. "Folks gen'rally don't bring that much with 'em when they come out here to settle."

"But that's not Clyde's intention," Laura explained. "You see, this is the first trip of the Mallory Freight Line."

Preacher's eyebrows rose in surprise. "I never heard of it before."

"That's because Clyde has just established it. Several settlements have been established between here and St. Louis. Clyde intends to provide freight service to all of them including this one, which is the westernmost settlement. As such, it will be one hub of the line, with St. Louis being the other, and I'll be staying here to keep an eye on Clyde's interests while he's gone on the long trips back and forth."

Preacher was dumbfounded. He had never heard of such a thing as a woman helping to run a business.

It was obvious to anyone who looked at her, though, that Laura Mallory wasn't a typical woman.

She must have seen his response and recognized it, because she went on with a new note of crispness in her voice. "I assure you, I'm up to the task. I've been well educated."

"Yes, ma'am, I reckon a whole lot better than me, more'n likely. I'm sure you can handle the job." Preacher didn't know what else to say.

Laura's attitude eased a bit. "You've gathered by now that Clyde and I aren't from around here."

"Yes, ma'am."

"Clyde is my father's second son, you see. You know about the law of primogeniture?"

Preacher nodded in understanding. "Yes, ma'am. I

never made much sense of it, but I've known some fellas who came over here because of it."

Most of the Englishmen who made their way to the American frontier were so-called remittance men. Because they weren't the firstborn sons, they could never inherit their fathers' estates. As he had indicated to Laura, that seemed like a mighty odd law to Preacher, but the Englishers hadn't asked his opinion before they came up with it.

And for some other equally odd reason, the Englishers seemed to be a mite embarrassed by those second sons and usually shipped them off somewhere. Out of sight, out of mind, as the old saying went. From what Preacher had heard, a lot of them went into the army and helped England preserve its far-flung empire. Others came to America to make new lives for themselves, often helped out in doing so by regular payments from home, the remittance that gave them their nickname.

Most of the Englishmen Preacher had met had been pretty good fellas, eager to learn the ways of the frontier and tough as nails when they had to be. Clyde Mallory looked like he might fit into that category.

"I'll introduce you," Laura said. She stepped to the edge of the porch and waved to attract her brother's attention. "Clyde!" she called. "Clyde, over here, darling!"

Where Preacher came from, gals didn't call their brothers darling, but he knew not to make anything out of it. For folks who shared the same language, those Englishers sure did talk funny some of the time.

Clyde Mallory turned to look toward the trading

post in response to his sister's summons, then spoke to one of the men who was unloading the wagons, probably giving him some instructions. Then he came toward the building, his long legs carrying him with confident strides.

"What is it, Laura?" he asked with a touch of impatience in his voice. "There's still a great deal to do, you know."

"Yes, of course," Laura said, "but I wanted you to meet Preacher."

"The local minister?" Clyde looked at Preacher's buckskins, broad-brimmed felt hat, and bearded face, and seemed puzzled. "I'm pleased to meet you, Reverend, but I must say—"

Laura's laughter interrupted him. "No, dear, not *a* preacher or *the* preacher. Simply Preacher."

"It's what they call me," Preacher said. He went down the steps to the ground and extended his hand to Clyde Mallory. "Mighty pleased to meet you. Your sister's been tellin' me about your plans to start a freight line runnin' betwixt here and St. Louis."

Clyde took Preacher's hand, and his grip had plenty of strength, as Preacher expected. "Those are my intentions," he said. He let go of Preacher's hand and turned slightly to gesture toward the wagons. "We'll have to wait and see how things work out, of course. But I'm encouraged by the welcome we've received here."

Corliss and Jerome Hart came out onto the porch in time to hear Clyde's words. Jerome said, "We were certainly glad to see you, Mr. Mallory. Our stock shows signs of running low soon. One of us was going to have to go back to St. Louis, arrange for more supplies, and then bring them out here. Instead, you arrive unexpectedly with everything we'll need to keep us in business for six months or more!"

Clyde smiled, although his eyes remained cool and reserved. "It was a gamble admittedly, but based on everything we heard back in St. Louis about what was happening out here, we felt that it was worth the risk, didn't we, Laura?"

"Otherwise, we wouldn't be here," Laura said. "Ah, is that my tea, Mr. Hart?"

"Call me Corliss," he said. He held out the paper-wrapped package to her. "This is all we have."

"And we didn't bring any more."

"You can learn to drink coffee like a proper American," her brother told her. "After all, that's what we are now."

Laura's chin came up in a slight show of defiance. "We'll always be citizens of the British Empire, Clyde, no matter what you say."

Clyde's mouth hardened under his sandy mustache. "We'll discuss that another time, Laura," he snapped. "I have to get back to the wagons." He turned to Preacher and nodded. "It was a pleasure meeting you, sir."

"Likewise," Preacher said, even though he hadn't really warmed up to Clyde Mallory. Something about the man said that he liked to keep his distance from folks and not get too friendly with them.

Mallory walked back over to the wagons. Laura watched him go and shook her head.

"I apologize for my brother's behavior," she said. "Clyde's been rather short-tempered since he . . . resigned his commission in the army."

Her slight hesitation told Preacher that maybe Mallory's resignation from the British army hadn't been entirely his own idea. Maybe he'd run into some trouble with a superior officer and been forced to leave.

"He seemed fine to me," Corliss said. He couldn't seem to take his eyes off of Laura, which didn't surprise Preacher all that much. Corliss Hart had an eye for a pretty girl, sure enough, even though he had a mighty good-looking wife of his own. A wife who was with child at that.

But Corliss's wandering eye was none of Preacher's business. He came back up onto the porch and said, "I reckon I'd better start gatherin' those supplies if I'm gonna put some miles behind me 'fore nightfall."

"You're leaving?" Laura asked. "But you just got here."

"Oh, Preacher never stays around here for very long," Jerome said. "He's too restless for that. Always on the move, eh, Preacher?"

"I reckon," Preacher drawled.

But as he thought about the fact that Laura Mallory was going to be here at the settlement in the future, he began to wonder if maybe it was time he stopped bein' so fiddle-footed . . .

Chapter 7

Preacher let the Hart cousins talk him into staying overnight again. To tell the truth, they didn't have to work very hard at it. Until a cabin could be built for Laura Mallory, she would be staying in one of the wagons that had been outfitted for her. She had traveled out here from St. Louis in it, and it would remain her home for the time being.

And those wagons would be parked next to the trading post until Clyde Mallory was ready to take them back east loaded with pelts. Over the past year, many of the trappers in the area had begun trading or selling their furs to the Hart cousins, rather than taking packhorses all the way back to St. Louis or paddling down the Missouri River in canoes. Corliss and Jerome, in turn, had an arrangement with one of the big fur companies to supply pelts. So far they had been doing so on a small scale, but if Mallory's freight operation was a success, they could expand their own business.

Preacher wasn't sure why he was making such a

fool of himself over Laura. Sure, she was a mighty pretty woman, but he hadn't been seriously involved with anybody since Jennie . . . and that relationship had come to a tragic end. Preacher had pretty much sworn off romance ever since then, except for an occasional romp with a willing Indian gal or one of the soiled doves who showed up at Rendezvous.

Of course, it wasn't like he had announced his intention to pay court to Laura or anything. He hadn't even paid that much attention to her during the day, choosing to keep his distance instead.

He'd spent his time getting another load of supplies together, buying a packhorse to replace the one that had been killed in the avalanche, and fending off Jake's efforts to talk him into taking him along when he left. The boy purely hated the idea of going to school once the teacher arrived.

One corner of the trading post's cavernous main room was where the mountain men congregated to eat, drink whiskey, and swap lies. Bouchard and Jock had pulled out the day before, same as Preacher, so he didn't have any close friends on hand at the moment. That didn't bother him. He was used to his own company. He sat there alone in the corner that evening, taking an occasional nip from a jug and wondering if Laura had turned in yet.

As if fate wanted to answer his question, both of the Mallorys walked into the trading post at that moment. Laura still wore the same dark green traveling outfit but not the matching hat. The light from the lanterns shone on her fair hair, making it glow like the sun, Preacher thought.

She spotted him in the corner and smiled, and he

thought she would have come over to say hello if Corliss hadn't intercepted her and her brother and practically dragged them over to the counter in the rear of the room. Deborah and Jerome were there, and all three of the Harts seemed to enjoy the conversation they carried on with the Mallorys. It had been a while since anybody except rough frontiersmen had visited here. Laura and Clyde were even better than fellow Easterners . . . they were *English,* Preacher thought as he chuckled to himself.

After a while, though, Laura extricated herself and came over to the corner where Preacher sat. He saw her heading in his direction, and for a second he felt the impulse to cut and run. That wouldn't look good, though, so he stayed where he was, setting the jug aside and rising to his feet to greet her as she came up to him.

"Howdy, ma'am," he said gravely. "How are you this evenin'?"

"I'm fine, Preacher," Laura replied. She nodded toward the barrel chair where he'd been sitting. "Please, don't inconvenience yourself on my account. Have a seat."

Instead, Preacher suggested, "Why don't you take the chair, Miss Mallory? You'll be more comfortable."

"Then where will you sit?"

"I'll just pull up this here keg," he said. It was more of a barrel and was filled with something heavy, but Preacher wrestled it over into place anyway.

"Preacher, I get the distinct feeling that you've been avoiding me this afternoon," Laura said with an accusing look on her face. "Did I do something to offend or insult you?"

That was the farthest thing from the truth. The reason he'd been steering clear of her was because he didn't want to try to talk to her and start stumbling over his words like a lovestruck youngster. He was way too old for that.

"Why, no, ma'am, Miss Laura, not at all. I've just been a mite busy, that's all. I had to get some supplies together for when I leave tomorrow."

She smiled. "I'm glad you decided to stay an extra night anyway. That gives me a chance to get to know you a little better."

Preacher wasn't sure why a lady like her would even want to know him at all, but he didn't say that. Instead, he sort of sat there like a bump on a log until Laura leaned toward him and spoke again.

"Mr. Hart tells me that someone tried to kill you by starting an avalanche. How perfectly dreadful."

"Well, it ain't like it was the first time," Preacher said without thinking. "A couple o' varmints tried to bushwhack me the day before that."

"Is life on the frontier always so . . . violent and unpredictable?"

"It can be," he said. "You got wild animals and wild Indians both out here, and some mighty bad weather at times, and even some bad men."

"Highwaymen, you mean? Brigands?"

"Cutthroats and murderers, sure enough," he told her. "Fellas who'll steal your pelts and kill you without even blinkin' to boot. I ain't tryin' to scare you, ma'am, but it'd be mighty smart o' you to stay right close to the tradin' post while you're out here."

"I assure you, that's exactly what I intend to do," she said. "But you can't do that, can you? You have your traps to check."

"That's right. I don't worry overmuch, though. I can take care o' myself, and I'm in the habit o' bein' careful."

"I hope you will be very careful." She smiled warmly at him. "I hope to see you again whenever you come back to the settlement."

Preacher wasn't sure how to respond to that, so he just said, "Yes'm. I'd like that, too."

Several men were sitting at a rough-hewn table closer to the front of the room. Preacher had noticed them earlier, but since he had seen them around the settlement on previous visits and they weren't exactly strangers, he didn't pay much attention to them. He didn't figure they were part of the mysterious bunch trying to kill him.

A big towheaded fella named Sanderson was the leader of the bunch. With him were a short, stocky man who sported a bristly mustache, a white-bearded, long-haired old-timer, and a couple of heavy-faced gents who looked like Dutchmen. Preacher didn't know their names, but he knew where they ran their trap lines and avoided them. A man didn't poach on another fella's territory unless it was by accident.

Now, as Preacher sat there and tried to think up something else to say to Laura Mallory, the old-timer pulled out a fiddle and began to play, sawing the bow across the strings with more energy and enthusiasm than talent. The raucous notes filled the trading post and made everyone look around.

Laura smiled and clapped her hands together

softly. "Music!" she exclaimed. "Do you know how long it's been since I heard any music, Preacher?"

"No, ma'am, but I'd say you're bein' a mite generous to call that music. Sounds more to me like somebody tied two cats' tails together and dropped 'em on either side of a fence."

"Oh, it does not," she said with a merry laugh. "I think it sounds just fine. Fine enough, in fact, that I'd like to dance." She stood up and held out a hand to him. "Would you be kind enough as to dance with me, good sir?"

Preacher's eyes widened in surprise. He had done some dancing before—there was always a lot of celebratin' that went on at a Rendezvous, including stomping around in rough approximations of the sort of dances that folks did back East—but he had never done anything like that with a woman as beautiful as Laura Mallory in his arms.

"Please, Preacher," she said when he hesitated. "It would almost make me feel like I was back home again."

No way in hell could he turn down a plea like that. He stood up, took hold of her hand—being careful not to squeeze it too hard—and said, "It'd be a plumb honor, ma'am."

She moved closer to him. "If you're going to take me in your arms and whirl me around the floor," she said, "I think you should stop calling me ma'am and just call me Laura."

Preacher swallowed hard. "All right, ma'am. I'll try."

He held her left hand with his right and slipped his left arm around her waist, being careful not to hold her too close. She wasn't much closer than arm's length, in fact. She rested her right hand on his shoulder, and he seemed to feel the warmth of her touch through his buckskin shirt. He definitely felt it in the hand he grasped. Their fingers twined together intimately. He took a deep breath—which reminded him that, Lord, she smelled good!—and began moving his feet in a rough waltz.

Whatever you do, he told himself, don't stomp on her toes.

There wasn't much room for dancing, but they made a fair job of it. Laura followed his steps, although Preacher sensed that she was holding back and could probably dance a whole heap better than he could. The Dutchmen had started clapping in time with the old fiddle player, and as Preacher and Laura turned in the waltz, he saw that everybody in the trading post was watching them. That sort of scrutiny made him uncomfortable, but he tried to ignore it.

Clyde Mallory's eyes had narrowed as he looked on while his sister and Preacher danced, and Preacher wondered if he disapproved. He didn't want to get on Mallory's bad side, but he had to admit that he was enjoying this dance with Laura.

The big trapper called Sanderson stood up and shuffled toward them, an intent look on his face. Preacher saw him coming and wondered what the man wanted.

It didn't take him long to find out.

Sanderson reached out and tapped Preacher roughly on the shoulder. "I'm cuttin' in on this dance, Preacher," he declared as Preacher and Laura came to a stop in their waltz. "That's my Uncle Dan providin' the music, so I reckon it's only fair that I get to dance with the lady, too."

Preacher hadn't known that the old-timer was Sanderson's uncle, and he didn't much care either. He didn't want to let go of Laura. However, it was her decision, so Preacher told her, "Whatever you want to do, ma'am."

She smiled at Sanderson and said, "I'm sorry, sir, but I'm dancing with Preacher right now. Perhaps another time."

Sanderson wasn't taking no for an answer. He said, "The hell with that," and reached out to take hold of Laura's arm. He pulled her away from Preacher. The fiddle playing came to an abrupt halt with a screech of the bow across the strings.

Preacher let go of Laura because he didn't want her to get hurt by being tugged back and forth between him and Sanderson. But that didn't mean he was giving in. He growled, "Let go o' the lady, Sanderson . . . *right now.*"

"She's dancin' with me now," Sanderson said. "Back off, Preacher."

With that, he jerked Laura against him and held her so tightly that she gasped.

"Play that fiddle, Uncle Dan!" Sanderson ordered.

The bow wailed on the strings, but only for a second. Preacher reached out, grabbed Sanderson's shoulder, hauled the man around, and crashed a fist into the middle of his face. Blood spurted as Sanderson's nose pulped under the blow's impact.

Laura let out a scream as Sanderson staggered away, crimson welling over the bottom half of his face. He caught himself, glared at Preacher, and launched himself forward with a furious roar. He tackled Preacher and both men went down, crashing into chairs and barrels.

Sanderson came flying backward as Preacher hit him again. Preacher scrambled to his feet just as the short man who'd been sitting at the table with Sanderson and the others yelled, "Get 'im!"

The two big Dutchmen lumbered toward Preacher, fists clenched. Their eagerness for a fight brought animation to their usually stolid faces. The little man was right behind them, egging them on. And Sanderson was climbing back up, his bloody face twisted by lines of rage.

Looked like the odds were going to be three or four to one, Preacher thought. He had faced worse. He stood there grinning and lifted one hand, crooking it mockingly.

"If you figure on whuppin' me, boys, then come ahead," he invited. "It's your job, and you've got it to do."

"Damn right we'll do it," Sanderson rasped. "You think you're the big he-wolf around here, but we're gonna whip you seven ways from Sunday!"

"You mean after you get through talkin' me to death?"

The four men came toward Preacher slowly now, closing in on him. Laura Mallory had fled to the counter, where Deborah Hart had her arms around her, trying to comfort her. Corliss and Jerome watched the confrontation, but didn't make a move to interfere. As the proprietors of this trading post, they had to stay neutral in the occasional brawl. Preacher understood that, even though the cousins owed a considerable debt to him for getting them here alive.

He didn't want any help. He always fought his own battles, and he wasn't inclined to change that now.

"Wait!"

The sharp-voiced command came from Clyde Mallory. The Englishman strode forward, putting himself between Preacher and the four men. He ignored his sister's plea to be careful and planted himself there with his fists on his hips.

"I say, this is hardly fair. You outnumber this man by four to one."

"Stay out of it, mister," Sanderson warned. "It ain't none o' your business."

"On the contrary," Mallory said, "that was my sister you were mauling, sir. It's very much my affair. An affair of honor."

And with that, he reached up and slapped Sanderson across the face.

Chapter 8

For a moment Sanderson was too stunned to do anything except stare at Clyde Mallory, the same thing that everybody else in the trading post was doing.

Then he howled, "What the hell did you do *that* for?"

Preacher had been around enough Englishers and highfalutin' Easterners to know the answer to that question. Mallory had just challenged Sanderson to a duel.

"I told you, this is an affair of honor," Mallory said. "As such, we shall settle it like gentlemen."

Sanderson sneered. "That's where you're wrong, mister. I ain't no gentleman."

And as if to prove it, he slugged Mallory in the jaw.

"Clyde!" Laura cried in horror as the unexpected punch drove her brother backward. Mallory would have fallen if Preacher hadn't been there to catch him. Laura started forward, but Deborah held her back.

"Don't worry," Deborah told her. "Preacher will take care of this."

Laura turned to look at her. "How do you know?"

"Because he always does."

Preacher had his arms hooked under Mallory's arms, holding him up as Mallory shook his head groggily. "I say," the Englishman mumbled, "wha . . . what happened?"

"Sanderson walloped you a good one," Preacher told him.

"But . . . but I challenged him to a duel. I told him it was an affair of honor . . ."

"Yeah, but he ain't got any."

"In that case . . ." Mallory straightened, getting his legs back solidly underneath him and squaring his shoulders. "I suppose there's no choice except to settle this with fisticuffs."

"Are we gonna fight or not?" Sanderson shouted.

Mallory put up his fists and cocked his arms in a boxing stance. "Come ahead, you insufferable ruffian."

"Clyde, you don't have to get mixed up in this," Preacher warned.

Mallory turned to look at him. "On the contrary, Preacher, I already—"

Sanderson lunged at him, swinging wildly. The other three men rushed Preacher.

Chaos ensued.

Mallory seemed to have recovered from the punch. He ducked under Sanderson's roundhouse swings and then straightened to pepper the trapper in the face with a series of short, sharp blows. None of the Englishman's punches traveled very far, but they landed with stinging force. Sanderson's head rocked back under the impact.

Meanwhile, the two Dutchmen grabbed Preacher's

arms and pulled him backward, lifting his feet off the floor so that his back slammed into the trading post's log wall. They pinned him there and the short man moved in, grinning as he prepared to hammer his fists into Preacher's belly.

He never got the chance. Since the Dutchmen were holding him up anyway, Preacher drew his knees up and then straightened his legs. His heels crashed into the chest of the man in front of him. The fella sailed backward and landed on a table that collapsed under him as its legs splintered.

Preacher heaved with both arms. There was an incredible amount of strength in his seemingly lean frame. The two Dutchmen blundered into each other and bumped heads pretty hard. That made them let go of Preacher, who seized the opportunity to grab each of them by the back of the neck. He rammed their heads together even harder.

Unfortunately, their skulls seemed to be made of solid rock. One of them wrapped his arms around Preacher in a bear hug and started spinning him around.

Meanwhile, Sanderson got lucky. One of his flailing punches clipped Mallory on the chin and knocked the Englishman back a step, interrupting the series of jabs that had made Sanderson's face even bloodier. Sanderson made the most of his chance and hooked a hard left into Mallory's brisket. Mallory staggered backward and gasped for breath as his face turned gray.

Sanderson closed in, fists cocked to smash the momentarily defenseless Englishman into oblivion. But at that moment, a dizzy Preacher, being whirled around by the Dutchman, saw what was about to happen and kicked as high as he could at the precise second when his opponent swung him past Sanderson. Preacher's foot hit Sanderson in the back of the head and sent him pitching forward. Mallory twisted away so that Sanderson ran head-on into the wall instead.

The other Dutchman was yelling something in his guttural lingo. The one holding Preacher stopped spinning, but Preacher's head didn't. The room tilted crazily, and he seemed to see three men coming at him, fists poised. He knew there was only one of them, but he ducked all three punches anyway, hoping the real one would miss him.

It did, grazing his ear but doing no real damage, at least to Preacher. The same couldn't be said of the man holding him. He caught the blow from his cousin or brother or whatever he was full in the face. His knees unhinged, and he let go of Preacher as he folded up on the puncheon floor.

That left Preacher free but still dizzy. He swayed backward just as the remaining Dutchman launched an uppercut. The punch might have taken Preacher's head off if it had landed, but instead, it whizzed harmlessly past his nose.

Before the man could try again, Clyde Mallory brought his clubbed hands down on the back of the Dutchman's neck. The man slumped to one knee. Mallory hit him again the same way, but still the Dutchman didn't go all the way down. He moved his shoulders like he was shaking off a troublesome insect and started to lumber to his feet again.

As the Dutchman came upright, Preacher said,

"Hey!" His head had finally settled down a mite, and he had his feet under him now as he pivoted slightly at the waist and threw a punch. It smashed into the Dutchman's jaw like a pile driver, and that finally did the trick. The big man's eyes rolled up in their sockets, and he toppled over like a felled tree crashing to earth in the forest.

That left Preacher and Mallory facing each other. Both men were breathing hard. Their clothes were disheveled, and their faces bore the marks of battle.

But as their eyes met they grinned, each feeling the bond that develops almost instantly between men who have shared the rigors of combat.

"Good . . . fight," Preacher panted.

"Splendid!" Mallory managed to gasp. He held out his right hand. "Shake!"

They shook, each man wincing a little because their hands were sore from punching their enemies.

Groans came from the other men, and as Preacher and Mallory turned they saw that Sanderson, the short man who had wrecked the table when he landed on it, and the first Dutchman were struggling to get to their feet again.

"This clash appears not to . . . be over . . . after all," Mallory said.

"Then we'll just have to . . . whup 'em again," Preacher said.

A shot blasted out just as Sanderson and his two allies made it to their feet. The roar was so loud that it froze everybody. A voice said, "Pete, that's enough, consarn your stubborn hide!"

The old-timer whose fiddle-playing had set off the brawl indirectly—Uncle Dan, Sanderson had called him—strode forward. He had set the fiddle aside and now his gnarled hands clasped a brace of pistols instead. Smoke curled from the barrel of the weapon he had fired into the ceiling.

"Damn it, Uncle Dan, stay outta this!" Sanderson said. "You seen with your own eyes what these fellas did!"

"Durned tootin' I seen it. I seen two men whup the hell outta four, and pretty handy they was about it, too! And you started the fight by disrespectin' that English gal to boot. I know damned well your ma didn't raise you to behave like that 'cause she was my sister." The old man drew a deep breath and blew it out in a gusty sigh, fluttering the long white beard. "Reckon this is the first time I've been glad that she's passed on, God rest her soul. She don't ever have to know that you act like a total jackass when you been drinkin', boy . . . that is, unless she's lookin' down from heaven and cluckin' her tongue over your antics right now!"

Sanderson couldn't stop himself from glancing toward the ceiling, as if worrying that his dear, departed mother could peer right through it from whatever heavenly mansion she occupied. He looked down again, all the way to the floor this time, and shuffled his feet.

"Aw, hell, Uncle Dan—"

"Don't aw-hell me. You been around here long enough to know what a durned fool stunt it was to go up agin Preacher. Now go over there and shake the hands o' those men and tell 'em they fought a good fight."

"I ain't a-gonna—"

Uncle Dan drew himself up to his full height, which still left him a good foot and a half shorter than his nephew. "Am *I* gonna have to whup you, too, to make you behave like a decent human bein'?"

Sanderson muttered and cussed and looked around, but he couldn't find any way out. Preacher saw that, and managed not to grin at the man's dilemma. Finally, Sanderson came over to him and Mallory and stuck out his paw.

"That was a good fight," he said with a curt nod. To Mallory, he added, "Mister, I'm sorry for disrespectin' your sister." He glanced back at Uncle Dan. "My ma taught me better."

Mallory shook hands with him. "Apology accepted, old man . . . that is, if my sister agrees."

"Of course, Clyde," Laura said quickly, obviously eager to get the trouble over with. "I'm sure this gentleman meant no harm."

He turned to look at her. "I surely didn't, ma'am. I was just, uh, overcome by your beauty. That an' the fact that it's been a hell of a long time since I danced with a white woman."

Laura blushed in the lamplight, which just made her prettier.

Sanderson shook hands with Preacher, too, and said with a hint of nervousness in his voice, "No hard feelin's?"

"No hard feelin's," Preacher agreed. Sanderson had been forced into the apologies, but Preacher sensed that he was mostly sincere. Like a lot of men who had come to these mountains, Sanderson was rough around the edges but basically a decent sort.

Sanderson gestured to the other men who had joined

in the fight and went on. "Same goes for Dennison and the Van Goort boys, I hope? Denny's like me . . . he don't think too straight sometimes when he's been drinkin'."

"That's the gospel truth, Preacher," Dennison agreed with a nod.

"And the Van Goorts, they don't speak much but that Dutchy talk o' theirs, so I ain't sure they even really knew what was goin' on."

Preacher nodded to the Dutchmen and said, "No hard feelin's, boys."

They returned the nod and smiled and said, "Yah, yah," which Preacher took to mean they were content to call a truce, too.

Corliss came forward and said, "All right, fellas, it's all over now . . . right?"

"Yeah," Sanderson said.

Uncle Dan added, "And since it was our fault that table got busted up, we'll pay for it."

For a second, Sanderson looked like he wanted to argue about that, but then he nodded and sighed. "Yeah, that's right, Mr. Hart. We'll pay for it."

Corliss clapped a hand on his shoulder. "Don't worry too much about it, Pete. We'll work out an arrangement the next time you bring in a load of pelts and get square that way."

"Sure, that'd be fine." Sanderson looked relieved that no money would be coming out of his pocket right now, but if Preacher knew Corliss Hart, and especially Jerome Hart, he suspected that the cousins would come out ahead in the long run on this deal.

Uncle Dan shepherded his charges back to their table. Preacher thought there probably wouldn't be any more fiddle-playing tonight, and he was right. The men left the trading post shortly after that.

Preacher sat down at another table with Laura and Mallory. The Englishman ran his fingers through his sandy hair, felt his jaw, and smiled ruefully.

"That big fellow could certainly hit. His fist felt a bit like the kick of a mule."

"You've been kicked by a mule?" Preacher asked.

"Indeed, while I was posted in India. All armies, I suspect, use mules for transport, and at times they can be recalcitrant."

"Not to mention downright ornery."

"Yes, that, too," Mallory agreed with a chuckle.

"You two should be ashamed of yourselves, brawling like that," Laura scolded. "You're acting now almost as if you enjoyed it."

"It *was* a rather exhilarating few minutes, wasn't it, Preacher?"

"It was," Preacher said.

"And we were merely defending you, my dear," Mallory pointed out to Laura.

"Yes, but I didn't ask you to . . . Never mind. I can see that this is an argument I stand little or no chance of winning, so I'll just say that I'm glad you're both all right." She looked back and forth between the two men. "You *are* all right, aren't you?"

"A bit battered and bruised, but no real damage, eh?"

Preacher nodded. "That's about the size of it."

Corliss came over with the jug Preacher had been drinking from earlier. "Lucky this didn't get busted in all the commotion. I assume you still want the rest of it, Preacher?"

"I sure do." Preacher took the jug and held it out toward Mallory. "Have a drink?"

"Don't mind if I do." The Englishman took the jug and tilted it to his mouth with the same sort of expertise that the mountain men demonstrated. The fiery liquor gurgled into his mouth and down his throat. Preacher watched the muscles working as Mallory swallowed. Mallory put away a hefty slug before he lowered the jug, said, "Ah," and wiped the back of his other hand across his mouth. "Splendid," he said as he pushed the jug back across the table to Preacher.

"You know, Clyde," Preacher drawled. "I may have misjudged you a mite."

"You don't know the half of it, my friend," Mallory said, and then hiccupped.

Laura just rolled her eyes, muttered something about men being just one step above the beasts of the fields, and laughed softly in spite of herself.

Chapter 9

As tempting as it was to prolong his stay at the trading post, Preacher headed for the high country the next morning. He had traps to check, and no matter how much he enjoyed the company of Laura Mallory, he was still a solitary man at heart. No woman was going to change that.

He felt a definite pang, though, as he looked back and saw her standing beside one of her brother's wagons. He had found her there a short time earlier and said his good-byes to her.

"Do be careful, Preacher," she had told him with heartfelt sincerity. "I would like to spend more time with you the next time you return to the trading post."

"I'd like that, too," he'd said. "I'd like it a whole heap."

For him, that was being pretty demonstrative, and the slight smile on Laura's face told him that she understood that. For a second, he'd gotten the feeling that she was going to come up on her tiptoes and brush a kiss across his grizzled cheek, but she didn't. She just shook hands with him instead, and then he mounted up and rode away, leading his new packhorse.

Now, as he glanced back, a couple of hundred yards away Laura lifted her hand and waved. Preacher returned the wave, then resolutely turned his gaze toward the mountains again.

The drumming of hoofbeats caused him to rein Horse to a stop and look around again. Clyde Mallory galloped after him, demonstrating considerable skill at riding. He slowed his horse as he came up to Preacher.

"Somethin' I can do for you, Clyde?" Preacher asked. He considered the Englishman a friend now, after they had battled side by side in the brawl the night before. They had shaken hands and said goodbye earlier this morning, too, before Preacher went to find Laura.

"Actually, there is," Mallory replied. "I've come to offer you a job."

Preacher's shaggy eyebrows rose in surprise. "I've got a job," he said. "I trap beaver and sell the pelts to the Harts."

Mallory waved a hand. "Oh, I'm aware of that, of course. But the talk around the trading post is that you've also guided a number of wagon trains out here."

"A few is more like it," Preacher said with a shrug.

"I'd like for you to take charge of my wagons. I need a good man to take them back to St. Louis and be in charge of making the return trip with a fresh load of freight."

Preacher frowned. "I figured you'd be doin' that yourself."

"That was the plan," Mallory agreed, "but I'm having second thoughts about leaving Laura here. Even if she stays close to the settlement, there could be danger."

"Sure there could," Preacher said. "Folks can run into trouble wherever they are. But you could always take her back to St. Louis with you."

"Which would also be hazardous. Indians might be more likely to attack the wagons than they would the settlement."

Seemed to Preacher like Mallory should have thought of all this before he ever brought Laura out here in the first place. But it wouldn't serve any purpose to point that out now, so Preacher kept the thought to himself.

Instead, he said, "You're right. You want me to take over the wagons so you can stay here with your sister and make sure she's safe?"

"Exactly! Will you consider it?"

Preacher didn't have to think about it for very long. He never had liked being saddled with the responsibility for other folks, even though he seemed to keep getting roped into situations like that. That was why he lived the isolated life that he did. And the settlement was plenty big for him to visit now and then; he had no desire to venture back to smelly, crowded St. Louis just yet.

"Sorry, Clyde," he said, shaking his head. "I don't reckon I'd be interested. But I'm obliged to you for makin' the offer. Reckon you wouldn't have if you didn't trust me."

A look of disappointment appeared on Mallory's ruddy face. "I certainly do trust you, Preacher. Are you sure I can't persuade you—"

He stopped as Preacher shook his head again. With a rueful smile on his face, the Englishman went on. "Ah, well, I tried."

"You might find somebody else at the tradin' post who'd be interested in the job," Preacher suggested.

It was Mallory's turn to shake his head. "There's no one else I'd offer it to. Laura and I will simply have to figure out the best way to proceed and go on from there."

"Sorry," Preacher said again.

"Think nothing of it, my friend. A man must follow his own drummer, you know. Sometimes, we have little or no choice in the roles we play in this production we call life."

"I reckon," Preacher said.

He lifted a hand in farewell as Mallory turned and headed back toward the settlement. After a moment, Preacher heeled Horse into motion again. Dog bounded ahead as Preacher rode toward the mountains.

Colin Fairfax paced back and forth across the camp, impatience and anger growing inside him. Five of the scouts he had sent out several days earlier to search for Preacher had failed to return, and he was growing worried that something had happened to them.

He didn't care that much about the men themselves, of course, but when the time came for him to confront

Preacher at last, he wanted the odds to be on his side as much as possible. Not only that, but he didn't want Preacher to have any idea that someone was after him until the proper time came. If those fools had attempted to kill Preacher and failed, that would certainly serve as a warning to the mountain man.

Because of that, Fairfax had sent out men to search for the missing scouts, and he expected them to report back at any time now.

His frustration grew until one of the sentries came into camp to tell him, "A couple o' riders comin' in, Mr. Fairfax. Looks like Harbin and Cranmore."

"It's damned well about time," Fairfax snapped. He walked to the edge of camp with the guard and watched the two men on horseback working their way down the side of a long hill toward them.

As they came closer, Fairfax realized the sentry was right. The two men were Harbin and Cranmore, the ones he had sent out to search for the missing men. As they rode up and reined in, Fairfax snapped, "Well?"

They didn't have to ask what Fairfax wanted to know. Harbin took off the coonskin cap he wore and wiped sweat off his forehead. "No sign o' Jubal or Wilcox," he said.

"What about Garroway, Hilliard, and Kent?"

"We found their bodies," Harbin said.

Fairfax stared at him for a moment, then exploded, "Son of a bitch! He killed them! They went after him despite my orders, and he killed them."

"You're talkin' about Preacher?"

"Of course I'm talking about Preacher! Who else would I be talking about?" Fairfax took off his beaver hat and ran his other hand over his bald scalp as he struggled to bring his anger under control. Ever since Schuyler's death and his own long ordeal in escaping the wilderness, Fairfax's emotions had been so raw, he might fly into hysterics if he didn't keep them tamped down. He took a deep breath and asked, "What about Preacher? Did you see any sign of him?"

"Nary a one, in fact." Harbin scratched his jaw and frowned in puzzlement. "Fact o' the matter is, if you asked me I'd say it looked like those fellas killed each other."

"Killed each other? That's insane."

Cranmore spoke up for the first time. "Not if you knew Hilliard," he said. "He flew off the handle mighty easy, especially if he'd been drinkin'. Garroway was almost as bad. And there was a busted jug there where they were camped. They got in some sort o' ruckus, somebody pulled a pistol and one o' the others grabbed a knife . . ." Cranmore shrugged. "'Fore you know it, they was all either dead or dyin'."

Fairfax put his hat back on. "And it didn't look like Preacher killed them?"

"Nope," Harbin said with a shake of his head. "I don't think Preacher was anywhere around."

"But you didn't find Wilcox or Jubal?"

"Not hide nor hair of 'em."

"So Preacher could have killed *them.*"

Fairfax saw the glance that Harbin and Cranmore exchanged. He knew they thought he was insane for automatically blaming Preacher for anything that happened, especially anything bad. Fairfax had overheard enough comments he wasn't supposed to hear to know that the feeling was prevalent among the men Beaumont had sent with him.

He didn't care. They didn't know Preacher. They didn't know how dangerous the mountain man really was.

"I suppose he could have," Harbin said after a moment. "No way of knowin' either way."

Fairfax nodded curtly, turned on his heel, and stalked back to the center of camp without saying anything else. He looked around at the men, who were cleaning their weapons or tending to their horses or playing cards. He raised his voice and said, "Listen to me, everyone!"

When he had their attention, he went on. "Tomorrow we're going to resume the search for Preacher. But we're not going to split our forces again. We'll all search together until we find him and dispose of him."

That announcement brought frowns from several of the men. One of them said, "But there's two dozen of us, Boss. It's hard for that many men to move around without makin' a hell of a lot of racket."

"That may well be true," Fairfax said, "but I'm not going to allow Preacher to whittle us down to nothing. If we're spread out, he'll pick us off by twos and threes until we're all dead. At least if we're together when we find him, we'll have a chance."

Harbin and Cranmore had followed him in from the edge of camp, leading their horses. Cranmore said, "But, Boss, you're talkin' about *one man*."

"No." Fairfax shook his head. "I'm talking about Preacher."

Let them think he was mad. They would see for themselves that he wasn't . . .

When they finally met Preacher.

Preacher rode through South Pass and on into the thickly wooded mountain fastnesses with their cold, swift-flowing streams where the beavers were so plentiful. He spent a couple of days riding a familiar route and checking his traps. When he had collected half a dozen of the critters, he stopped at one of his regular camping spots, skinned the beavers, scraped the insides of the hides, and staked out the pelts to dry. He would stay here for a day or so, letting Horse rest and waiting for the pelts to dry enough so he could roll them up and stow them on the packhorse.

He had stayed busy enough that he didn't think too much about Laura Mallory, but the image of her beautiful face stayed in the back of his mind anyway. Any time he had a few free moments, memories of the time he had spent with her at the trading post came back strongly, reminding him of how much he had enjoyed her company and how strongly he had been drawn to her.

Not since Jennie had he given any thought to marrying someday. He might have married Jennie if he'd ever had the chance. The fact that she was a whore and had known hundreds of men besides him didn't really matter. Preacher was the only one who had ever known her heart.

But that was a long time ago, and after she'd died, he had figured there would never be anybody else he wanted to get hitched to.

Now, though, maybe that had changed, he mused as he sat next to a creek with his back propped against the rough bark of a pine tree and smoked a pipe. He knew it was mighty early to even be thinking about marryin' Laura Mallory. Shoot, he had only known her a few days. And she was English as well, a lady through and through, even if she didn't carry the actual title like some Englishwomen did.

Horse was grazing peacefully on the creek bank a few yards away. Dog dozed with his chin resting on his paws in the shade of the same tree. Preacher looked over at the big cur and said, "Dog, I reckon I've gone plumb loco. No way in hell could I ask a lady like Laura to marry a dirty, smelly, ol' varmint like me . . . is there?"

Dog didn't open his eyes, but he flicked one ear and sighed, as if to wonder why in the world Preacher was asking such a question of him.

The next second, however, Dog's head came up and his eyes snapped open. Preacher knew that Dog had smelled something he didn't like even before a menacing growl rumbled deep in the big cur's throat. Horse lifted his head as well and pricked his ears, standing stock-still now.

Preacher knew those warning signs . . . knew them all too well, in fact. He leaned over to pick up the long-barreled flintlock rifle lying on the ground nearby.

As he moved, something hummed past his ear like a giant insect and smacked into the tree trunk. Pine bark splinters stung Preacher's cheek as they exploded outward from the impact of a rifle ball. He snatched up his own rifle and rolled across the ground, trying to get behind one of the other trees before whoever had just tried to kill him reloaded and drew another bead on him.

That might have worked . . . if the peace and quiet of the day hadn't been suddenly shattered by the roaring reports of a dozen or more rifles.

Chapter 10

Preacher hugged the ground as the lead balls buzzed through the air over his head like a swarm of angry bees. "Dog!" he roared. "Horse! Get out of here!"

The two animals took off running. Horse wasn't wearing a saddle or bridle, so he looked like a wild mustang as he dashed through the trees. Dog halted after a short distance, looked around, and whined.

"Go!" Preacher shouted at the big cur. He winced as one of the shots came close enough to kick some dirt into his eyes.

This was gettin' downright annoyin', he thought as he blinked his vision clear again.

A ball burned across the back of his right leg. He knew he couldn't stay where he was. He was damned lucky they hadn't ventilated him already. He was going to have to risk getting up. Either that, or lay there and wait for the sons of bitches to start aiming better.

With a powerful lunge, he was up and running. He darted between a couple of trees. The ground dropped away from him into a gully. He tried to maintain his balance as he slid down the side of it, but he was moving too fast to do it. He fell, tumbling down the slope and scattering the pine needles that carpeted it.

Of course, falling in the gully was probably the best thing that could have happened, he realized as he came to a stop at the bottom of it. It gave him some cover. The men who were trying to kill him couldn't hit him down there.

But he couldn't fight back either, and that was like a big rock stuck in his craw.

He lay there for a moment, catching his breath and thinking about what had just happened. The back of his leg hurt where the rifle ball had scraped across it, tearing his buckskins, but he didn't let himself think about that. His instincts told him that the wound was painful but not serious.

The tree under which he'd been resting and thinking was only a few yards from a stream, and on the other side of that stream were thick woods. The men who'd tried to kill him had snuck up over there through those trees. He should have heard them, he thought bitterly. No matter how good they were, he should have heard them.

And he would have if he hadn't been so preoccupied with thoughts of Laura Mallory, he told himself. Pondering marriage to the Englishwoman had damned near gotten him killed.

It wasn't Laura's fault he'd been mooning over her. He'd known better than to let his guard down. It had only been a few days since two attempts had been made on his life. He should have been ready for the next ambush.

If he hadn't leaned over when he did, he'd be dead now. There had been just one shot at first, as if the man who had fired had told his companions to hold off.

He's mine, Preacher could imagine the man saying. *I'm going to kill the bastard.*

Only he hadn't. He had missed, and that had served as the signal for the other men with him to open fire. Preacher had escaped death by a whisker.

And that whisker might get shaved off any minute now, because he could hear shouts coming closer.

"He went this way, I tell you!"

"No, I saw him over here!"

"Be careful!" There was something vaguely familiar about that voice, but Preacher couldn't place it. "You don't know what he's capable of!"

The man sounded like he had run into Preacher before. Preacher had made plenty of enemies during his adventurous life, but most of them were dead.

He could worry about the man's identity later, he decided. Right now, the important thing was to keep from winding up dead himself.

His enemies had crossed the creek, and were now spreading out through the trees on this side of the stream. Preacher had heard their feet splash through the water, and now he could track their movements by the racket they made. Whoever they were, they weren't experienced frontiersmen. They couldn't move around quietly, and they weren't very good rifle shots either, or else he'd be a sieve by now.

One of them was getting close. Preacher heard the man moving along the edge of the gully above him. He crawled upward, using some brush for cover, until he was within arm's length of the edge. He placed his rifle beside him and reached down to his waist to draw the heavy-bladed hunting knife.

When the hunter was right above him, Preacher moved with blinding speed. He lunged up, grabbed the man's shirt, and jerked him off his feet. The man fell and started sliding down the slope into the gully. He opened his mouth to let out a yell, but before any sound could emerge, Preacher landed on top of him and his left hand clamped over the man's mouth. His right drove the knife into the man's body. By the time they came to a stop at the bottom of the gully, the hunter was dead with Preacher's cold steel buried in his heart.

Preacher pushed himself up and studied the man's pain-twisted face for a second. Just as he expected, the fella was a stranger, just like the ones who had tried to kill him a few days earlier. However, the familiar voice he had heard giving orders told him that not everyone involved was a stranger. Somebody had a grudge against him.

Well, the odds had been cut down by one anyway, he thought with a glance at the dead man.

Preacher retrieved his rifle and began making his way along the gully, moving as stealthily as an Indian. A wind sprang up and soughed through the branches of the pines, making them rustle and covering up any small sounds he might make.

Unfortunately, it also kept him from hearing all the noises the men were making as they searched for him. He could still hear some of them blundering around, but he worried that others might be moving a little more quietly.

That proved to be the case as a man somewhere

nearby suddenly called, "Hey, maybe he's in this gully over here! I'll take a look!"

With that, the man stepped over the edge and slid down the slope maybe ten feet in front of Preacher.

Preacher still had the bloody knife in his right hand. The man barely had time to register the mountain man's presence and try to lift his rifle, before the knife left Preacher's hand and flashed across the intervening distance. It was thrown so hard that the razor-sharp blade went all the way through the man's throat and stuck out a couple of inches from the back of his neck. He staggered against the side of the gully, and made choking sounds as he dropped his gun and pawed at the knife's handle, finally ripping it free. That was a mistake. Blood fountained from the wound.

Not that it really mattered. The varmint was a dead man either way. He dropped to his knees and then pitched forward on his face.

Preacher hurried to the man's side. He had fallen on the knife. Preacher rolled him onto his back and picked up the weapon, then wiped the blade clean on the corpse's shirt. Two down, he thought grimly . . . but Lord knows how many there were left.

A rifle roared somewhere behind him. The ball clipped a branch from one of the bushes that grew out of the gully wall only a couple of feet from Preacher's head. Preacher slid the knife back into its sheath as he whirled around. His right hand closed around the rifle's stock as he brought it smoothly to his shoulder and peered over the long barrel. He saw a man about thirty feet away frantically trying to reload. The man glanced up, and then his eyes widened in horror as he saw Preacher squinting and drawing a bead on him.

Preacher fired. The man's head snapped back as the ball caught him in the forehead and bored on into his brain. He fell against the side of the gully and slid down it like a puppet with its strings cut.

For half a second before pressing the trigger, Preacher had considered running over there and killing the man with his hands, rather than risking the sound of a shot.

But even if he had done that, he couldn't have gotten there in time to keep the fella from shouting for help from his friends. This way, there was at least a chance that the others would think one of them had fired the shot.

"Did you get him? Did you get the bastard?"

The shouted question came from at least fifty yards away. Roughening his voice, Preacher called a reply. "Naw, I thought it was him, but it was just a damn badger!"

"Be careful! He's around here somewhere! He has to be!"

That was the fella who knew him. Preacher wished he could figure out who the voice belonged to.

He didn't let the fact that he had killed three of his enemies make him overconfident. In listening to them search for him, he had revised his estimate of their numbers upward. There were at least twenty of them, maybe more. His luck wouldn't stay with him forever. Sooner or later, those odds would catch up to him.

The thing to do was to slip out of this trap and live to

kill more of them later. To that end, he continued making his way along the gully in close to absolute silence.

As the minutes passed, the sound of the voices calling back and forth grew fainter. He was leaving the hunters behind, slowly but surely. To go with all their other failings, they weren't very good trackers either.

Only one thing made sense, Preacher decided as he continued making his way up the side of the mountain that loomed above him. Somebody with a grudge against him had hired a gang of killers back east somewhere—St. Louis, more than likely, but they could have come from someplace else—and come out here looking for him. They had planned on hunting him down like a dog.

They had discovered today, though, that this dog had teeth, just like on the other occasions when they had come after him. He had no doubt the same bunch was responsible for the earlier attempts on his life.

What the motive could be, he had no idea. Right now, it was enough to know that somebody hated him enough, wanted him dead badly enough, to go to so much trouble. He wouldn't underestimate them in the future, not that he had so far.

He wouldn't just stand around and give them an easy target either. From now on, he would be on the move, always on the alert for trouble. He'd been getting soft, he told himself. Thinkin' too much about beautiful gals and gettin' married.

He wouldn't make that mistake twice.

Runoff from the snowmelt every spring had carved the gully into the mountainside, so naturally it led upward. Preacher followed it until it petered out, and when it did, he judged that he was a good mile above the valley where the men had ambushed him. He knew he had left his pursuers far below him. He climbed out onto a rocky knob that had a commanding view and sprawled on his belly to study the beautiful but rugged landscape below him. He saw the green expanses of trees, the grassy parks, the winding streams sparkling in the sun. Finally, movement drew his keen-eyed gaze, and he spotted a line of horsemen riding across a broad clearing. He wished he had a spyglass so he could get a better look at them, but he was able to count them before they disappeared.

Twenty-two. Twenty-two varmints who wanted to kill him . . . because he had no doubt this was the same bunch that had ambushed him earlier.

Twenty-two-to-one odds.

He could whittle that down some, Preacher thought.

He waited until the men were completely out of sight before starting down the mountainside. It was possible that they had left someone behind to keep an eye out for him, but he considered that unlikely. He didn't believe they would even think of that. Three of them had died today, mostly in silence, and he figured they were considerably spooked and just wanted to get away so they could try for him another day.

He hadn't seen Dog or Horse since the shooting started, and he hoped his trail partners and old friends were all right and hadn't been hit by any of the wild shots. He headed back toward the spot where the ambush had taken place. Before he even got there, he heard Horse's excited neigh of greeting. A moment later, the stallion came trotting through a grove of trees, followed by Dog.

They were as glad to see him as he was to see them. Horse nudged his arm while Dog reared up, placed his paws on Preacher's shoulders, and proceeded to lick the mountain man's lean, bristly face. Preacher laughed, rubbed Dog's ears, and patted Horse on the shoulder.

"Sure is good to see you fellas again," he told them. He looked them over good to make sure that neither animal was wounded. The inspection quickly confirmed that they had escaped without a scratch. They were a little luckier in that respect than Preacher was. He had that bullet burn on his leg, and branches and brambles had clawed at his skin and left him bleeding in several places.

He would be all right, though. He had been banged up a lot worse than this many times. He wouldn't even need any time to recover before he set off on the important task that lay before him.

Namely, tracking down those bastards, finding out who they were, and why they wanted him dead.

They didn't know it yet . . . but the hunters had just become the hunted.

Chapter 11

As the group of men rode back toward their camp, Colin Fairfax couldn't remember ever being so angry. Preacher had been right there—*right there!*—across the creek, unaware of the danger he was in, with two dozen rifles lined up on him, and still, somehow, he had escaped with his life.

Fairfax had passed along the orders in a whisper. He was to take the first and hopefully only shot. The honor of killing Preacher would go to him, and only if he failed would the others open fire.

Well, he had failed, all right, because that damned dog and horse had caught wind of the men skulking on the other side of the stream and known instinctively that they meant to harm Preacher. That had caused the mountain man to move just as Fairfax pressed the trigger, and instead of Preacher's brains being splattered all over the tree trunk, the only damage the ball had done was to pulverize some pine bark.

Then, to make matters worse, Preacher had

managed to avoid all the other shots when the rest of the men opened up. At first glance that seemed impossible, but Preacher had been moving so fast that it was hard for the eye to follow him.

Not only that, but none of the men with Fairfax were experienced frontiersmen. Brutal and ruthless, yes, and not men to shy away from murder, but their killings in the past had been done in smoky taverns and dark back alleys, with pistols or knives or bare hands. Shad Beaumont had made a tactical error by not sending with Fairfax at least a few men who knew the ways of the West, men who knew better how to handle a rifle.

However, Fairfax was well aware that he would have to play the hand that had been dealt him. With the odds still overwhelmingly on his side, he was confident that sooner or later he would have the pleasure of watching that damned Preacher die.

"He sure is a lucky son of a bitch."

The words brought Fairfax out of the hazy vision he was having of Preacher's bloody corpse stretched out on the ground. He looked over at Sherwood, who had spoken, and feeling contrary, said, "Luck has nothing to do with it. He's good, that's all. Very good at what he does, and very dangerous. I won't underestimate him again."

"Shad wants him dead."

"I'm well aware of that," Fairfax snapped, "but he doesn't want Preacher dead any more than I do. He couldn't possibly."

"I'm just sayin', that's all. Shad Beaumont ain't a good man to disappoint."

"Neither am I. You'd do well to remember that."

Anger flared in Sherwood's eyes. "It ain't my fault you missed with that first shot."

"We *all* missed," Fairfax pointed out. "And three of us paid the price for that."

Sherwood grimaced at the reminder that Preacher had killed three of them before slipping completely out of the trap. They had come out here with thirty men, and now eight of them were gone. Everyone assumed that the two men who vanished had done so because they'd run into Preacher.

"We'll get him," Sherwood vowed. "This was just a job to me at first, to be honest with you, Boss, but now I'm gonna take particular pleasure in watchin' that bastard die."

"Soon," Fairfax said between tightly clenched teeth. "Very soon."

For a man of Preacher's instincts and experience, picking up the trail of the men who had tried to kill him was no problem. He found the park where he had seen them riding away and followed them from there. That many men on horseback left so much sign that a blind man could have followed it, Preacher thought.

The odds against him didn't bother him. He'd had entire tribes of Indians after him in the past, and he had managed to survive. Not without some bumps and bruises along the way, of course, but he was still drawing breath and that was all that mattered. So the idea of facing twenty or more white men—none of whom appeared to be very good shots with a rifle—wasn't all that intimidating.

All he had to do was cut those odds down . . . one at a time if necessary.

He stayed on their trail all day as they moved northward through the valleys between the snow-capped mountains. It was magnificent country, and Preacher wondered if the men he was following appreciated its beauty as much as he did. He doubted that. If they came from back East somewhere as he suspected, they were probably more accustomed to the squalor of the cities. Accustomed to the press of crowds and the stink of smoke, unwashed flesh, and rotting garbage. He couldn't imagine how folks could live like that all the time. He didn't want to imagine it.

Late in the afternoon, the group of riders reached a large clearing where they appeared to have been staying for several days, judging from the size of the campfire that had burned there. By that time, Preacher was only about a quarter of a mile behind them, skillfully using all the cover he could find to close in on his quarry without any of them being aware that he was anywhere nearby. When he smelled the smoke, he dismounted and stole forward on foot, taking Dog with him.

A few moments later, when he parted some brush to peer through the tiny gap, Preacher saw the men moving around the clearing. Some were still unsaddling and tending to their horses. A couple of others had rekindled the fire. They talked loudly and profanely, several of them complaining about their failure to kill him earlier in the day.

Considering the size of that fire and the amount of racket they were making, Preacher thought that maybe he should just steal away and leave them here. Sooner or later, a war party of hostiles would come along and wipe them out, just on general principles.

That might take too long, though, and the varmints might get up to other mischief or cause more damage before then. Hell, they might start a forest fire, the way the flames were leaping so high in their campfire. It would be better, Preacher decided, to go ahead and deal with them now.

Not at this exact moment, of course. He would wait until nightfall. Under the cover of darkness, he could slip into the camp and kill several of them. He had used that tactic before with the Blackfeet, which was one reason they hated and feared him. His ability to get in and out of camps like a phantom and leave dead men behind always spooked his enemies. Maybe after he paid a visit to this bunch, the ones who were left would be so afraid that they'd hightail it out of the high country without him having to kill the rest of them.

He was mulling that over when he suddenly stiffened at the sight of one of the men stalking across the clearing. The man was a little under medium height and not impressive physically. He had a beaver hat shoved back on a head that appeared to be mostly bald.

It was the bald head and the beaver hat that struck a chord of recognition in Preacher. Dog must have known him, too, because the big cur growled softly until Preacher rested a hand on the back of his neck and said, "Shhh."

The previous year, Preacher had had several run-ins

with a man who looked like that, first in St. Louis and then later out here on the frontier. The fella had been partnered up with a tall, skinny, gawky gent. Neither of them looked very threatening, but they had caused Preacher and the Hart cousins no end of trouble before a final showdown in which the tall man had been killed.

After that battle, Preacher had looked for the body of the man in the beaver hat but hadn't found it. He'd assumed that such a man wouldn't be able to survive for very long in the wilderness on his own. If the Indians didn't get him, the bears would. If the bears didn't, the mountain lions would. If the mountain lions didn't, the weather—

Preacher remembered that line of reasoning very well; there was no need to rehash it all now. And even though the conclusion he'd reached had been a logical one, obviously it had been wrong.

Because there the man was, big as life and twice as ugly, an angry expression on his pinched face as he confronted one of the other men.

"I thought I told you to post guards all around the camp as soon as we got back."

The other man, who was huskier and younger than the man in the beaver hat, nodded and said, "I'm goin' to, Boss. Just hadn't quite got around to it yet."

"Do it now, damn it. Preacher could be out there somewhere. He could have followed us."

"After nearly gettin' his head blowed off and then bein' lucky enough to get away, I'll bet he's still runnin'," the second man said.

"You don't know Preacher."

That was for damned sure, Preacher thought as he continued to look on from the brush.

"I wouldn't put anything past him," the man in the beaver hat went on. "He ruined every plan that Schuyler and I had."

Schuyler would have been the tall, gawky gent, Preacher told himself. He had never heard the man's name, despite all the time they clashed.

"All right, Mr. Fairfax," the burly subordinate said. "I'll get those guards posted right now."

Fairfax jerked his head in a curt nod, but still didn't look happy. He struck Preacher as the sort who never looked happy, except maybe when he was causing somebody some misery.

Preacher was still surprised that the fella had made it back to civilization alive. He had to be stronger and tougher than he looked.

And he hated Preacher, that was for sure. Probably blamed him for Schuyler's death. Even so, Preacher wouldn't have expected the gent to come back out here with more than two dozen men just to try to settle the score with him. That was some powerful hate, if that was all there was to it.

As the burly man began picking out sentries, Preacher faded back into the woods, taking Dog with him. He didn't want to take a chance on being discovered just yet.

When he was well out of earshot of the camp, he said aloud, "I didn't ever expect to see that bald-headed polecat again, Dog. Fairfax, his name is, accordin' to that other fella. I could've done without seein' him, too. He's been nothin' but trouble ever since the first time I run into him."

Dog looked up at him.

"Yeah, I know, you wanted to kill him. But if I'd let you go chew his throat out, then I'd've had to fight all the rest o' them fellas, and there might've been too many of 'em, even for me. Best we wait and try to improve the odds a mite."

He went back to the place where he had left Horse. Grass and water were nearby, so it was as good a place as any to wait for night to fall. Preacher found a comfortable spot to stretch out underneath a tree, and with a frontiersman's ability to snatch sleep whenever he got a chance, he dozed off right away, confident that Dog and Horse would let him know if anyone came around.

Hell, they had already saved his life once today.

Preacher's light but restful sleep continued until after dusk had settled down over the rugged landscape. His eyes opened as he came awake, but otherwise he didn't move for several minutes as he let his vision adjust to the darkness and listened for anything unusual nearby. The only sounds he heard were the usual nighttime rustlings of small animals in the brush. He turned his head, saw Dog lying nearby with his head on his paws and Horse contentedly cropping at some grass.

Time to get up and get busy, Preacher told himself.

A rumbling in his midsection reminded him that he hadn't eaten since breakfast that morning. It would be a hell of a note if he was sneaking up on some bastard to cut his throat and a growling belly gave him away. So he took the time to eat a biscuit and some jerky from the meager supply in his saddlebags, washing the food down with clear, cold water from the stream.

Then he patted Horse on the shoulder, said, "Stay here, old boy, I'll be back in a while," and set out on his mission.

His killing mission.

Chapter 12

The sentries belched and farted, scratched themselves, muttered complaints under their breath . . . in short, each of them might as well have been shouting *Here I am!* to Preacher.

Fairfax's lieutenant had posted six men around the camp. Normally, that might have been enough to guard against any intruders, but Preacher wasn't just any intruder. Like a living shadow, he drifted through the darkness and came up behind the man he had chosen as his first target.

The luckless bastard didn't know Preacher was anywhere around until the mountain man's arm looped around his neck and clamped across his throat like an iron bar. Preacher could have choked him to death or even broken his neck, but he ended it even quicker and cleaner than that, with nearly a foot of cold steel that drove easily into the man's back and pierced his heart. The man gave one spasmodic jerk as he died, but didn't let out a sound or cause any other racket.

Preacher lowered the body to the ground, grimacing a little as he did so. He didn't like killing in cold blood like that, but he had done it before when necessary and would again. This varmint had done his damnedest to kill Preacher earlier in the day, so Preacher wasn't going to lose any sleep over what he'd just done.

Moving through the darkness like a ghost, Preacher closed in on the next sentry and disposed of him in the same manner, with the same results and lack of noise. The third man was stronger and managed to struggle a little, but in the end he died, too.

Preacher let the other three guards live. It always made a man nervous when the fella beside him died and he knew good and well it could have just as easily been him.

He entered the camp itself then. He'd waited until everything quieted down for the night. The men had been drinking and playing cards and talking, and some of them didn't crawl into their blankets until well after dark. Now, however, they all seemed to be sound asleep. Raucous snoring came from some of the figures on the ground.

Dog had stayed behind in the woods, even though a tiny whine showed that he didn't like it. If Preacher got in trouble, though, all it would take was a whistle and a thickly furred bundle of fury and slashing teeth would descend on the camp.

For now, Preacher crawled among the sleeping men, selecting his targets. Time and again he struck, clamping his left hand over a man's nose and mouth or around his throat and then driving the blade in with his right. A couple of them thrashed in their death throes, but no more than a man would who was having a vivid dream. The whole thing was so quiet and discreet, there wasn't even much blood.

And when he had killed three more men, Preacher drifted out of the camp like a wisp of smoke from the still-smoldering campfire. He knew that he could have disposed of more of them, but such mass slaughter went beyond what he was prepared to do. He would rather just frighten off the others, and he hoped that the discovery of the bodies in the morning, if not sooner, would have that result.

He rejoined Dog in the woods, and they both went back to the spot where Horse waited. Horse tossed his head when Preacher came up, and then shied away, something Preacher wasn't used to.

"What's gotten into your fool head?" he asked the stallion, then glanced down toward the hand he had reached out with and realized why Horse was spooked.

Preacher's hand was dark with blood. Horse must have smelled it on him. He had wiped the knife blade, but hadn't realized that the gore was on his hand as well.

"Sorry," he muttered. He bent over and wiped his hand on the grass. Dew was already beginning to form. It helped wash away the crimson stain, but Preacher knew not all of it would wipe off. What was left behind would just have to wear off.

Too bad the stains on a man's soul wouldn't wear off the same way.

Angry shouts jolted Colin Fairfax out of a restless slumber, haunted as usual by dreams—no, nightmares—of Preacher. At first, he thought some of the men were probably arguing with each other about something, most likely something trivial.

But as he sat up and rubbed sleep out of his eyes, he realized that the shouts contained a note of fear, too. Something had happened that had the men spooked.

Preacher.

Fairfax didn't doubt for a second that the mountain man was involved. He grabbed his pistol and bolted out of the small tent where he slept. He was the only one in the group to have such a luxury, and he knew the men resented it. He didn't care. After everything he had been through, he deserved a modicum of comfort.

He pulled his suspenders up over his shoulders as he looked around the camp in the gray, predawn light. Most of the men were up, standing around looking stunned. Three of them still lay wrapped up in their blankets, though, evidently sleeping soundly through the commotion.

"What's going on here?" Fairfax demanded. "What's happened?"

Sherwood lumbered over to him and reported in a sullen voice, "Berryman just come in from guard duty and says that Johnson, Wilmont, and Deever are layin' out there in the woods dead."

"Dead!" Fairfax repeated. "What happened to them?"

Even as he asked the question, he knew the answer.

"They were all stabbed in the back," Sherwood said heavily. "Looked like with a big huntin' knife. And that ain't all, Boss . . ." Sherwood gestured toward the men who were still in their blankets. "The son of a bitch was here, too. Somebody tried to shake Hawkins awake and . . . well, see for yourself."

Fairfax walked over to the man Sherwood indicated. He bent down to pull the blanket aside, but his hand stopped before he reached it. The blanket was draped across the man's face so that his right eye was visible, and even in the poor light, Fairfax could tell there was no life in it. The man stared up sightlessly.

Grimacing, Fairfax flicked the blanket back anyway. What he saw only confirmed his initial judgment. Hawkins was dead, with his features set in lines of agony. Fairfax noted the rent in the blanket now, surrounded by a small bloodstain. The wound hadn't bled a lot because the knife had penetrated the man's heart, stopping it almost immediately.

"The other two are just like that," Sherwood said from behind Fairfax. "He was here. You know it was him."

Fairfax nodded and pulled the blanket over Hawkins's face again. "Yes," he said as he straightened. "I know it was him."

"What are you gonna do about it?"

Fairfax turned to face his angry second in command. "We're going to kill him, of course," he declared. "That's why we came out here, after all. This is just more proof, as if we needed any, how dangerous Preacher is. He must be disposed of."

"He was right here in the camp! He could've killed us all in our sleep!"

"I doubt that. He would have been discovered if he'd stayed here much longer. He did his dirty work and then ran, like an animal."

Sherwood shook his head and said, "You're wrong." He didn't seem to be worried about offending Fairfax anymore. "Nobody knew he was here. Six men on guard, and he kills half of them without anybody noticin', then sneaks in here and kills three more men. The man's a damn ghost! He can't be killed!"

Angry, frightened mutters of agreement came from some of the other men.

"Don't be ridiculous. He's as human as anybody, and he'll die just like anybody else."

Even as Fairfax spoke, though, a nagging doubt was in the back of his mind. He thought of all the times Preacher had come within a hairbreadth of death, and yet the man was still alive. Maybe there *was* something mystical about him . . .

Fairfax forced that thought out of his head. It was bad enough that Sherwood and the other men were starting to think such things. He couldn't allow himself to give in to that. If he did, he was as good as beaten.

One of the men stepped forward. "I say we get the hell out of here and head back east. This Preacher fella is too much."

"Do you want to go back to Shad Beaumont and tell him that you failed?" Fairfax asked coldly. "Because I don't."

The man looked uneasy at the thought of reporting failure to Beaumont. But then he said, "Maybe I won't go back to St. Louis. Maybe I'll head someplace else, like down to New Orleans. I never been there."

Mutters and nods of agreement came from several

of the men. Fairfax sensed how tenuous the grip he had on them was. They would desert him in an instant, and that was exactly what would happen if he didn't do something to put a stop to this brewing mutiny.

"All right," he said as his mind worked to come up with a desperate ploy. "I wasn't supposed to tell you this, but . . . Beaumont put a bounty on Preacher's head. Five hundred dollars to the man who kills him, and a thousand to be split among the rest of the group who make it back alive with proof of Preacher's death."

No such bounty existed. It was a figment of Fairfax's imagination. But the men didn't have to know that until they got back to St. Louis, and by then Preacher would be dead. That was all Fairfax really cared about. At this moment, all that mattered was keeping the men from bolting.

"The boss didn't say anything about no bounty to me," Sherwood said with a suspicious frown.

"Of course not," Fairfax replied, making himself sound supremely confident. "It was going to be a surprise when we got back. A reward for work well done."

Another man spoke up, saying, "No wonder you kept wantin' to kill Preacher yourself. You wanted that five hundred dollars!"

That prompted more angry muttering, and for a second Fairfax worried that his hastily conceived lie was going to backfire on him.

But he said calmly enough, "Not at all. I'm more interested in seeing Preacher dead. If I killed him, I planned to add the five hundred to the pot we'll all split. That only seems fair."

He wasn't sure they believed him, but he saw enough doubt in their eyes to embolden him to continue. "So you see, Preacher's actually done us a favor. Once he's dead, the bounty will be split into larger shares now."

Again, it seemed like he might have misstepped as resentment sprang up on the faces of several men, but then greed overwhelmed any anger they might have felt at his callousness. They began talking among themselves and nodding.

Sherwood said, "I still ain't sure I believe it, but I reckon anything's possible."

"You'll believe it when you've got the coins in your hand."

"Yeah, I guess." Sherwood rubbed his heavy, beard-stubbled jaw. "So what do we do now?"

"We bury these men," Fairfax said, "and then we start looking for Preacher again."

Sherwood grunted. "We may not have to look very hard." He nodded toward the blanket-wrapped corpses. "He's liable to come to us again."

"Indeed he will," Fairfax said as an idea suddenly began to form in his brain. "Indeed he will . . . because we're going to have something that he wants."

Laura Mallory stepped into the cabin and looked around. It was newly built and freshly furnished, with a puncheon floor, furniture that had been brought out from St. Louis on the wagon train, and even curtains hanging over the windows, something that couldn't be found in any of the other cabins in the settlement.

"It's lovely, Clyde," she said with a smile on her face. "Thank you."

"Only the best for you, my dear," Clyde Mallory said. "It's not what you're accustomed to, obviously, but perhaps it will suffice while we're forced to remain here in this godforsaken wilderness. I'm not sure why Lord Aspermont is so interested in this territory."

Laura's smile disappeared, a frown taking its place. Her eyes turned chilly. "You know how important the fur trade is," she snapped, "but more than that, these mountains have some of the most abundant natural resources on earth. My God, you've seen the forests. Can you imagine how much lumber could be cut from those trees? Not to mention the minerals that may be here." She shook her head. "Besides, do you want those damned Americans to have it? They've already taken so much from us."

A faraway look appeared in her eyes as she thought about the father who had gone away to war and never come back. He had fallen in the Battle of New Orleans, a victim of the raw barbarians who had opposed the king's forces there.

Only later had the truth come out: That battle was fought after the war itself was over. The news of the treaty simply had not reached either side in time to prevent the bloody clash. So all the deaths suffered there had been pointless.

But they wouldn't have happened if not for the upstart Americans, and Laura Mallory would never forgive them for that, nor for what her father's death had done to her mother. Stricken by grief, the poor woman had wasted away and finally died, leaving Laura and her brother alone in the world.

Alone and penniless . . . until Lord Aspermont, one of their father's old friends who held some mysterious high position in His Majesty's Government, had contacted them and offered them a job. It would require some special talents, and a certain degree of ruthlessness, but Lord Aspermont believed that Laura and Clyde could handle it because they possessed the most vital quality of all.

A deep and abiding hatred for the Americans.

"Of course I'll do whatever is necessary to thwart their expansion," Clyde said now. "If they're allowed to settle this vast territory, their grip on the continent will never be shaken loose. We have to stop them before they control everything from the Atlantic to the Pacific."

"We will," Laura said with a solemn nod. "The rifles are all right?"

Mallory sounded impatient as he said, "You keep asking me that. The guns are fine. No one will find them, concealed as they are in those false bottoms of the wagons. As soon as the man who's supposed to put us in contact with the Indians arrives, we'll get in touch with the savages and strike a bargain with them, just as Lord Aspermont planned. It won't be long until this whole part of the country is overrun with well-armed redskins who want nothing more than to drive the Americans from their land."

"The king's land," Laura corrected him, "once the Americans have abandoned it. Then we'll deal with those savages properly." She stepped to the door and looked out across the settlement and the neighboring fields all the way to the snowcapped mountains that ringed the lush valley. "It's only a matter of time, Clyde . . . only a matter of time until the streams are running red with American blood."

Chapter 13

Lying at the top of a giant, slab-sided rock, Preacher watched as several hundred feet below him the line of horsemen wound through the trees, heading east. He tried to count them, but the vegetation was too thick to determine the exact number. He was confident, though, that there were either fifteen or sixteen of them.

"Should be sixteen," Preacher said to Dog, who lay beside him. "There were twenty-two yesterday, and I did for six of 'em last night. I ain't the best in the world at cipherin', but I can count that good anyway."

Dog's tail brushed against the rock as it wagged back and forth.

"Of course, there may be sixteen," Preacher went on. "I can't rightly tell. But if there's one fella missin', it don't have to mean anything. He could've got sick and died, or struck out on his own when the rest of the bunch turned back."

Even as he mulled it over, though, Preacher felt uneasy. Survival on the frontier often depended on the little things, the sort of details that folks often overlooked . . . like whether there were sixteen men or only fifteen.

The one thing Preacher was sure of was that Colin Fairfax was leading the group of men down below. He could see the beaver hat on the man riding in front with the burly second in command next to him. The riders were striking almost due east, heading for one of the passes that led out of the valley. It appeared that Preacher's nocturnal visit had had the desired effect.

The men who had been trying to kill him were now cutting and running, and they weren't wasting any time about it either. At the rate they were going, they would be through the pass and out of the valley by the end of the day, on their way back to St. Louis or wherever they came from.

Preacher wasn't going to just assume that they were leaving, though. He intended to follow them until they were well away from his stomping grounds. He didn't like neglecting his traps, but some things were more important.

He slid down the rock. Dog bounded down with him. Horse waited at the bottom. Preacher picked up the reins and swung into the saddle. He rode east, too, following a trail that roughly paralleled the one the men were using.

From time to time during the day, he swung closer to the group of riders to check on their progress and make sure they were still heading out of the valley. They didn't seem to be deviating from their course.

Preacher imagined there had been quite a ruckus in their camp that morning when they discovered the dead men. The survivors must have realized that it could have just as easily been them lying there growing cold, and they had risen against Fairfax's leadership and insisted on going back.

Either that or Fairfax himself had decided to give up his vengeance quest. Maybe he had figured out that killing Preacher wasn't worth his own life or the lives of the men with him. From what he had seen of Fairfax in the past, the man didn't care that much about anybody else, so it must have been concern for his own hide that sent him scurrying . . . if indeed it was even his idea to leave.

Late that afternoon, the men rode through the pass. Preacher was a quarter of a mile away in the top of a pine tree as they did so, watching them depart from the valley.

When they were gone, he shinnied back down the tree, mounted up, and rode hard for the pass. He scouted it on foot when he got there to make sure the varmints hadn't doubled back, but there was no sign of them except what they had left going through the opening in the mountains. When Preacher studied the far side of the pass, he saw that they were out of sight.

He was glad they were gone, gladder still that he hadn't been forced to kill all of them. It didn't bother Preacher to take the life of some no-good bastard who had it comin', but he didn't believe in wholesale slaughter.

When he got back to the place where he had left Horse and Dog, he told his old friends, "Well, I reckon this trouble is all over. We can go back to what we were doin' before it started."

* * *

Colin Fairfax's heart pounded in his chest. He had a hard time believing that once again he was alone out here in the wilderness . . . and that it was his own choice this time.

More than that, it was even his idea. He had sent the rest of the men away this morning with orders to head east out of the valley. One of them, a weasel-faced killer named Campbell, wore the beaver hat in which Fairfax took so much pride. He hated to give it up, but he was convinced that Preacher would be keeping an eye on the group, and he wanted the mountain man to think that he was leaving along with the others.

Instead, he had lain low in some brush for a couple of hours after the others pulled out, until he was convinced that Preacher was nowhere around. Preacher would have followed the rest of Beaumont's men to make sure they left the valley. Fairfax felt certain that Preacher wouldn't take their departure at face value. He would want to see for himself that they really were gone.

At least, that was what Fairfax was counting on . . .

He tramped along, carrying his rifle and heading south from the place where the group had been camped. The Hart cousins' trading post lay in this direction, he knew. He couldn't go all the way to the post because Corliss, Jerome, and Corliss's wife Deborah all knew him and would recognize him. Deborah had even been his prisoner for a short time the previous year, when he and Schuyler were trying to stop the cousins from ever reaching this area where the fur trade was proving so lucrative.

His plan called for him to get close to the place, close enough to keep an eye on it until the opportunity arose for him to slip into the settlement and kidnap Deborah again. By that time, Sherwood and the other men would have turned back, entered the valley again, and if all went as it was supposed to, they would be close by so that he could rendezvous with them.

Then, using Deborah Hart as the bait, they would lure Preacher into a trap from which he would never escape. Fairfax didn't have all the details figured out yet, but he knew he could come up with something foolproof. The first and most important step was to get his hands on Deborah again.

That thought put a faint, fleeting smile on his face as it went through his head. Deborah Hart was a damned attractive woman. He would enjoy having her in his power for a while. He didn't care what happened to her in the long run. She was just a means to an end.

And that end was Preacher's death.

That evening, a stranger showed up at the trading post, which was nothing unusual in itself. Newcomers were common. There seemed to be no limit to the number of men who wanted to come west to make a new start for themselves or amass a fortune or simply to avoid something—or someone—unpleasant back east.

So not many people paid much attention to the

bearded man with the long black hair hanging down around his shoulders under a flat-crowned hat. He wore a beaded buckskin jacket, rode a paint pony of the sort that the Indians preferred, and had a squaw trailing him on another pony and leading a packhorse. The stranger balanced a long-barreled flintlock across the saddle in front of him. The barrel had a couple of eagle feathers tied to it.

The pair rode through the open gates and headed for the trading post. They drew their ponies to a halt in front of the building. The man dismounted and spoke to the Indian woman in a low voice. She stayed where she was while he climbed the steps to the porch and went inside.

Jerome Hart was behind the counter at the rear of the big room. Corliss and Deborah had gone to their quarters behind the main building for supper. There had been a time when Jerome harbored romantic feelings for Deborah himself, but he had accepted the fact that she was married to his cousin now and wished them both well.

Lifting a hand in greeting to the tough-looking stranger who had just come into the trading post, Jerome called, "Hello! Welcome, friend. Come right on in. What can we do for you?"

Moving with an easy, catlike grace, the man strolled back to the counter. He had the flintlock cradled in his left arm. With a nod to Jerome, he said, "Howdy, mister. You the boss around here?"

"I'm one of the proprietors, yes," Jerome answered. He introduced himself. "Jerome Hart." He didn't offer to shake hands. The stranger was a bit too intimidating for that.

The newcomer didn't extend his hand either, but he nodded and said, "Name's Ezra Flagg. My squaw and me are lookin' to pick up some supplies."

Jerome smiled and waved a hand at the shelves full of goods. "We have everything you might need, Mr. Flagg. This is the finest trading post between St. Louis and the Pacific Ocean."

Flagg grunted. "Damn near the only one, ain't it?"

"Well . . . the only one in these parts. What sort of supplies do you and your, ah, wife require?"

A thin smile curved Flagg's lips for a second. "She ain't my wife. She's my squaw. Weepin' Willow, I call her, 'cause that's the kind o' tree I caught her under."

"'Caught . . . her?'" Jerome repeated with a frown.

"That's right. She'd gone down to a stream to do some wash, and I come ridin' along and seen how comely she was, so I decided to take her with me." Flagg chuckled. "She put up a fight at first, but I beat that outta her pretty quicklike. She jus' does what I tell her to now."

Jerome kept the revulsion he had begun to feel off his face. He had learned early on that the frontier was a rough, violent place. Many of the men were unsavory types who were accustomed to taking whatever they wanted, by force if necessary. But as long as they didn't cause any trouble here at the trading post, Jerome and Corliss didn't judge them. What their customers did away from here was none of the cousins' business.

"I'll, uh, start putting together an order of staples for you," Jerome said. "If that's all right."

"Yeah, I reckon."

"The supplies will be ready in about half an hour."

Flagg nodded. "Gimme a jug o' whiskey first. Got to have somethin' to kill the time whilst I'm waitin'."

Lips pursed, Jerome took a jug from the shelf underneath the counter and set it on top. Without offering to go ahead and pay for the whiskey, Ezra Flagg picked up the jug and strolled toward a table in the corner. "I'll just count that in the total with the supplies," Jerome called after him, but Flagg didn't give any sign that he'd heard. Glaring in disapproval now that Flagg's back was safely turned, Jerome started putting together the order.

Flagg sat down at the table, propped one foot on another barrel chair, laid the flintlock across the table, and used his teeth to work the cork out of the jug's neck. With his forefinger through the loop and the jug's weight resting on his forearm in mountain man fashion, Flagg lifted it and took a long swallow of the fiery liquor.

When he lowered it and thumped it onto the rough-hewn table, he let out a sigh of satisfaction and wiped the back of his other hand across his mouth. Then he glanced up as a man stepped into the doorway of the trading post and looked around the room.

Flagg didn't know the man's name, but it was Clyde Mallory who had just entered the trading post. Mallory looked around the room, spotted the rifle with the eagle feathers tied to its barrel, and gave the weapon's owner a curt nod before withdrawing from the doorway.

Flagg took another long drink from the jug, then stood up and moseyed over to the counter. "I'll be back," he told Jerome.

When he stepped out onto the porch, he saw the

man who had just nodded to him. The man lounged near the back of a parked wagon. He moved out of sight. Flagg ambled in that direction. He put his right hand on the butt of the pistol tucked behind his belt. If this was a trick or a trap of some sort, the son of a bitch would be sorry he had tried to fool Ezra Flagg.

Even though a faint crescent of orange remained in the western sky above the mountains, thick, dark shadows had already gathered behind the wagon. As Flagg stepped around it, he drew his pistol and eared back the hammer. He froze as he heard the unmistakable sound of another flintlock being cocked.

"For king and country," Clyde Mallory said.

"For five hundred dollars," Ezra Flagg said.

Both men lowered their weapons. The phrases they had just exchanged confirmed their identities to each other.

"You've got the rifles?" Flagg asked.

"Of course," Mallory replied. "You've made the arrangements with the Indians?"

Flagg said, "Yeah, the Blackfoot war chief Walks Like a Bear is chompin' at the bit to get 'em. You can be sure that him and his bucks'll raise holy hell once they get their hands on those guns."

"Splendid," Mallory said. "My wagons will leave tomorrow. We'll meet at some spot you select, well away from the trading post, and transfer the rifles to this Chief Walks Like a Bear and his men."

"And transfer my money to me," Flagg said.

"Of course. You'll be amply rewarded for your services as arranged. That goes without saying."

Flagg shook his head. "Nothin' goes without sayin' where money's concerned."

Mallory rubbed his hands together in satisfaction. "Very well. I think that concludes our business for tonight. I'll see you tomorrow."

"You don't want to know my name?" Flagg asked with a sneer.

"Frankly, sir," Mallory said, "I don't care what your name is. All that matters to me is that you're willing to betray your countrymen for the sum of five hundred American dollars."

Flagg laughed. "Beats thirty pieces o' silver, don't it?"

Chapter 14

The next morning, the men who worked for Clyde Mallory got busy early hitching up the teams of mules to the wagons. Corliss Hart spotted the activity and walked out of the stockade to talk to Mallory, who was standing near the wagons overseeing the work.

"Leaving so soon, Mr. Mallory?" Corliss asked.

The Englishman smiled and nodded. "No need to stay longer," he said. "The furs you and your cousin are sending back to St. Louis are loaded, and it's time to return for more supplies. By the time we get back here in a couple of months, you'll be ready for more supplies."

"We sure will," Corliss agreed. "The way the settlement is growing, you can probably have wagon trains coming and going all the time before much longer."

"A lucrative arrangement for all of us, eh?" Mallory chuckled.

"Darned right." Corliss shook his head. "I've got to

admit, though, that I'll miss having your sister around here. A lady like that always brightens a place up."

"Oh, Laura isn't going back to St. Louis with us. She's going to stay here to look after our interests."

"Really? I'd heard rumors that she might stay behind, but I wasn't sure that was what you planned to do. You don't have to worry about her, Mr. Mallory. We'll see that she's well taken care of."

Mallory knew how Corliss Hart would like to take care of Laura. The lust was apparent in the boorish American's eyes every time he so much as glanced at Laura. Mallory wasn't sure why Corliss's wife put up with it.

Deborah Hart was quite an attractive woman herself, even with her delicate condition beginning to show. Perhaps he would take steps to see that she was spared from the bloody Indian uprising to come, Mallory mused. If he saved her life, she might be properly grateful to him . . .

Laura emerged then from the cabin where she would be staying and walked toward them. Corliss's eyes followed her avidly. *Why don't you just lick your lips in anticipation, you bloody fool?* Mallory thought. He wished that he could take his pistol and blow a hole in the American.

That day was coming, Mallory assured himself. He probably wouldn't have the privilege of killing Corliss Hart himself, but he could rest comfortably in the knowledge that Corliss was doomed, along with the rest of the settlers.

"Good morning," Laura greeted the men. Her smile was brilliant as she turned it toward Corliss. "I suppose Clyde told you that he's leaving today, Mr. Hart?"

"He certainly did," Corliss replied. "He also told me that you'll be staying here with us while he returns to St. Louis. Let me assure you, Miss Mallory, we'll do everything we can to make your stay here pleasant and safe."

"I never doubted that." Laura turned to her brother. "Are the wagons almost ready, Clyde?"

Mallory nodded. "We'll be leaving within the hour."

She put a hand on his arm and said, "I'll miss you, but don't worry about me. I'm sure I'll be fine."

"And I'm sure that I'll be back before you know it."

As if sensing that the siblings wanted some privacy to say their farewells, Corliss said, "I'd better get back to the trading post." He extended his hand. "Good luck on your journey, Mr. Mallory."

The Englishman shook hands with him, concealing his distaste for the American with consummate skill. "Thank you, sir," Mallory said.

He kept the smile on his face until Corliss had vanished back into the trading post. Then Mallory turned away, scowled, and muttered under his breath, "Lecherous fool. You be sure and keep your distance from him, Laura. And don't let yourself be caught alone with him."

She laughed. "Stop being the protective brother, Clyde. You know perfectly well that I'm just as capable of taking care of myself as you are."

"Yes, perhaps, but still . . . I'll be glad when this is all over."

"So will I." Laura frowned slightly. "I don't look forward to the bloodshed. There are quite a few women and children here."

"I know what you mean," Mallory said with a sigh.

"Certain losses are inevitable, though. I'm glad that Preacher fellow isn't here. It's difficult to fight side by side with a man and then betray him. I rather liked him, despite the fact that he's an American."

"So did I," Laura said. "There's something about him . . ." She let her voice trail off, then gave an abrupt shake of her head. "But we're here to carry out an assignment, and we cannot let anything deter us from it."

"We won't." Mallory's voice was strong and confident again. "If all goes as planned, before the day is over, those rifles will be in the hands of the Blackfeet . . . and in the end the blood will be on their hands."

He only wished he believed that as strongly as he made it sound that he did.

True to Mallory's prediction, the wagon train pulled out of the settlement less than an hour later with the shouting of drivers, the rattling of harness chains, the creaking of wheels, and the plodding of hooves. Most of the people who were around the trading post turned out to watch the wagons leave. Their arrival had been a welcome break from the monotony, and so was their departure.

Corliss, Deborah, Jerome, and the boy Jake stood on the porch of the trading post and waved through the open gates as the wagons rolled past. Other people lined the walls of the stockade, and still others stood outside their cabins and shaded their eyes against the sun. It was still fairly early in the day, and the wagons were heading east, into the sun.

Laura stood by herself, the only one remaining

at the settlement who knew that her brother would be back much sooner than anyone else expected. She lifted a hand in farewell, but Clyde wasn't looking back.

Mallory felt better once the settlement was out of sight. He had known when he came here that the plan devised by Lord Aspermont included arming the savages and stirring them to attack the settlement.

Once this American foothold in the wilderness was wiped out, Lord Aspermont was certain they would abandon their plans to settle this vast territory. Then British settlers could come down from Canada and establish their own trading post and community.

By the time the Americans came back again, this would be de facto British territory. New boundary lines could be negotiated then. The Americans would have no choice except to concede part of the territory they had acquired from France in that damned Louisiana Purchase, and their greedy, grasping overreaching would be blunted at last.

There was room for only one empire in the world, Mallory told himself . . . and that was the British Empire.

Rule Britannia.

He didn't know exactly where Ezra Flagg and the Blackfoot chief Walks Like a Bear would rendezvous with the wagons. Somewhere east of the settlement and well away from it, Flagg had said. His instructions had been for Mallory to take the wagons east as if he were really heading back to St. Louis, and they would be met.

Mallory didn't trust Flagg as far as he could throw

the man. Anyone who would betray his own countrymen for money would certainly betray a foreign agent for more money.

But Mallory had taken precautions to see that that didn't happen. Without going into detail, he had warned Flagg not to double-cross him. Flagg had denied that he would ever do such a thing, of course, but his word meant nothing to Mallory.

Mallory rode alongside the lead wagon. A man named Vincent handled the reins. Like all the other drivers and workers who had accompanied the wagon train west from St. Louis, they had been well paid to follow orders and keep their mouths shut. They had to know that something underhanded was going on, but they didn't care as long as they got their money.

The sun was overhead at midday as the trail the wagons were following skirted a long, wooded ridge to the north. Mallory held up a hand in a signal for the wagons to halt as he spotted two riders descending that ridge.

He recognized Ezra Flagg, even at a distance. The telltale eagle feathers fluttered at the end of Flagg's rifle barrel.

The man with Flagg sported feathers, too, but they were tied in his hair. A small shiver went through Mallory as the riders drew closer and he was able to make out the ruthless cast of the second man's copper-hued face. Mallory had seen a few Indians in St. Louis, but they had been what the Americans called "friendlies."

The warrior riding at Flagg's side appeared to be anything but friendly.

Vincent called from the seat of the stopped lead wagon, "That's a redskin comin', Boss. Where there's one o' those devils, there're likely to be more."

"I'm well aware of that," Mallory snapped. "Your job is to drive the wagon, Vincent, not to offer advice."

Vincent shrugged, but his hand moved closer to the butt of the pistol at his waist. "Maybe so, but I'll be damned if I'm gonna sit by and let some painted, feather-wearin' bastard take my scalp."

"For God's sake, there's not going to be any scalping! We're here to do business with the Indians, not to fight them."

Understanding dawned on Vincent's face. "Those rifles hid in the false bottoms o' the wagons . . . you're gonna sell 'em to the redskins?"

Mallory turned his head to give the man a hard stare. "Do you have any objections to that?"

Vincent looked back at him for a long moment, then finally shook his head. He said, "As long as I get my money, mister, you can sell anything you want to anybody you want."

"You'll get paid, have no fear of that." Mallory turned to look at the approaching riders again. "But as a matter of fact, we're not *selling* those weapons to the Indians. We're going to give them away."

A surprised expression appeared on Vincent's face, as if he thought that the Englishman he was working for had lost his mind. Mallory knew exactly what he was doing, though. The money to purchase those rifles and to outfit the wagons to carry them in concealment, as well as to buy the supplies that furnished the ostensible reason for the journey west, had come from Lord Aspermont, which meant that it came from high levels of the British government.

Which meant, in the most basic terms, that it came from the king, although quite possibly William himself knew nothing about it. This king had never been much more than a figurehead. A circle of influential men, including Lord Aspermont, determined policy, trying to strengthen the Empire in anticipation of the inevitable ascension to the throne of the young Princess Victoria.

Flagg and Walks Like a Bear were only about fifty yards away now. Mallory composed his thoughts and kept his expression carefully neutral as the two men approached and drew rein to halt their horses. Mallory walked his horse forward to greet them, not stopping until only a dozen feet separated him from Flagg and the Blackfoot chief. He wasn't sure how he was supposed to greet them, so he just sat there and waited for Flagg to say something first.

Flagg smiled coldly and said, "Howdy, Mallory. Looks like you didn't have any trouble gettin' away from the settlement."

"Of course not. Everyone accepted my story that the wagons were returning to St. Louis for more supplies."

Flagg nodded toward his companion. "This is Walks Like a Bear, war chief of the Blackfeet."

Mallory gave the chief a solemn nod and asked, "Does he speak English?"

Flagg chuckled. "Not a lick. He hates white men so bad he won't have nothin' to do with 'em, includin' learnin' their lingo. I figure he'd like to kill you right now, just 'cause you're white."

"He seems to tolerate you without any difficulty," Mallory pointed out.

"That's 'cause I'm helpin' him get somethin' he wants."

"I thought perhaps your, ah, wife was one of his people."

Flagg shook his head. "Nope. She's Crow. And she ain't my wife, I told you. The Crow hate me 'cause I stole her, and that's another reason Bear here puts up with me. The Blackfeet an' the Crow been fightin' and killin' each other for years, and the Crow bein' my enemies makes ol' Bear like me a mite better. Or hate me a mite less, dependin' on how you want to look at it."

"That's all very interesting, but let's get on with it, shall we? I take it that the chief knows about the rifles?"

"I told him all about 'em," Flagg replied with a nod. "He can't wait for him and his bucks to get their hands on 'em."

Mallory turned in the saddle and called to his men, "Open those false bottoms and get the rifles out!" He turned back to Flagg and the Blackfoot and added, "I'm surprised that the chief doesn't have his men with him."

"Oh, they're here," Flagg said, a sly smile on his face. "You can't see 'em, but they're up there in that timber. Bear don't trust you. You try to trick him or double-cross him, and you'll see his men fast enough. They'll be the last thing you see," Flagg added.

"There'll be no tricks or double crosses . . . on either side."

Flagg shrugged. "I got no reason to cross you,

Mallory. And these redskins, well, they'll kill you straight out, or they'll torture you for a few days if they're in the mood to, but they won't lie to you."

Vincent and Mallory's other men unloaded the wagons, using iron bars to pry up the false bottoms in the vehicles and then wrestling out the crates containing the new flintlocks. Mallory dismounted and took a rifle from one of the crates when Vincent had wrenched the lid off. He carried the weapon over to Flagg and Walks Like a Bear and held it up to the war chief.

The Blackfoot took the rifle and studied it for a minute or so, finally grunting in approval. Flagg leaned over in the saddle to take a closer look and said, "Wait just a damned minute. That gun's got no flint. It won't fire."

"Of course not," Mallory said. "I'm not going to turn over functioning weapons to a bunch of savages. The flints have been removed from all of them."

An angry flush darkened Flagg's face. "That was the deal, Mallory."

"Don't worry, we have the flints," Mallory assured him. "But it will take some time to make the rifles workable. That will give my men a chance to get away before the savages can decide to try out the weapons on them."

"They weren't gonna do that," Flagg said, but Mallory thought the man was lying. The Blackfeet had planned on killing them all and taking the rifles.

"Well, now they won't have to resist the temptation."

Frowning, Flagg went on. "You said somethin' about your men gettin' away. What about you?"

"Oh, I'm not going anywhere," Mallory said.

"Vincent and the other men will return to St. Louis with the wagons, but I'm staying here."

"Here?" Flagg repeated. "Where?"

"With you and the chief." Mallory smiled. "I'm going to be there when those damned American upstarts learn to their everlasting regret that they never should have come out here in the first place."

Chapter 15

Preacher found beavers in several of his traps, so by the next day after the gang of would-be killers left the valley, he had a good start on another load of plews. He was glad that Fairfax and the rest of the men were gone, but doubt still plagued him a little.

Why had they come after him to start with? It had to be more than a desire for vengeance on Fairfax's part, he thought, no matter how much the man in the beaver hat hated him. Bringing that many men west cost a considerable amount.

With that uncertainty in mind, Preacher's senses remained at a high level as he made the rounds of his trap lines. Of course, there was nothing unusual about that. He always stayed alert. Best way to stay alive, he had learned.

So when Dog suddenly stiffened, his hackles lifting, and let out a deep-throated growl, Preacher instantly lifted his eyes to search for a threat. He had been scraping the hide from one of the beavers he had skinned, but he put the knife aside and reached for his rifle instead.

Horse was grazing a few yards away on the tree-shaded bank of the stream where Preacher had found the beaver in one of his traps. The stallion lifted his head and peered off into the woods. His ears twitched.

Horse was looking in the same direction as Dog. Preacher knew the animals smelled something that he couldn't, and they didn't like it.

"All right, Dog, go see what it is," he said in a low voice as he straightened to his feet.

Without hesitation, Dog streaked off into the brush.

"Stay, Horse," Preacher told the stallion. Then he followed Dog, moving at a more deliberate pace. His eyes moved constantly as he threaded his way through the trees.

After a few moments, he heard Dog growling again. The sound held an added urgency now. Preacher broke into a run as Dog barked. Running made more noise, but Preacher had a hunch there was no time to waste.

He broke out of the trees in a small clearing at the foot of a bluff. He'd made camp in this spot a time or two, he recalled.

Somebody else occupied the clearing now. An Indian, Crow by the looks of the decorations on his buckskins, had his back pressed against the bluff's granite face. He had a tomahawk gripped in one hand, and he waved the weapon back and forth in front of him as if he were trying to fend off the big cur.

Dog wasn't trying to attack the Indian, though. He just stood there, growling and barking, keeping his quarry pinned against the bluff.

Not that the man was going to run off, Preacher saw. The Indian was hurt. His shoulders were hunched over like he was in pain, and the tomahawk's movements were slow and feeble. His left arm was pressed across his belly. Blood dripped onto the ground at his mocassined feet.

It must have been the blood Dog smelled, Preacher thought. That, along with the distinctive odor of the rancid bear grease that the Indian had rubbed on his hair, was enough to tell the big cur that something was wrong.

Preacher saw all of that in a heartbeat when he entered the clearing. The wounded man looked up, saw Preacher, and snarled. He spat out some words.

Preacher spoke the Crow lingo pretty well. He understood what the wounded man was saying. It was a challenge and a warning at the same time, a defiant vow to kill the white man if Preacher came a step closer . . . after, of course, killing the white man's devil wolf.

"He's not a wolf," Preacher said in the Crow tongue, surprising the man. "He's a dog . . . and I mean you no harm, friend."

Calling any Crow warrior "friend" was stretching things a mite where Preacher was concerned. He had killed a heap of them, and they had tried to kill him plenty of times.

But Preacher had never encountered this particular Crow before and had nothing against the man, who seemed to be alone. Not only that, but the way the fella was bleeding, he didn't represent much of a threat. He seemed to be unarmed except for the tomahawk.

"Who . . . are you?" the man asked.

Preacher hesitated before answering that. If he

admitted who he was, the wounded warrior might try to kill him, just on general principles.

But Preacher wasn't in the habit of lying, also on general principles, so he said, "Some call me Preacher."

The man's eyes widened. "Some call you . . . Crow Killer!" he grated.

"I've been called lots of things. The point is, I don't have any reason to kill you. I'd like to help you."

The man shook his head and said, "You cannot help me. The hated Blackfeet have . . . stolen my life . . . and the lives of my friends."

Preacher wasn't surprised to hear that the man wasn't out here alone. He wasn't painted for war, so he'd probably been part of a hunting party. This area was shared on a tentative and often bloody basis by the Blackfeet, the Crow, the Shoshone, and the Sioux. The Crow were usually a mite farther east, the Blackfeet more to the north. But they ran into each other from time to time, usually with violent results.

"Where are the others?" Preacher asked.

"All . . . dead," the wounded man panted. "Their bodies lie . . . I do not know . . . somewhere not far . . . I no longer know where I am . . ."

It was quite an admission for an Indian to say that he was hurt so bad he didn't know where he was. Preacher knew that was what this man meant. The fella had lost a lot of blood and probably wouldn't last much longer. He sure as hell wouldn't if he didn't let Preacher help him.

That decision was out of the wounded man's hands, along with the tomahawk. With a groan, he slumped forward and the weapon slipped from his fingers. He landed on his knees, caught himself with the hand that had held the tomahawk, and with the last of his strength lifted his head to glare murderously at Preacher.

"Stay . . . back!" he gasped. "I will kill . . ."

He pitched forward on his face, the rest of the threat unvoiced.

Preacher hurried forward. He kicked the tomahawk well out of reach, just in case the Crow warrior found some unguessed-at strength somewhere, and then knelt at the man's side. He found a pulse in the man's neck. It was fast and irregular but still there.

Carefully, Preacher rolled the wounded man onto his back. He lifted the buckskin shirt and saw the arrow shaft protruding a couple of inches from the man's belly. He hadn't been able to see it before because of the way the man had kept his arm pressed to his midsection. The arrowhead was buried deep in the man's gut. Either he had snapped off the rest of the shaft himself, or he'd fallen and broken it off that way.

Didn't really matter. The fella was as good as dead. Nobody recovered from a belly wound like that.

The Crow stirred and groaned. His eyelids flickered open. Preacher saw the agony in the man's eyes. The Crow's lips moved. Preacher leaned closer to make out the words.

"If you would . . . help me . . . end my suffering."

Preacher nodded. A quick slash across the man's throat with his razor-edged hunting knife would usher him into the next world with swiftness and a lot less pain than he was going through now.

But first, something prodded Preacher to ask, "What happened to you and your friends?"

The man blinked and looked confused, as if puzzled why Preacher would be asking him such a question at a time like this. But if there was a Blackfoot war party in the valley, Preacher wanted to know about it.

More importantly, the folks back at the trading post and settlement needed to know about it.

"We were . . . hunting," the wounded Crow managed to say. "A party of . . . Blackfeet . . . attacked us."

"A war party?"

"They were . . . painted for war."

A chill went through Preacher at those words. He had suspected as much, but hearing it confirmed brought home the danger that the settlers faced. He wasn't worried about himself; a man alone could easily avoid a larger group. He could probably even pick off a few of them if he wanted to.

But there wasn't time for that. He needed to get back to the settlement and warn the folks there. If everybody forted up inside the stockade at the trading post, they would have a chance to fight off the attack. Anyone caught outside the fence would probably be slaughtered, though.

The wounded man drew Preacher's attention back to the here and now by saying, "You said . . . you would help me."

"That's right, I did." Preacher reached for his knife.

But before he could draw it, the Crow's back arched and his eyes opened wide. His breath came out of him in a long sigh as he sagged back to the ground, and when the last of the air left his body, his life went with it. His dark eyes, open and staring, began to glaze over.

Preacher took the time to press the man's eyelids closed. If things had been different, he would have honored the warrior's spirit by seeing that his body was laid to rest properly, in the Crow fashion.

But there was no time for that now. As he straightened, he glanced up through the trees at the sky and judged the amount of light remaining. Even going back to fetch Horse right now and riding as hard as he could, it would probably be dark before he could reach the settlement.

All he could do was hope that he would be in time, he thought as he said, "Come on, Dog," and broke into a run through the trees.

It would have been all right with Colin Fairfax if he never had to spend another night alone in this wilderness. The terrors he had experienced during his long trek back to St. Louis the year before had come back to him with the fall of darkness.

Even though the situation was much different—he had a horse now and was well armed, with plenty of provisions—as night closed in he had felt again like the cold, starving, miserable wretch he had been for long weeks during his journey. Unwilling to build a fire since he didn't want to give away his continued presence in the valley, he sat in the dark, eyes wide with fear, hands clutching his rifle, until exhaustion finally claimed him.

His sleep wasn't very restful, but even so, he felt

much better once the sun was up the next morning. He had set off toward the trading post again. In the light of day, he was able to think about his plan, rather than the nameless horrors that lurked in the night.

He had reached the vicinity of the settlement around midday and positioned himself atop a small, wooded knoll where he could keep an eye on the place. He had a spyglass in his pack, but used it sparingly because he didn't want anyone to notice the sun reflecting off the lens.

Even without it, he could see that the wagons that had been at the trading post a couple of days earlier were gone now. He hadn't seen the wagons himself, but some of his scouts had reported that they were there.

Fairfax was glad the wagon train had departed. He didn't need any extra people around the trading post when he kidnapped Deborah Hart.

He could see through the open gates from where he was, and he spotted Deborah a couple of times during the afternoon. Training the spyglass on her momentarily, he saw that she was as lovely as ever.

Her stomach was definitely rounded, though. Fairfax frowned as he thought about that. If Deborah was with child, that might complicate things.

On the other hand, her condition might mean that Preacher would be that much more desperate to rescue her. Maybe that urgency would make the mountain man reckless.

As the sun lowered toward the mountains, Fairfax made up his mind. He would go to the trading post this evening. He could ride in through the gates at dusk, just before the guards closed them.

Chances are, no one there would recognize him except the Harts and Deborah. He was dressed like a fur trapper now, in buckskins and a coonskin cap he had gotten from Campbell when he gave the man his beaver hat to wear on the way out of the valley. No one would pay much attention to him.

Once inside, he would avoid the trading post itself until he'd had a chance to scout out the situation. Once it was good and dark, he would get into the building somehow and kill Corliss and Jerome Hart. Getting his revenge on the cousins would be quite satisfying. Then he would take Deborah and vanish into the night.

He wasn't worried about Preacher being able to follow him. The mountain man had demonstrated an uncanny ability to follow a trail.

This time, however, the trail would lead Preacher to his death, Fairfax thought with a smile of anticipation.

Finally, the sun slipped below the mountains to the west. Though the sky remained rosy, shadows began to gather quickly in the valley.

It was time, Fairfax told himself. He mounted up and rode toward the settlement, confident that before this night was over he would be well on his way to accomplishing his goal.

Chapter 16

"This is as far as I go," Ezra Flagg said as he reined in. "The settlement's not more'n a quarter of a mile from here."

Clyde Mallory brought his mount to a halt as well, as did Walks Like a Bear and the other members of the Blackfoot war party. Mallory said, "You're not going to take part in the attack?"

The renegade white man shook his head. "There's only so much I'll do for money, mister. Slaughterin' women and kids ain't part of it."

Mallory felt a twinge of misgiving, but forced it far back into his mind. He wasn't going to think too much about what was going to happen tonight. Instead, he would concentrate on everything that England would gain in the long run.

But there *was* one pressing concern that had to be dealt with.

"I'm sorry, but you have to accompany me," he said to Flagg. "I don't speak the chief's tongue, and I may need to communicate with him. If you don't choose to take part in the actual attack, that's your business, but I still have need of you."

Flagg stiffened in the saddle. "I ain't used to bein' talked to like that," he spat out. "We had a deal, but it didn't include you givin' me orders!"

Mallory saw that he had made a mistake. Perhaps a more reasonable approach would be more effective.

"It's just that I have to reach my sister and make sure that she's safe," he said. "I'm afraid that in their, ah, bloodlust, the savages may harm her."

Flagg sounded a little mollified as he said, "I can explain all that to the chief."

"But he won't be right there beside every one of his men during the entire battle," Mallory pointed out. "I need someone who can make himself understood to go with me while I find Laura and make sure she's safe. Surely you can see that."

Flagg sat there for a long moment, frowning in the light from the millions of stars that floated in the dark night sky overhead. He scratched his bearded jaw, grimaced, and finally said, "All right, damn it. I'll come with you. But I'm stayin' out of the fight if I can."

"Fair enough," Mallory agreed. "Is the chief ready?"

Flagg turned to Walks Like a Bear and spoke briefly in the Blackfoot tongue. The chief grunted something in response, clenched his right hand into a fist, and thumped it hard against his chest.

Mallory took that to mean that Walks Like a Bear was indeed ready to attack the settlement.

He turned his head to look at the Indians bunched behind them. He wasn't sure how many of them there were, but at least sixty warriors had ridden out of the trees at the rendezvous point.

They had looked at the departing wagons with savage expressions on their faces, and Mallory knew they wanted to attack the vehicles that represented the white man's inexorable advance into territory that had always belonged to them. Walks Like a Bear had spoken sharply, though, and instead of going after the wagons, his men had dismounted and begun taking the rifles from the now-open crates.

After that, it was simply a matter of turning over the flints to them and waiting while the weapons were armed. Mallory knew he was taking a chance. They might decide to go ahead and kill him.

Flagg had spoken at length to the chief, though, and Mallory suspected he knew what the turncoat was saying. If they spared Mallory's life, he might help them again in the future in their war against the white men. He could prove to be more valuable alive than dead.

Whatever Flagg had said, it worked, and now Mallory, Flagg, Walks Like a Bear, and the rest of the war party sat on their horses in the thick shadows of the trees along a ridge overlooking the settlement. Flagg had called a halt there to announce his intention of leaving the group. Now that Mallory had persuaded him otherwise, there was no need for any further delay.

"Well, then, gentlemen," Mallory said, "shall we go?"

Laura looked out the door of her cabin at the lights in the trading post and wished for a moment that she could go over there. The cabin was as nicely furnished as it could be in this wilderness, but it was still a squalid hovel compared to the house in London where she had lived as a child.

That was before the death of her parents, of course. After their mother passed away, she and Clyde had been shuffled about between various relatives, and often they had been treated more like servants than members of the family.

The resentment Laura had felt at that treatment had festered within her, growing into the hatred she directed at the Americans for taking her father away from her and starting the chain of events that had ruined her life.

As bad as things had been back then, she'd still always had people around her. She hadn't experienced the sort of isolation she felt here. Of course there were people here, too, but not the sort whose presence gave Laura any comfort. They were oafish American louts, and she despised them all.

So even though she longed for lights and sounds and human company, she closed the cabin door and stayed where she was. Anyway, she told herself, if she went over to the trading post, she would have to put up with the lecherous stare of Corliss Hart, the annoying nervous mannerisms of his cousin Jerome, the simpering sweetness of Deborah Hart, and even the stupidity of that boy Jake, who was usually with them. Better to just stay here.

And of course, by morning they would all be dead, she added mentally. At least, they would be if the attack took place tonight as she and Clyde had planned.

Something might happen to delay it, she thought.

In which case, the next night would be the fatal one, or the night after that. Laura was prepared to wait for however long it took.

And this would be only the first step in a long campaign of revenge . . .

She walked over to the table and picked up one of the pistols that lay there. They were loaded and primed but not cocked.

Clyde had assured her that he would keep the savages away from her cabin, but sometimes things happened that were beyond anyone's control. If she had to, if any of the Indians burst in here intent on harming her, she wouldn't hesitate to shoot them . . . or anyone else who threatened her.

She thought about Preacher then. She was glad he had left the settlement in time to avoid the attack. Although he wasn't handsome, at least not in the way to which she was accustomed, he had a certain rough charm about him. He had been as quick to defend her honor as any British gentleman would have been.

And he was much more dangerous than any British gentleman she had ever encountered. It was a good thing he was gone. Even though she doubted that his presence could make any difference in the outcome of the battle, that was a chance better not taken.

She stiffened as the sudden drumming of hoofbeats came in through the windows from somewhere in the night. With a gasp, Laura swung around, still clutching the pistol in her hand.

Was the attack starting? She rushed to the door and flung it open to peer out into the darkness. Her heart pounded in her chest. Vengeance was at hand!

But something was wrong, she realized a moment later. Instead of dozens of horses rushing toward the settlement, she heard only one.

One man, riding hell-bent through the night . . . Even though she had no idea how it was possible, a single thought burned its way through Laura Mallory's brain at that moment.

Preacher!

A short time earlier, as dusk was settling in, Colin Fairfax had ridden in through the gates in the sturdy stockade fence around the trading post. The coonskin cap was pulled down tightly on his head, concealing the fact that he was mostly bald.

Anyway, he told himself, plenty of men were bald. It wasn't a sign of guilt. As long as he avoided the Harts, no one would suspect that he was up to no good.

"Howdy, mister," one of the guards at the gates greeted him. "New hereabouts, ain't you?"

"That's right," Fairfax replied with a nod. "Just got here."

"Well, welcome to . . ." The man's voice trailed off, and he looked over at the other guard. "We gotta give this place a name."

"That ought to be up to Corliss and Jerome," the other man said. "Wouldn't even be no settlement here if it wasn't for their tradin' post."

"Yeah, I reckon. Anyway, welcome, mister. If you're lookin' for a drink, the Harts got the best whiskey in these parts."

Fairfax nodded again and said, "Much obliged." He had no intention of going to the trading post for a drink, but he rode in that direction anyway, so the guards wouldn't be suspicious of him.

He tied his horse at the very end of the hitch rack, as far away from the trading post door as he could. Then he stepped up into the shadows at the end of the porch and pressed his back against the rough log wall of the building.

The trading post had no windows, but there were chinks between the logs and rifle ports as well. Fairfax found a tiny opening and pressed an eye to it.

From this angle he couldn't see much, only some shelves where pelts that the Harts had taken in on trade were stacked. Fairfax grimaced and stole along the wall, looking for another chink. He hoped no one saw him lurking around like this.

The second opening he found afforded him a better view, even though it was a narrow one. He could see all the way to the rear of the trading post where Corliss and Jerome Hart moved around behind a counter. They came in and out of Fairfax's sight several times as he watched. He didn't see Deborah, but surely she was in there, he thought.

Approaching footsteps and men's voices made him straighten hurriedly from his crouch. He sat down on the porch with his back against the wall and drew his knees up in front of him. He leaned his head forward and rested it and his arms on his knees as if he were either drunk or sleeping or both. The men walked past, paying no attention to him.

Fairfax looked up as he heard a scraping noise. Several men were closing the gates for the night. Once they'd been swung shut, thick beams were lowered onto hooks to bar them. Fairfax wouldn't be getting out again that way, at least not easily. He would have to find some other way out with Deborah Hart.

Which meant she would have to be unconscious when he left with her; otherwise, she was bound to raise an alarm. He planned to kill Corliss and Jerome before he left if he could, but Deborah was more of a problem. He wanted her alive.

Live bait always worked best.

He would figure it out as he went along, Fairfax told himself. He had always been good at improvising, at seizing whatever opportunities fate presented to him. If he hadn't been, he wouldn't have lived as long as he had.

He sat there in the shadows, thinking, as the darkness deepened. People were still moving around the trading post, but not many now. Fairfax stood up, thinking that the time had come to try to get in there somehow and find Deborah . . .

That was when he heard the swift rataplan of pounding hoofbeats somewhere outside the stockade, racing closer with each passing second. Anyone riding that fast in the night usually carried trouble with him, and Fairfax caught his breath as a horrible thought occurred to him. He didn't know why, he didn't know how . . .

But he was convinced that was Preacher thundering through the night toward him.

Preacher had made many a fast ride in his life, but few had been faster or more urgent than the one he made this night. He was reminded of stories his mother had told him about Paul Revere, back in the days before he had left the family farm to find adventure in the West.

That Revere fella had ridden to warn the patriots around Boston that the British army was coming. The fate of nations had depended on him. Nothing so earth-shaking depended on Preacher tonight . . .

Only the lives of his friends.

For Preacher, that was more than enough.

So he sent Horse lunging ahead, riding over hills, through valleys, across streams. Thickets of brush and brambles sometimes clawed and tore at them, but Preacher lowered his head and forged on, ignoring the painful scratches. The big stallion was just as determined, and slowed down only when he had to in order to keep his footing.

Dog ran after them, falling behind but stubbornly staying on their trail. If nothing happened to slow them down, Preacher and Horse would reach the settlement before the big cur did, but Dog wouldn't be very far behind them.

As darkness fell, Preacher hauled back on Horse's reins. He couldn't afford to have the stallion fall and break a leg. Afoot, he would never reach the settlement in time to warn everyone about the Blackfoot war party. So they eased back to a pace that was still fast, but not as breakneck as before.

Every minute that passed gnawed at Preacher's vitals. He thought about Deborah Hart and the new life growing within her; about Corliss and Jerome, who, for all their bickering and annoying habits, were good men at heart; about Jake, who might grow into a fine man someday if given the chance; and about all the other settlers and trappers who were at the trading post. If the Indians took them by surprise, they might all be wiped out.

Finally, he entered the valley that led to the trading post. Snowcapped mountains loomed on his right, starlight glittering on the snow that stayed there all year round.

The Blackfoot war party had to be ahead of him somewhere, between him and the settlement. He veered as close to the foothills as he could in hopes that he could get past them before they knew he was anywhere around.

It was inevitable that they would hear the rolling thunder of Horse's hoofbeats, though, so Preacher wasn't surprised a few minute later when several riders galloped out of the darkness toward him. The Blackfoot war chief had sent a few of his warriors to see who was riding so desperately through the night, but he hadn't split his main force by much.

Preacher leaned forward over Horse's neck and patted the stallion's shoulder. "Give it all you got, big fella," he urged.

The Indians whooped in excitement. They couldn't resist the thrill of the chase. Angling sharply across the valley floor, they moved to intercept Preacher.

They underestimated Horse's speed, though, even after the hard run the stallion had already made. Reaching down deep inside, Horse found the strength to surge ahead and sweep past the Blackfeet. Angry yells came from them as they whirled their ponies to take up the chase.

But before they could even get started on the pursuit, a large, thickly furred shape came flying out of the darkness and slammed into one of the Indians, knocking him off his mount. The warrior landed on the ground with stunning force, and before he could move, Dog's sharp teeth had torn his throat out. Blood spurted high in the air.

Dog whirled away from the man he had just mauled. One of the Blackfeet tried to skewer him with a lance, but the big cur twisted out of danger. Just like the wolves he so strongly resembled, he darted in and hamstrung one of the ponies. It went down with a shrill scream, throwing its rider. Dog was on him in a flash. His jaws locked around the Indian's arm and clamped down, breaking bones with a crunching sound.

Up ahead, Preacher heard the screams and the angry shouts and figured that Dog had made his presence known. The cur was buying time for him . . . buying time for everyone at the settlement, in fact . . . and Preacher hoped that his old friend got away from the Blackfeet safely.

But if he didn't, it would be a proud death, fighting his enemies until the last breath.

Preacher and Horse raced on, the stallion giving everything he had. Preacher worried that he was riding Horse to death, but he couldn't afford to slow down. He was confident that he was ahead of the war party now, and the trading post was only a couple of miles away. The settlers wouldn't have much warning, but maybe it would be enough.

The valley's grassy floor swept by under Horse's flashing hooves. Preacher saw the yellow glow of lights up ahead, along with a dark shape that he knew to be the stockade wall. He was only a hundred yards from the closest outlying cabin when he used his left hand to pull one of the pistols from behind his belt.

He cocked the weapon, pointed it into the air, and fired. The booming report rolled out and echoed from the foothills. Preacher bellowed, "Indians! Indians! Everybody into the stockade!"

Chapter 17

Preacher didn't know how far behind him the main body of the war party was, but they had to be pretty close. The settlers had only minutes to get to safety inside the stockade.

From the corner of his eye, he saw a man rush out of the first cabin as Horse flashed past it. The man had a flintlock in one hand, and was using the other to pull up his suspenders as he stared in alarm at Preacher riding by.

More people scurried out of the other cabins to see what all the commotion was about. Preacher kept shouting, "Indians! Head for the stockade!"

Men grabbed their wives and kids and hustled them through the night toward the trading post. There were quite a few youngsters at the settlement, some white, some half-breed children of trappers and their squaws. Their Indian blood wouldn't save them from the marauding Blackfeet, though.

Preacher was close enough now to yell to the men inside the stockade, "Open the gates! Folks comin' in! Open the gates!"

For a moment, he thought the guards were going to ignore him, thinking that this might be some sort of trick on the part of an enemy who wanted to get inside. He was about to shout out to them who he was when he saw the gates begin to swing back slowly. He hauled back on the reins, pulling Horse into a tight turn.

He wasn't going to dash inside to safety when there were folks out here trying to reach the stockade. He saw them running toward the trading post and heard their frightened yells. He waved an arm at them and called, "Hurry! No time to waste!"

His eyes searched the darkness for any sign of the war party. He listened intently, and after a moment he heard hoofbeats in the night like the sound of distant drums.

They were closing in. A matter of minutes now, Preacher thought.

The trading post was ablaze with light. Every lantern in the place looked to be burning. Torches placed at intervals along the stockade wall were set ablaze so that they cast their glare over the surrounding area. That light would help the defenders on the parapet aim their rifles when the enemy rushed the walls.

Right now, that light showed frightened settlers hurrying frantically toward the stockade. Several of them ran past Preacher, and he began to think that maybe they were all going to make it inside before the Blackfeet struck.

Then guns began to roar on the outskirts of the settlement, followed by shouts and screams, and

Preacher knew that despite his desperate race, not everyone was going to make it.

Colin Fairfax huddled in the shadows next to the trading post wall as he heard the roar of the shot and then the deep, powerful voice shouting its warning. That familiar voice confirmed his worst suspicions.

Preacher had somehow come out of nowhere to threaten his plans yet again!

Alarmed yells came from inside the trading post. People who ventured out this far from civilization knew that they were living on the knife-edge of danger all the time, so they remained alert.

The Harts had been warned now, Fairfax thought with a bitter grimace. There was no way he could get into the trading post and kidnap Deborah Hart.

Instead it was going to require some luck just to live through the Indian attack and not be recognized by any of the people here who knew him. As men began to run toward the ladders leading up to the parapet, Fairfax leaped down from the porch and hurried to join them. He wanted to keep his face turned away from the trading post itself.

Of course, that meant he would have to help fight off the Indians, and he would be risking his life doing that, too.

But if he could survive tonight's battle and slip away, perhaps he would have another chance later to even the score with Preacher.

Torches placed along the top of the wall flared up as Fairfax slung his flintlock over his shoulder and ascended the nearest ladder. When he reached the top he hurried to a spot halfway between two of the torches where their light wasn't quite so bright.

A burly man came up beside him and asked, "What do you reckon's happenin' out there, friend?"

"It sounds like someone's warning that an Indian attack is imminent," Fairfax replied, thinking that the man was a dolt for not realizing that. Preacher's voice rang loud and clear through the night, ordering the settlers to hurry into the stockade.

The man beside Fairfax clutched a rifle and licked his lips nervously. "I figured there'd be some trouble with the redskins sooner or later," he said. "I knew that when I come out here. But it's different somehow. You think you know what it's gonna be like, but you don't. You don't ever know until it's rushin' straight at you, like it is right now."

Fairfax wanted to tell the man to stop his damned babbling, but he held his tongue. He might need this dullard to save his life before the night was over.

The gates had been opened and people hurried in, most of them either half-dressed or clad in night-clothes. Pale-faced men shepherded along half-hysterical women clutching infants.

Fools, Fairfax thought. Damned fools. What had they hoped to accomplish by coming out here? Did they actually think their lives were going to be better? It was only a matter of time before *something* bad happened to them.

And evidently, tonight was the night for that something to happen.

Suddenly, the sight of a buckskin-clad man on a horse caught Fairfax's eye. Man and horse were at the very edge of the light cast by the torches, but with a shock of hate that went all the way through him, Fairfax recognized them.

Preacher, riding that big ugly stallion!

In that moment, as gunshots began to roar on the northern edge of the settlement, a maddened impulse rushed through Fairfax. He jerked his rifle to his shoulder and shouted, "Look, there's one of the Indians!" as he thumbed back the hammer.

Then his sights settled on Preacher and he pulled the trigger.

A surge of instinctive fear went through Laura Mallory as she heard the pounding hoofbeats, the roar of gunshots, the terrified screams. She had already blown out the lamp, and now she stood in darkness, both pistols clutched in her hands. The weapons were loaded, primed, and cocked.

If one of those painted, red-skinned savages came crashing through the door, he would get a surprise. A lead surprise right in the middle of his howling face.

Laura didn't think it would come to that, though. She had confidence in her brother. Clyde planned to accompany the war party so that he could protect her, and she knew that nothing would stop him from carrying out his plan.

Still, hearing the shots and those terrible cries grated on Laura's nerves. She hoped that Clyde would show up soon.

One thing puzzled her. Just before the violence broke out, she would have sworn that she heard Preacher's voice shouting somewhere nearby.

That should have been impossible. He had left the

settlement a couple of days earlier to return to the mountains and his traps. He should have been gone for a week, probably longer.

Why would he have returned so soon, tonight of all nights?

With a shake of her head, Laura put that possibility out of her mind. It didn't really matter, she told herself. If Preacher was here, he would be wiped out with the rest of the Americans. Laura had no sympathy for him . . . no matter how ruggedly attractive he was.

No, Preacher would just have to take his chances like everyone else in this world.

The shots were louder and closer now. Laura couldn't stand it any longer. She had to see what was going on.

She went to the front window, unbarred the shutters, and opened one of them a few inches so she could peer out into the night. She saw a sudden spurt of orange about a hundred yards away and recognized it as the flame from a gun muzzle.

In that instant of illumination, she caught a glimpse of figures rushing past on horseback and men on foot running for their lives. Then the darkness closed back in, only to be split again and again by more muzzle flashes.

Laura became aware of a shifting, reddish light coming from the direction of the trading post. Was the place on fire already?

She leaned forward to check, but she couldn't see the trading post from this angle. Torn by indecision, after a moment she went to the door, set the bar aside, and opened it, too. If the trading post burned down, then even if all the Americans weren't killed, surely the survivors would abandon the settlement.

She stepped outside and turned toward the stockade. A twinge of disappointment went through her as she saw that the light came from torches set along the walls. The buildings inside weren't ablaze at all.

A frenzied, high-pitched yipping assaulted her ears, causing her to jerk around. Her eyes widened in horror as she saw one of the Indians mounted on a swift pony charging straight toward her. The savage howled in glee and pumped a rifle above his head triumphantly.

It had been a mistake for her to step outside, Laura realized, a terrible error.

Quite possibly, the last mistake she would ever make.

But she was damned if she would just stand there and allow that redskin to trample her without even trying to fight back.

She thrust both of the pistols toward the Indian and pulled the triggers.

Clyde Mallory had had no idea who the lone rider could be, but when the man came up behind the war party and then tried to sweep past, Flagg and Walks Like a Bear had taken quick action to deal with the problem, sending a small group of warriors to intercept and kill him.

Unfortunately, things hadn't quite worked out that way. The man had gotten past them and raced ahead to the settlement. His mount obviously possessed a great deal of speed.

Then had come the warning shot and the shouts of

alarm, and Mallory had uttered the shocked exclamation, "Preacher!"

It didn't seem possible. The man had left the settlement and wasn't expected back any time soon.

And yet here he was, threatening to ruin everything! Mallory had no doubt that Preacher was the man who had raced past the war party in the darkness.

The number of men in the settlement was roughly equal to the number of Blackfoot raiders. Mallory had tried to make a rough count of them while he was there. There were a few boys like Jake who might be old enough to fight as well.

But with the element of surprise on their side, Mallory had had no doubt that he and his allies could kill most of the settlers who were outside the stockade before anyone knew what was going on, and then they would be able to overwhelm the relatively few defenders inside the walls.

But if Preacher's warning allowed the majority of the Americans to get inside before they were wiped out, that could change everything. Even well armed with the new rifles, the warriors might not be able to overrun the stockade. The plan was on the verge of ruin, and the Blackfeet would have to act swiftly and ruthlessly if they were going to succeed.

Luckily, the savages were capable of doing exactly that. As they reached the edge of the settlement and opened fire, Mallory saw several of the fleeing settlers fall, shot in the back as they ran. Others were trampled under the hooves of Blackfoot ponies.

Mallory hung back and watched the fighting. He didn't want to get close enough to be spotted and recognized, just in case any of the settlers survived.

Ezra Flagg was with him, and when Mallory glanced over at the man, he saw that Flagg's expression was taut and grim.

"Having second thoughts, old boy?"

"I took your money," Flagg snapped. "I don't back out on a deal. I don't have much stomach for killin' women and kids, though."

"You mean you don't have much stomach for observing it. You knew what would happen when you agreed to help me arm the savages."

Flagg's head turned sharply toward Mallory, and for a second the Englishman thought that he had pushed Flagg too far. Mallory's hand was on the butt of his pistol in case he needed to pull it in a hurry and blow the American out of the saddle.

That moment passed, though. Flagg's tension eased. He said, "Yeah, I reckon a deal's a deal. Hadn't we better go see about your sister?"

"Indeed," Mallory agreed. "That's a splendid suggestion."

He urged his horse into motion again, heading for the cabin that Laura occupied. He had selected it specifically with tonight's raid in mind. It was on the eastern edge of the settlement, farthest away from the trading post. Mallory thought he and Flagg could reach it without any of the settlers seeing them.

Anyway, the Americans were too panic-stricken to notice much of anything except their impending deaths as they rushed hysterically toward the stockade.

Mallory and Flagg circled the fighting, which had become fierce as some of the settlers rallied and tried to mount a defense around the cabins rather than making for the trading post. The almost constant flare of muzzle flashes split the night, flickering like lightning. That and the garish red glow from the torches atop the stockade wall gave the two men enough light so that they could see.

That light suddenly washed over a sight that struck sheer terror into Clyde Mallory's heart. The very thing he was trying to protect against looked like it was about to happen.

One of the Blackfoot warriors, caught up in the bloodlust of battle, yelled savagely and rode his pony straight toward the tall, fair-haired woman who stood just outside the cabin door. *Laura!* He had told her to stay inside, Mallory thought wildly. What was she doing out of the cabin?

The answer wasn't important. The only thing that was important to Mallory was somehow saving his sister.

He hauled his horse to a skidding, sliding halt and shouted to Flagg, "We've got to stop that Indian!"

At the same time, he lifted his rifle to his shoulder. He was a good marksman, but this was the most important shot of his life.

Laura's life depended on it.

Mallory pressed the trigger.

Chapter 18

At the sound of high-pitched yipping behind him, Preacher whirled Horse around to confront one of the Indians charging toward him.

Even as he did so, he felt as much as heard the wind-rip of a rifle ball past his ear. If he hadn't moved when he did, he would be dead now.

But close didn't count and Preacher had a more pressing problem: a hate-maddened Blackfoot drawing a bead on him and pulling the trigger.

Luckily, the warrior was firing from the back of a running pony. Preacher didn't know where the shot went, but it didn't hit him or Horse, and that was all he cared about at the moment. He raised his own rifle and fired. The Indian flipped backward off his mount as the heavy ball plowed into his chest.

As Preacher lowered the rifle, he had already forgotten about the man he'd just killed. Another thought had occurred to him, and it crowded everything else out of his brain.

Where was Laura Mallory?

He remembered Laura's brother Clyde saying that she was going to stay here at the settlement while Clyde returned to St. Louis with the wagons to outfit them for another trip west. Preacher knew that Clyde was gone; the torches cast enough light for him to see that the big covered wagons were no longer parked where they had been.

That meant Laura would be staying in one of the cabins, but Preacher had no idea which one. She might even be in the trading post right now, since it was still fairly early in the evening.

That was what he hoped for since she would be safer there, behind the stockade walls and inside the sturdy building, than anywhere else in the valley right now.

But there was just as good a chance she was among the terrified settlers trying to reach the stockade as the Blackfeet dashed among them on their killing spree. Preacher hadn't seen her so far, but that didn't mean she wasn't out here in all this commotion.

He urged Horse away from the stockade now, instead of toward the walls. He had to check the outlying cabins and make sure Laura hadn't been cut off and trapped.

Another Blackfoot on horseback rushed him from the side. The Indian's rifle must have been empty, because he used it like a club, holding on to the barrel and swinging the stock at Preacher's head.

Preacher ducked under the sweeping blow. His own rifle was empty, but that didn't stop him from thrusting it out like a lance and driving the barrel into the Blackfoot's belly.

The Indian doubled over and toppled off his horse. Preacher jerked Horse to the side. One of the stallion's steel-shod hoofs landed smack-dab in the middle of the warrior's face. Blood spurted and bone crunched under the impact, and then Preacher was past the man.

The raiders had set one of the cabins on fire. It blazed up, casting even more flickering, hellish light on the scene. Preacher raced past it, hoping that the burning cabin hadn't been Laura's. He wasn't going to allow himself to even think that.

He swung Horse in a wide curve toward the cabins along the eastern edge of the settlement. As he did so he spotted movement in front of one of the log structures. Firelight glinted on fair hair . . .

Laura!

And one of the marauding Blackfeet was bearing down on her, obviously intent on trampling her under his pony's hooves.

Preacher yanked Horse to a stop and grabbed one of his pistols from behind his belt. It would be a long shot for a short gun, but he didn't have time to reload his rifle. He thrust his arm out from his body and sighted along the pistol barrel in the uncertain light.

Just as he pulled the trigger, he saw twin plumes of flame erupt from Laura's hands and realized that she was armed with a brace of pistols, too. And from off on Preacher's left, another pair of muzzle flashes winked redly, with enough distance between them that Preacher knew two men had just fired rifles.

The Blackfoot flew off his pony like he'd been slapped by a giant hand. Preacher almost felt sorry for the bloodthirsty son of a bitch as lead tore through his body from three or four directions at once.

The varmint was killed good and proper, that was for sure. He crashed to the ground and didn't move again.

That still left the matter of getting Laura to safety. Preacher heeled Horse into a run again, intending to sweep her up on the stallion's back as he rode past her and carry her back to the trading post as fast as he could get there.

The defenders were going to have to close the gates pretty soon or risk the Indians getting inside. Preacher didn't want to get caught on the wrong side of those gates.

On the other hand, he thought suddenly, maybe he ought to just grab Laura and take off for the tall and uncut. They could slip off into the foothills, away from the battle.

But that would mean deserting the Harts and Jake and all the other settlers and just leaving them to their fate, whatever it might be.

Preacher knew he couldn't do that. Not even to save Laura Mallory.

So his mind shifted back to his original plan, to grab her and make for the stockade . . .

That thought was going through Preacher's mind when something crashed into his head and sent him spiraling off into a darkness deeper than even the darkest night.

Damn the man's luck!

Once again Preacher had moved just as Colin Fairfax drew a bead on him and pulled the trigger. It was maddening the way Preacher managed to dodge death again and again, often when he wasn't even trying to, as if he had some sort of beneficent fate guiding his actions.

Or a guardian angel, Fairfax thought, even though he had seen too much evil in his life to truly believe in such heavenly beings. Hell might well exist, but Fairfax had his doubts about Heaven.

Preacher dashed away on horseback, obviously unhurt, as the man on the parapet next to Fairfax yelled, "You damn fool! That weren't no Injun! That was Preacher!"

Fairfax played dumb as he crouched down below the level of the wall made of sharpened timbers and began to reload his rifle. "Are you sure? It looked like an Indian to me."

"Yeah, I'm sure. What the hell do you think you were doin'? Preacher's on our side!"

Fairfax shook his head. "Sorry. I didn't know."

The stubborn bastard wouldn't let go of it, even in the middle of a battle against marauding Indians.

"You had to have seen him," he argued in a loud voice. "There was enough light. Looked to me like you were *tryin'* to kill him."

Fairfax's lips drew back from his teeth in a grimace. This idiot was going to ruin everything if he kept yelling like that. People were liable to start paying attention to his accusations. Fairfax still had some faint hopes of salvaging his plan, but he couldn't do it unless the man beside him on the parapet shut up.

Or unless someone shut him up.

"Listen," Fairfax said as he stepped closer to the

man, holding his rifle in his left hand and reaching behind him with his right, "I tell you it was an honest mistake . . ."

The settler glared and shook his head.

Fairfax brought the knife around and shoved it in the man's belly, driving it deep. When the blade was buried all the way to the hilt, he twisted it and ripped to the side with it.

The man's eyes opened wide and bulged out as the agony of his wound hit him. He didn't let out a sound, though, as he sagged against the wall. Fairfax caught hold of his shirt and braced him as the man slid down the logs and came to a stop in a sitting position.

Other defenders weren't far away on the parapet, but all their attention was focused outward on the attackers. Fairfax didn't think any of them had noticed what he'd done, but as he straightened from the dying man, another settler called, "What happened?"

"He's hit," Fairfax answered without hesitation. "Nothing we can do for him. It's too late."

The man who'd asked the question gave Fairfax a grim nod of acceptance. Losses were inevitable in a fight like this. Probably, no one would even check on the dead man's body until after the battle was over. Then they'd discover that he had been killed by a knife to the belly rather than a gunshot wound.

And if the Indians won . . . well, no one in here would *care* how the man died. No one would be left to care.

That was starting to look more and more likely. The fighting had spread all over the settlement. A cabin was on fire, and as Fairfax watched, another dwelling was put to the torch by the redskins.

He didn't see Preacher anymore. Maybe the mountain man had been killed in the fighting. Fairfax wasn't going to believe that unless he saw Preacher's body, though, and that seemed unlikely.

In fact, it was beginning to seem unlikely that he would get out of here alive himself, unless he did it soon. The gates were still open, with riflemen trying to defend them as a few stragglers fled frantically into the stockade, but the Indians were coming closer. They might soon be inside the walls . . .

Fairfax looked over his shoulder at the trading post. The Hart cousins were standing on the front porch holding rifles. He couldn't get in there and grab Deborah. It was just impossible, Fairfax realized.

He had to abandon the plan and concentrate on saving his life instead.

He began to move along the parapet as if looking for a suitable target, but he was really looking for a place where the fighting wasn't as fierce. Most of the Indians were on the east side of the stockade, so when Fairfax reached the southwest corner he saw only darkness out there. No muzzle flashes.

And no other defenders close by either.

He slung his rifle over his shoulder and grabbed hold of the tapered end of one of the upright logs that formed the wall. He drew himself up and threw a leg over. The sharpened ends were supposed to make it difficult to climb over the wall, and Fairfax had to be careful not to impale himself.

But he managed to make it, awkwardly, and started climbing down the outside of the wall, using the rawhide lashings that held the logs together for handholds. When he was low enough, he let go and dropped the rest of the way.

His booted feet thudded on the ground. He almost fell, but caught his balance and stayed upright.

It was dark back there, wonderfully dark. Fairfax loped away from the wall, not really caring where he went as long as it was away from there.

Behind him, the battle continued to rage. Flames leaped high, guns roared, men shouted and screamed and killed and died.

Fairfax didn't care about any of it. They could all wipe each other out as far as he was concerned. The only death that mattered to him was Preacher's.

And if the mountain man somehow survived the bloody chaos behind Fairfax—as Fairfax fully expected him to—then he would be dealt with another day.

The fleeing man disappeared into the shrouding shadows.

As Preacher galloped toward her, Laura Mallory saw that she'd been right earlier when she thought she heard his voice. The lean, rugged mountain man was unmistakable. Even though he wasn't supposed to be here, he was.

Then she let out a startled cry as Preacher's hat flew off his head and he fell off the stallion to land in a limp sprawl, rolling over a couple of times on the ground before coming to a stop with his left arm bent under him at an awkward angle and his head covered with blood. He didn't move after that.

Clearly he'd been shot, and from the looks of it, he

was either dead or badly wounded. Even though she had known him for only a short time, somehow that seemed impossible to Laura. Preacher wasn't supposed to get shot. He was the sort of man who always managed to cheat death.

But maybe not anymore.

Then more hoofbeats drew her attention, and she turned to see who was riding toward her now. If it was more Indians, she would dash back into the cabin, slam the door, and try to reload before the savages could break in.

A feeling of relief washed through her as she recognized her brother. "Clyde!" she cried. She didn't know the man riding with him, but she assumed he was the one who had arranged the alliance with the Indians.

Mallory raced up to the cabin, brought his horse to a stop, and swung down from the saddle. He caught Laura up in his arms and hugged her tightly.

"Are you all right, dear?" he asked as he stepped back a moment later.

She nodded. "I'm not hurt at all, just scared. What do we do now?"

Mallory turned and for a moment studied the battle going on around the settlement, then said, "We're going to get you out of here."

She clutched his arms. "Clyde, I saw Preacher—"

"I know. I saw him, too, and heard him trying to rally the settlers." A look of regret passed briefly across Mallory's face. "That's why I had to shoot him."

"*You* shot him?"

Mallory nodded. "That's right."

"But why?"

"We can't afford to have him turning the tide of this battle. I've heard enough about him to know that he's capable of incredible things. He might make a difference all by himself."

He was right, of course, Laura told herself. She drew a deep breath and nodded. "I understand. But it's a shame. I rather liked him, you know."

"So did I," Mallory said. "But in the end, he's just an American, like all the others." He took his sister's hand and tugged her toward his horse. "Let's get you out of here before anything else happens."

He mounted first and then pulled her up behind him. She put her arms around his waist to hang on.

At that moment, several Indians raced up on their ponies. Laura stifled a scream as she saw their fierce, painted faces surrounding them.

"Don't worry, darling," Clyde said. "These are our friends. This is Chief Walks Like a Bear. You don't know Mr. Flagg yet either."

"Ma'am," Flagg said as he gave her a curt nod. Then he spoke to the chief for a moment and went on. "Bear says they're about to storm the stockade. You want to wait around for that?"

Mallory considered it for a second, then shook his head. "No, I want to get Laura to safety. That's more important right now."

"All right. I'll ride with you folks."

The whole group turned their horses and rode away from the cabin, which other Blackfeet dashed up to and set on fire behind them. Laura glanced back once. She couldn't see Preacher anymore, but she knew his body lay there not far from the cabin.

Even though she hadn't argued with her brother, she

knew that Clyde was wrong about one thing . . . Preacher wasn't just like the other Americans. Preacher wasn't just like anyone else.

There was only one Preacher, and Laura felt a pang of loss at the knowledge that he was dead.

Chapter 19

Searing pain was the first thing Preacher became aware of as consciousness seeped back into his brain. At first, it was one overwhelming agony, but gradually it split into two. He realized that part of the pain was centered in his head, and the rest of it came from his left arm, which was doubled underneath him.

When he shifted slightly, the pain in both places grew worse. His head swam, and he thought he was going to pass out again.

But then he heard a peculiar thudding sound, and managed to lift his head and open his eyes. The sound was hoofbeats as several horses trotted away. The light wasn't good, but Preacher saw fair hair . . .

"Laura," he croaked, too low for anyone to hear him.

His eyesight sharpened a little, enough for him to see Laura Mallory riding on the back of a horse, behind a man who looked like her brother Clyde. Preacher couldn't figure out what Clyde was doing here at the settlement when he was supposed to be on his way back to St. Louis with the wagons.

But that didn't matter. What was important was that Laura and her brother were surrounded by Indians. The Blackfeet had captured them and were taking them away, probably intending to torture them to death!

Preacher groaned and tried to push himself to his feet. If he could find his rifle and reload it, he might be able to stop the savages from escaping with the Mallorys.

As he put weight on his left arm, though, fresh agony shot through it, as if imps from Hell were hacking away at it with knives. It collapsed underneath him, causing him to sprawl on his belly again. A black fog rolled through Preacher's brain for several seconds.

By the time he could lift his head again, Laura, Mallory, and their Indian captors were gone.

When the Good Lord was putting Preacher together, He'd left out the capacity for despair. But at that moment Preacher came mighty near to experiencing it.

He fought off the feeling. Something was wrong with his left arm, no doubt about that, but his right one still worked. If he was careful about it, he could get to his feet, find Horse, go after those damned Blackfeet . . .

Somebody grabbed his long, tangled black hair and hauled up hard on it, sending fresh waves of agony through his head. He heard a startled cry from above him as he swung his right arm up and back and drove the elbow into something yielding.

The Blackfoot warrior who'd been fixing to scalp

him must have thought he was already dead, Preacher realized.

That was a bad mistake for the varmint to have made.

Instinct, anger, and determination combined to give Preacher the strength he needed to ignore the pain and twist onto his back. At the same time he lashed out with a foot and caught the startled Indian in the belly with it. The Blackfoot went over backward.

Preacher kept rolling and got his right arm under him. He levered himself up with it until he could get his feet on the ground. Surging upright, he kicked the Indian again, this time in the jaw. Bone shattered, and the Blackfoot went down and stayed down.

Swaying as a wave of dizziness hit him again, Preacher managed to stay on his feet until it passed a few seconds later. His left arm hung limp and useless at his side. He lifted his right hand to his head, and found a patch of sticky wetness just above his right ear.

He had been creased by rifle balls in the past, and knew that was what had happened to him a few minutes earlier when he was knocked out of the saddle. He prodded the wound with his fingers and it hurt like hell, but he didn't figure his skull was busted.

The cabin that he supposed had been Laura Mallory's was burning now, and by the garish light of the blaze, he saw that his left arm was broken about halfway between the elbow and the wrist. It hung crooked, and he could see the lump where the broken bone was pressing up against the skin.

At least the bone hadn't torn all the way out of the

flesh. If he could find somebody to set it and splint it, it might heal up all right.

That would have to wait, though, because right now there was still a battle going on. He looked toward the stockade and saw that the gates were shut.

Muzzle flashes flickered along the walls as the defenders on the parapet fired down at the Blackfoot attackers. The Blackfeet had found all the cover they could and were pouring lead at the stockade.

Preacher wondered fleetingly where the attackers had gotten so many rifles, and good ones at that. Indians had adapted quickly to the firearms brought to the frontier by the white men. In fact, it had been an avid interest by a Blackfoot brave in a rifle belonging to one of Lewis and Clark's men that had led to the Indian's fatal shooting, that incident being the wellspring of the hostility that the Blackfeet had felt toward the whites ever since.

But usually, the only guns they had were ones they had stolen or taken off the corpses of their victims, and many of those were older trade muskets that weren't particularly accurate or reliable. Fact is, some of those muskets were prone to blowing up in the hands of anybody who tried to use them.

Preacher could tell by the crisp sound of the firing that the rifles being used by the Blackfeet in this raid were of much higher quality. That was going to make defeating them even harder.

Harder . . . but not impossible. Preacher looked around until he found the pistol he had dropped when he tumbled off Horse. His other pistol was still tucked behind his belt. He started limping toward the stockade.

Funny, he thought with a bleak grin, he hadn't even realized that he'd hurt his leg, too, until now.

Reloading a flintlock pistol one-handed was a right difficult chore, but Preacher managed. He stayed in the shadows of the cabins as he approached the Blackfeet from behind, but they weren't looking in this direction anyway. They thought all their enemies were in front of them.

Again, that was going to be a bad mistake, at least for some of them.

Preacher grimaced as he passed the body of a woman who had been shot in the back. A few yards further on lay the body of a girl about ten years old. Probably the woman's daughter, Preacher thought. She had sent the little girl running on ahead of her, but then she'd been killed and the girl was next.

Fury seethed like fire inside Preacher. He tamped it down. Killing took a steady hand and cold nerves.

He pressed his back against a cabin wall. Twenty feet away, a couple of Blackfeet warriors crouched behind a wagon and fired toward the stockade.

Preacher could see the rifles being used by the Indians and knew his guess had been right. The weapons looked new.

He took a deep breath and then stepped out and walked quickly toward the Indians. He was within five feet of them before something warned them of his approach. One of them started to turn, his mouth opening to shout a warning.

Preacher shot him in the side of the head. The ball crashed through the Indian's brain and exploded out the other side of his skull.

Even as the dead warrior was slumping against the

wagon with half his head gone, Preacher lunged at the other one and swung the now-empty pistol. The barrel crashed against the man's head with a satisfying crunch of bone. The Indian folded up.

That was two of the bastards done for, Preacher thought.

And one of them had just reloaded his rifle.

Preacher grinned as he picked up the long-barreled weapon. He knelt and rested the barrel on the wagon tongue. Firing one-handed like this, he wouldn't be able to control the recoil, but he didn't care about that.

He aimed at one of the Blackfeet who was crouched at the corner of a cabin, and squeezed the trigger. The rifle blasted, and the recoil tore it out of Preacher's hand just as he'd expected.

His target was now staggering around, trying futilely to reach the wound in his back where Preacher's shot had struck him. After a moment, he collapsed, kicked a couple of times, and then lay still.

Three.

Too damned many still to go.

But Preacher still had a loaded pistol and a belly full of rage.

He braced his right hand on the wagon tongue and pushed himself to his feet. So far, the Blackfeet hadn't noticed that they were under attack from the rear, but Preacher knew that kind of luck couldn't last. He needed something to help turn the tide . . .

He looked down at the bodies of the two Indians behind the wagon. Each of the warriors had a powder horn slung over his shoulder. Preacher reached down and tugged them free. Each powder horn was at least half full, he judged. And his horn had even more powder in it.

A grin pulled at the corners of his mouth.

Carrying the powder horns, he turned and ran back along the path he had followed. The bodies of several settlers lay on the ground, and most of the men had been carrying powder horns when they died. Preacher gathered up six more of the horns, each of them at least half full. A couple were almost completely full of black powder.

He tore the shirt off a man who had been scalped and wrapped it around all the powder horns, using the sleeves to tie the bundle closed.

Earlier, he had noticed more than a dozen members of the war party clustered behind one of the cabins. He limped toward them now, pausing to light one of the shirt sleeves on fire as he passed the smoldering remains of a burned cabin that had collapsed. The heat coming off the debris was painful against his face, but he ignored it.

With the shirt sleeve burning up closer and closer to the bundle of powder horns, Preacher broke into a run toward the largest group of Blackfeet. One of them saw him coming, yelled a warning, and swung a rifle toward him.

Preacher threw the flaming bundle as he dove forward. At the same time, the Indian fired. The ball sizzled through the air above Preacher's head.

The Blackfeet stood there, evidently so puzzled by what was happening that they didn't think to move. As the powder horns landed among them, the fire reached the volatile powder and ignited it.

The result wasn't actually an explosion, more like

a ball of fire that suddenly bloomed among them, spraying burning powder in their faces and over their bodies. They screamed and yelled, and some of them clapped hands over blinded eyes.

Preacher scrambled up and dashed past them. His presence outside the stockade walls was no longer a secret, so his hope now was that he make it to the gates while the Blackfeet were still confused by what had happened. If the defenders saw him coming, maybe they could open the gates just enough for him to slip inside.

That wasn't going to happen, he saw almost right away. More of the Indians ran to cut him off from the stockade. Infuriated, they didn't try to shoot him, but rather closed in around him, obviously intending to hack him to pieces with knives and tomahawks.

Preacher jerked out his remaining pistol. This one had a double-shotted load in it, and when he fired, the balls cut down two of the savages who were rushing at him side by side.

That created a little gap, but it closed before Preacher could leap through it. He slammed the empty pistol into the face of the nearest Blackfoot. Blood spurted as the impact crushed the warrior's nose and drove shards of bone into his brain, killing him.

Preacher dropped the gun and snatched his knife from its sheath, slashing a circle around him with the razor-sharp blade. He felt the fiery kiss of cold steel himself as Blackfoot knives found him.

Then one of the Indians screamed and went down, a shaggy gray shape atop him. His scream died in a gurgle as Dog ripped his throat out. The big cur spun and grabbed another man.

Dog wasn't the only one coming to Preacher's aid. A furious neigh announced Horse's arrival. The stallion reared up on his hind legs and lashed out with his front hooves. The bone-crushing power of the blows dropped two of the Indians, their skulls shattered.

Preacher was aware that his loyal trail partners had shown up to help him, but he didn't have time to watch what Dog and Horse were doing. He whipped the knife in his hand across the throat of a Blackfoot warrior, and felt the hot splash of blood on his knuckles. He twisted, drove the blade into another man's belly, and ripped it free with a savage stroke that opened the man's stomach and let his entrails spill out.

Despite the damage that Preacher, Dog, and Horse were doing, there were still too blasted many of the Indians. The mountain man and his companions were bound to be pulled down and killed in a matter of seconds . . .

But then, more men were suddenly among them. Guns blasted, knives flashed, rifle butts rose and fell. The brutal tide of hand-to-hand combat buffeted Preacher back and forth.

He caught a glimpse of Corliss Hart's face, pale and scared but resolute, as Corliss fired a pistol into the chest of a Blackfoot warrior. Jerome Hart, an unlikely battler if ever there was one, yelled incoherently as he drove a rifle butt into the face of another Indian.

The men who had been holed up inside the stockade had come out when they saw Preacher surrounded by the Blackfeet. He had already killed so many of the Indians that the odds were now on the side of the settlers. The battle ebbed and flowed fiercely for a couple of minutes, but then the final few shots rang out, the last death rattle sounded, and it was over.

Preacher was bleeding from half a dozen knife wounds, and he was already dizzy from being grazed on the head earlier. He would have collapsed if Corliss Hart hadn't grabbed his arm to hold him up.

Jerome took hold of Preacher's other arm, and Preacher let out a bitter curse.

"Take it easy . . . with that wing . . . Jerome," he panted. "It's . . . busted."

"My God! I can see that now. Corliss, we need to get him inside. He looks like he may be badly hurt."

"Wait!" Preacher said. "The Blackfeet . . ."

"All dead, or the next thing to it, except for the ones who ran with their tails between their legs," Corliss said. "They didn't expect us to come out again and bring the fight to them." He tried to steer Preacher toward the now-open gates. "Come on, we need to get you to the trading post. Deborah can patch you up—"

Preacher tried to pull away, but he was too weak from loss of blood and the shock of his injuries. "Got to . . . got to go . . ."

"You're not going anywhere," Jerome told him. "You need medical attention, and then a lot of rest."

"No time," Preacher insisted. "Laura . . ."

"You mean Miss Mallory?" Jerome asked. "We haven't seen her, but I'm sure she's around here somewhere—"

"No! The Blackfeet . . . had her . . . took her off somewhere . . ."

"Good Lord!" Corliss said. "You mean she's a prisoner of those savages?"

Preacher managed to nod. "That's right . . . We got to . . . go after 'em . . ."

But he wouldn't be going anywhere, at least not now. His eyes rolled up in their sockets and darkness closed in around him once again, a darkness this time shot through with the red glare of flames as several of the cabins continued to burn.

Then that faded as well, and Preacher knew no more.

Chapter 20

For the second time tonight, pain was the first thing Preacher was aware of as he regained consciousness. As his brain began to function, he reminded himself that he didn't *know* it was the same night.

No telling how much time had gone by since he passed out.

He heard voices, discerned the play of light and shadow against his eyelids. People were moving around him. He forced his eyes open, even though the lids felt as if they weighed a ton each.

The harsh glare of lantern light made him wince. Fresh pain shot through his head. He started to lift his left hand to his temple, but that arm wouldn't move.

He remembered that it was broken. The image of the bone pressing up against the skin in a grotesque lump was still vivid in his mind.

"Preacher's awake," a woman's voice said. For a second, Preacher hoped it was Laura Mallory's, but then he realized that it belonged to Deborah Hart as she went on. "Don't move, Preacher. You're badly hurt."

Her pretty face swam into view above him, frowning down in concern. Corliss and Jerome leaned in, too. Preacher figured out that he was lying in a bed somewhere, probably in the living quarters back of the trading post.

He was worried about Laura and wanted to get after her, but first he had to find out just what the situation was. After licking dry lips, he whispered, "You reckon a fella could . . . get a drink around here?"

"Of course," Jerome said. "Wait just a minute."

He disappeared from Preacher's sight, then came back a moment later carrying a tin cup that he handed to Deborah. She sat on the bed beside Preacher, put a hand behind his head to help him lift it, and held the cup to his lips.

He took a sip and felt the bracing burn of the whiskey. It helped dull the pain in his head and arm. After another sip, he was able to ask in a fairly strong voice, "Is this the same night?"

Deborah nodded. "That's right. You've been unconscious for a little more than an hour."

"How bad am I hurt?"

"Your left arm is broken," Deborah told him. "It's been set and splinted, and now it's strapped down so it can't move." She smiled. "It's probably a good thing you were unconscious for that, Preacher."

"Even out cold we had to hold you down," Corliss added.

"Who done the . . . settin' and splintin'?"

A weathered, bearded face came into Preacher's view. "I did," the old-timer said. Preacher recognized him as the trapper called Uncle Dan. "Weren't the first busted wing I ever set neither, so you don't need to worry that I didn't know what I was doin'."

"I'm much obliged," Preacher said with a nod. He didn't know Uncle Dan all that well, but he knew the man had been in the mountains a long time and had been to see the elephant. Preacher trusted that he'd done a good job.

"You have a head injury, too," Deborah said. "I'm not sure what happened there. It looks like someone hit you."

Preacher said, "Nope. Got creased by . . . a rifle ball."

"You mean you were shot in the head?" Jerome asked in amazement. "And you're still alive?"

"Not really shot," Preacher explained. "Just nicked a mite. Takes more'n that to . . . hurt this ol' noggin o' mine."

"Well, from the looks of the blood all over your face, the wound bled a lot," Deborah said. "I'm sure you're very weak from it. You also have nearly a dozen cuts on your arms and torso, and you lost blood from them, too. And your right knee is swollen. You must have wrenched it somehow."

"Is that . . . all?"

"Is that all?" Jerome repeated. "My God, Preacher, those injuries are enough to keep you laid up for a month!"

Preacher shook his head. "Not hardly. Some o' those Blackfeet rode off and took Laura Mallory and her brother with 'em. We got to get after 'em."

"No offense, but you must have been seeing things," Corliss said. "Clyde Mallory left here yesterday with his wagons. He's miles away by now, heading back to St. Louis."

Jerome added, "It is true, however, that we, ah, haven't been able to locate Miss Mallory. But I'm sure she's around somewhere. Her . . . body wasn't among those who were killed."

"How many folks . . . didn't make it?" Preacher asked.

"Twelve men, five women, and seven children," Corliss replied with a grim expression on his face. "And at least a dozen more people suffered fairly serious wounds. The attack took a terrible toll on the settlement."

But as bad as it was, it could have been a lot worse, Preacher thought. If the war party had swept in with no warning at all, more of the settlers would have died. It was possible that the whole settlement could have been wiped out.

"I'm mighty sorry I didn't get here in time to warn folks sooner."

"Good Lord, Preacher!" Uncle Dan said. "You saved our bacon, comin' outta nowhere yellin' and shootin' like that."

Jerome nodded. "He's right. We owe you a huge debt of gratitude, Preacher."

"Yeah, well, some o' you can repay by goin' after those Blackfeet with me. We got to rescue Laura and her brother, and there ain't no time to waste."

Deborah put a hand on his shoulder. "You're not going anywhere for at least a week," she insisted. "In fact, you won't even be getting out of that bed for that long."

She was wrong about that, Preacher thought. In a week's time, Laura and Clyde Mallory would be dead, if they weren't already.

But he was enough of a realist to know that he couldn't ride tonight. He was too weak, and if he tried, he would probably fall off of Horse and just hurt himself even worse. He had to have a little rest, and anyway it would be hard to track the Indians at night . . .

But come morning, Preacher told himself, he would feel better. He could pick up the trail then, and however many men he could round up to go with him would set out after those savages.

The Good Lord willin', they would catch up in time to save Laura and Clyde from whatever terrible fate awaited them.

"*Damn* the man!" Clyde Mallory said as he stalked back and forth beside the fire.

A short time earlier, Chief Walks Like a Bear had ridden into the camp where Laura, Mallory, Ezra Flagg, and Flagg's Indian wife were spending the night. The chief had eight warriors with him, the only survivors from a war party that had started out more than six times that size.

Flagg and Walks Like a Bear had spoken for several minutes in rapid, heated Blackfoot. Then a grim faced Flagg had turned to the Mallorys and reported, "They weren't able to take the stockade. Fact is, the rest of the war party was wiped out. Bear says that the Ghost Killer walked among them."

"What the bloody hell is the Ghost Killer?" Mallory had demanded.

Flagg's mouth quirked as he replied, "That's one o' their names for Preacher."

Over the next few minutes, Flagg had explained to them everything Walks Like a Bear had told him, from Preacher's seemingly magical ability to make fire explode in the midst of the war party, to the in-the-nick-of-time appearance of the savage dog and horse that helped save him.

"Accordin' to Walks Like a Bear, they ain't even real animals," Flagg had said. "They're spirit animals. They're bad medicine, like Preacher himself. He wishes he'd never heard of you folks, even though you brought him all those new guns. Most of his young warriors are dead now." Flagg had smiled coldly. "And he ain't too happy with me for bringin' you to him."

That had made Laura and Mallory nervous. Walks Like a Bear might want revenge for all the men he had lost, and the two British agents and the renegade American were the handiest targets for the chief's anger.

Flagg had assured them, though, that Walks Like a Bear wouldn't kill them.

"If you can get more rifles," Flagg had said, "then Bear will probably be willin' to make another deal once he cools off. He's really more interested in killin' Preacher than anything else."

"I thought I *had* killed him," Mallory said now as he paced beside the fire. His brief moment of regret at shooting Preacher had long since passed. "For God's sake, I shot the man in the head! What more could I have done to kill him?"

Flagg paused in filling a pipe to say, "From everything I've heard about him, Preacher's got a habit o' dodgin' the reaper. You must've just grazed him.

Even a head wound that ain't too bad'll bleed like a man's dyin'."

Mallory glared into the flames. "Well, then," he declared, "the first thing we have to do when we put the next plan into operation is to make sure that Preacher is dead!"

"Easier said than done. How about them rifles? You never said whether or not you can get more of 'em."

"Of course we can," Mallory snapped. "We have the wealth and power of the British government behind us. This is just a temporary obstacle in our path. All we need to do is get back to St. Louis."

"That's a long way," Flagg pointed out. "Plenty could go wrong betwixt here and there."

Mallory rubbed his angular jaw as he frowned in thought. "That's true. Do you think that the chief and his men would be willing to escort us part of the way?"

Flagg stared at the Englishman for a moment, then gave a bark of laughter. "You got the balls of a brass monkey, don't you, Mallory? The chief loses fifty warriors followin' your plan, and you want him to help you some more?"

"The Blackfeet have been fighting the Americans for more than twenty years," Mallory replied coldly. "I'm sure the warriors who were lost tonight aren't the first losses they've suffered. And it's hardly the fault of Laura or myself that Preacher showed up out of nowhere to warn the settlers."

Flagg shrugged. "I'll ask him. He can't do any worse'n say no." He laughed again. "Well, actually, I reckon he can. He can have all of us scalped. But I don't think he will."

Mallory swallowed hard and tried to look reassuringly at Laura while Flagg spoke to Chief Walks Like a Bear. The chief glowered at the two British agents and spat out a reply. Mallory didn't find that reaction encouraging.

After a few minutes of more discussion, however, the chief finally gave Flagg a curt nod. His voice was a bit less harsh as he spoke again.

Flagg turned back to the Mallorys. "He says he'll do it. He'll take you to the edge of the territory the Blackfeet claim as their hunting grounds. After that, though, you're on your own."

"Very well. We'll take whatever aid we can get. What about you, Flagg? Will you go with us?"

"I reckon I'll get paid for my services?"

Mallory nodded. "Cooperate with us, help us accomplish our goals, and I can assure you that you'll be a rich man."

"That's what I wanted to hear," Flagg said with a smile. "Count me in."

Colin Fairfax heard the metallic clicking of rifles and pistols being cocked as he stumbled into the clearing. It had taken him most of the night to reach the place where his men had been camped before.

He and Sherwood had agreed that they would return here after leaving the valley and making Preacher think they were on their way back to St. Louis. This was the spot where Preacher had stolen into the camp during the middle of the night and killed six men. Fairfax was convinced that Preacher wouldn't believe the rest of the group would ever return here.

The fire had burned down to embers and most of the men were asleep, but Sherwood had been smart enough to post guards. These men had their guns trained on Fairfax now. It was too dark for them to see very well, but they knew someone had just walked into camp.

"Who the hell's there?" one of the sentries demanded, and the loud, harsh voice woke other men and caused them to roll out of their blankets and grab for their guns.

"It's only me," Fairfax said. He could hear the weariness in his own voice. He had gotten lost a time or two during the night, and considered it nearly a miracle that he had made it back here at all.

"Boss?" Sherwood asked, his voice thick with sleep. He had been one of the men rolled up in blankets. "That you?"

"I just said it was, didn't I?"

"Put those guns down," Sherwood snapped at the guards and the other men who had lifted their weapons. "It's just the boss." He came forward, and there was eagerness in his voice as he asked, "You got the Hart woman with you?"

Fairfax didn't answer right away. It should have been obvious to Sherwood that he didn't have Deborah Hart with him. Where would he have hidden her, inside that damned coonskin cap on his head?

Instead, he sat down next to the fire, picked up a branch from the stack of wood near it, and stirred up the embers until a tiny flame leaped up and grew stronger. He was chilled to the bone, and he held out his hands toward the flame to get some of its feeble warmth.

"Our plans have changed," he said after a moment. "I wasn't able to kidnap the woman because Indians attacked the settlement while I was there."

"Indians!"

Fairfax nodded. "I heard someone say it was a Blackfoot war party, but I don't know for sure about that."

"How'd you get away?"

"By the skin of my teeth," Fairfax replied with a humorless smile.

"What happened to the settlers? Did the redskins wipe 'em out?"

"No. I stayed close enough to watch what happened before I started back here. I'm sure the savages killed quite a few of the settlers, but in the end the attackers were routed. And the man who made that possible," Fairfax added bitterly, "was Preacher."

That drew startled exclamations from the men. Sherwood said, "I thought Preacher was supposed to be off somewhere checkin' his traps."

"That's what we assumed he would do. Somehow, he found out about the war party on its way to attack the village and got there first to warn the settlers." Fairfax shook his head. "I don't see how he does the things he does. It shouldn't be possible for a man to always be in the right place at the right time. I had a bead on him again—"

"Let me guess," Sherwood said. "He moved just as you pulled the trigger."

Fairfax's head went up and down in a slow nod. He

had trouble believing what had happened, even now. If he hadn't seen it with his own eyes . . .

"Well, what do we do now? Are you still determined to kill him, or is it time to give up?"

"I'll never give up!" Fairfax said, surprising himself with the vehemence of his answer. "Not until Preacher's dead!" He reached over, picked up a jug that was sitting on the ground nearby, uncorked it, and took a long swig of the fiery whiskey inside. "We'll pick up his trail at the settlement somehow. Maybe we can still get our hands on Mrs. Hart and use her as bait in a trap. Somehow, we'll find a way . . ."

Fairfax tried to sound confident, but doubt gnawed at the edges of his mind. After everything that had happened, he couldn't help but wonder if it was even possible to kill Preacher. Perhaps the man was immortal.

That idea was insane, of course, and Fairfax knew it. But when he thought about all the times he'd had Preacher in his sights, only to have the mountain man escape . . . well, it was enough to make him despair.

It was a good thing he had his hate to keep him going, he thought as he stared into the fire.

Chapter 21

The pain in Preacher's arm, head, and knee kept him from sleeping well that night. He would have been even more restless if not for several long swallows from the tin cup full of whiskey that he put away.

When he woke up in the morning, his headache had subsided to a dull throbbing, as had the pain in his knee. And the way his arm was strapped down, he couldn't move it enough to make it hurt very much. He was able to sit up on his own.

He had learned the night before that it was Jerome's bed he was occupying. Jerome had fixed himself a pallet in the front part of the trading post. Preacher didn't like to put anybody out, but in this case he hadn't had any choice.

Now he'd had a night's rest and things were different. He pushed the blanket off him, then swung his legs off the bunk and started to stand up.

The sudden dizziness that hit him almost knocked him down. He put his good hand on the bed to brace himself, and managed not to fall. In doing so, though, he bumped the little table beside the bed and knocked the empty tin cup onto the floor.

The clatter that it made when it fell brought Deborah Hart to the door. "Preacher!" she scolded. "You're not supposed to be up. You should lie back down right now."

He became uncomfortably aware that he wore only the bottom half of a pair of long underwear, although all the bandages wrapped around his arms and torso covered him up almost as much as if he were wearing clothes. He said, "Deborah, you skedaddle on outta here whilst I find my buckskins and put 'em on. Ain't fittin' for you to be in here like this."

"Oh, pshaw," she said. "I'm not going to see anything I haven't seen before. Who do you think found all your wounds and cleaned them last night?"

Preacher felt his face growing warm. "Mebbe so, but I'd still feel a heap better with my buckskins on."

"Well, you can't have them for a while. One of the Indian women who live here in the settlement is cleaning and mending them. She'll bring them back here when she's finished with them. It may be a few days, she said."

Preacher shook his head. He picked up the blanket and draped it around his shoulders as he said, "I can't wait that long. Reckon I'll have to come up with somethin' else to wear."

"Why can't you wait that long?" Deborah asked. "You're not going anywhere."

"No offense, but that's where you're wrong, ma'am," Preacher drawled. "I'll be ridin' out soon's I've had somethin' to eat and gathered some supplies. The longer I wait to take up the trail o' them Blackfoot what stole Miss Laura, the better chance they'll have o' gettin' away. I'd appreciate it if you'd pass the word to any of the fellas who want to go with me that I'll be leavin' in half an hour or so."

Deborah just stared at him for a moment, then turned away without saying anything else to him. *"Corliss!"* she called as she started back into the other part of the trading post. "Come and see if you can talk some sense into Preacher!"

Now *that* was going to be a chore, Preacher thought with a grin.

By the time Corliss came into the room a few minutes later, Preacher had gone through Jerome's clothes and given up on finding any that might fit him. He didn't even try them on because he knew he'd rip out the seams.

"Deborah tells me you've lost your mind," Corliss said with a chuckle.

"She's a good woman and means well, but she just don't understand. Time's a-wastin'."

Corliss nodded as his expression grew serious. "You really did lose quite a bit of blood, Preacher," he said.

"I'll make more."

"And riding a horse is going to hurt like hell with that broken arm."

"I've hurt before. It'd be worse if it was my leg that was broke. Anyway, Uncle Dan's got it splinted good and wrapped up nice 'n' tight, so I don't reckon I can hurt it more'n it's already hurt."

"You can't use a rifle with only one hand," Corliss pointed out.

"I can fire a pistol just fine, though." Preacher

remembered the shot he had made the night before to down one of the raiders. "And I can use a rifle if I've got somethin' to rest the barrel on."

Corliss sighed. "You're not going to let anyone talk you out of this, are you, no matter how crazy it is?"

"Nope," Preacher said.

"All right, wait here. I think some of my clothes might fit you. I'm not quite as broad through the shoulders as you, though, so they may be a tight fit."

"I reckon they'll do," Preacher said.

Corliss found a pair of whipcord trousers that fit Preacher fairly well. The shirt was more of a problem because of the broken arm, but eventually they got one on him by slitting the sleeve of the left arm and then binding it in place.

Preacher's boots were all right, and his rifle, pistols, knife, and tomahawk had been brought into the trading post. He had blown up his powder horn along with the others he had used against the Blackfeet, but the Harts had others, along with kegs of powder and shot.

Jerome came into the room, saw that Preacher was dressed, and snapped, "You were supposed to talk him out of this, Corliss."

"Yeah, well, you try to talk sense to Preacher," Corliss shot back. He glanced at Preacher. "No offense."

"None taken," Preacher drawled. "Been called loco plenty o' times in my life."

"I wasn't saying—" Jerome began hastily, then stopped and shook his head. "Well, yes, I suppose I was. You need rest, Preacher. You're in no shape to chasing off after the Blackfeet, no matter who they've taken prisoner."

Preacher managed to cinch a belt around his waist. "I don't reckon Miss Mallory and her brother would agree with you."

"That's another thing," Corliss said with a frown. "Are you *sure* you saw Clyde Mallory with them? I don't understand that at all."

"Well, the light wasn't too good," Preacher admitted, "and I'd just been shot in the head . . . but I'm pretty damn sure that was Clyde I saw. Miss Laura was ridin' behind him on the same horse, and there was half a dozen Blackfeet around 'em." Preacher frowned. "Might've been another man, too. I ain't sure about that. Like I said, the light wasn't too good."

"And you'd been shot in the head," Corliss added.

Preacher shrugged.

Jerome said, "If you're bound and determined to do this, you'll need a hat, too. Let me go and find one for you."

He bustled out of the room. Corliss laughed and said, "Jerome believes in being dressed properly for any occasion . . . even chasing Indians."

Preacher wasn't limping much when he emerged from the room a few minutes later. He found about a dozen men waiting for him in the trading post's big front room.

He recognized Pete Sanderson, Sanderson's Uncle Dan, stubby little Dennison, and the hulking Van Goort brothers among them. Several of the men had bloodstained bandages tied around arms, legs, or heads, but they seemed to be in fairly good shape.

"We're goin' with you, Preacher," bearded Uncle

Dan said as he stepped forward, evidently the spokesman for the group. "We want to help you settle the score with them damn redskins."

"The reason I'm goin' after the Blackfeet is to rescue Miss Laura and her brother," Preacher said. "Revenge ain't the main thing I'm after."

"Yeah, but it'll be a heap easier to help the lady if all them savages are dead," Uncle Dan pointed out.

"You got a point there," Preacher said. "I'll be glad to have you boys with me, but we'll be ridin' hard and fast, and there's liable to be plenty o' blood spilled before we're done."

"Long as it's Blackfoot blood, we're fine with that," Uncle Dan declared. He jerked a thumb over his shoulder. "Our horses are saddled and waitin' outside. We're ready to ride whenever you are, Preacher."

"Got plenty o' supplies? No tellin' how long we'll be on the trail."

The bearded old-timer nodded. "Don't worry none about that. You know we can live off the land if we have to."

That was the truth. Game was abundant, and you couldn't hardly go a mile in the mountains without running across a stream.

"Speaking of food," Deborah said as she came up to the group, "if we can't talk you into going back to bed and resting like you should, at least you can have a good meal before you leave. I have flapjacks and bacon and plenty of hot coffee."

Preacher smiled and gave her a nod of thanks. "I feel better just hearin' about it, Miss Deborah. I expect I'll feel like a whole new man once I've had a mess o' that grub."

Deborah looked at the men gathered in the trading post and said, "You're all welcome to eat. I'll get started cooking some more."

Despite the grim, dangerous chore awaiting them, the invitation brought smiles and laughter from the men. The big meal took longer than Preacher expected, stretching out to an hour, so it was later than he had hoped it would be when the men trooped out of the trading post to mount up.

Even so, the sun wasn't very high in the sky yet. The Blackfeet had only a twelve-hour start. That was quite a bit of time to make up, but Preacher was confident that he and his companions could do it.

Corliss shook hands with him and started to say, "I wish I was going with you—"

Preacher stopped him by shaking his head. "The folks here in the settlement are gonna need leaders while they're buryin' their loved ones and gettin' started on rebuildin' their homes. That's you and Jerome. There wouldn't even be a settlement here without you two."

"There wouldn't be a settlement here without *you*, Preacher," Corliss said. "I know that a man like you doesn't ever stay put for very long, but if there's any place you'd ever call home, we'd be honored if it was here."

"That's right," Jerome said as he shook hands with the mountain man, too. "You know the settlement doesn't have a name yet. We'd be honored if you'd let us call it Preacherville."

"Or Preacher City," Corliss said.

Preacher grimaced. "I reckon I appreciate the sentiment, fellas, but I'd be mighty pleased if you'd sorta forget about that idea."

"You're sure?" Jerome asked. "We really don't mind—"

"I'm *sure,*" Preacher declared.

Deborah insisted on giving him a hug. "Be careful," she told him. "If you jostle that arm around, it won't set properly. And you can't afford to open up any of those wounds and lose any more blood."

"I'll be careful," Preacher promised. "As much as I can anyway."

"That's what I was afraid you'd say." Deborah hugged him again. "Come back to us safely, you hear?"

"Yes'm," Preacher said.

Some of the men who were coming with him were leaving family members behind. Quite a bit of handshaking, hugging, and crying went on before everybody was mounted up and ready to ride.

The men lifted hands in farewell and heeled their horses into motion. Preacher gritted his teeth against the twinges of pain that went through his broken arm with every stride that Horse took . . . and the big stallion had a smooth gait. He hated to think about what a rough ride would feel like.

After a while, he sort of got used to it, though, and learned how to hold his arm so that the pain wasn't as bad. His head spun every now and then, but the food and the hot coffee had done a lot to brace him up. He suspected that Deborah had snuck a slug or two of whiskey into the coffeepot, too.

It was easy enough to pick up the trail near the burned-out hulk of Laura's cabin. The Blackfeet and their prisoners hadn't been trying to hide their tracks. Preacher figured at that point the raiders had still believed that they would wipe out the settlement, so there wouldn't be anyone left to pursue them.

It hadn't worked out that way, as the Indians would soon learn to their regret, Preacher hoped.

Pete Sanderson and Uncle Dan rode beside him with the other men spread out behind them. Sanderson said, "I heard that that Englisher who sided you in that ruckus we had was one o' the prisoners. Is that right?"

"I'm convinced I saw him with Miss Laura," Preacher said. "I know he was supposed to have left with those wagons of his, but I saw what I saw."

Uncle Dan ran his gnarled fingers through his beard. "Mighty strange, if you ask me."

"Well, I reckon when we catch up to 'em, we can ask Mallory what he's doin' back in this part o' the country."

The other trappers let the subject drop after that, but something else odd cropped up. The group of riders they were following split up, with most of them turning toward the settlement and two sets of tracks going on north up the valley.

"What the hell?" Preacher muttered as he reined in to study the sign. "That bunch headed back to the fight, but those two went on."

"Those are shod hooves," Uncle Dan pointed out. "Looks like the Blackfeet let the prisoners go."

"Why in blazes would they do that?" Sanderson asked. "And if those folks weren't captives anymore, why didn't they come back to the settlement?"

Preacher thought that over for a moment and then

said, "Maybe they didn't think there was a settlement to go back to. The cabins were on fire, the Blackfeet were layin' siege to the stockade . . . They may have figured that their best chance to survive was to just keep goin'."

"But that means them two Englishers are out there somewhere in the wilderness on their own," Uncle Dan said. "They're still liable to get in a heap o' trouble."

"That's why we're gonna follow them anyway," Preacher declared. "They may still need our help."

Under his breath, Sanderson said, "Some o' these fellas only came along so they could kill Blackfeet and settle the score for what happened back at the settlement. They may not like it if they don't get the chance."

Preacher raised his eyes to the mountains and said, "I got a feelin' that before this is all over . . . they'll get the chance."

Chapter 22

Fairfax called a halt around midday when the group was about a mile from the settlement. They dismounted and he motioned his second in command over to him.

"You'll go in and see if Preacher is there," he told Sherwood.

"Why me?"

"Because I was there last night, and it's possible someone might recognize me."

"What's wrong with that?" Sherwood wanted to know.

Fairfax made a face and snapped, "I had to kill a man while I was there. I don't think anyone saw me, but I don't want to take that chance."

Sherwood let out a low whistle of surprise. "You didn't say anything about that."

"The bastard saw me take a shot at Preacher—"

"And miss," Sherwood couldn't resist adding.

"And miss," Fairfax agreed with a grimace. "I tried to convince him that it was an honest mistake, that I mistook Preacher for an Indian in the bad light, but he wouldn't accept that explanation. The damn fool tried to raise a commotion about it."

"So what did you do, plant a knife in his belly?"

Fairfax gave his second in command a cold stare. "Exactly."

After a second, Sherwood shrugged. "I reckon you're right. The fella was a damn fool. I can see why you don't want to go into the settlement. What am I supposed to do?"

"Like I said, find out if Preacher is there. If he's not, try to find out where he's gone."

"He might be dead," Sherwood pointed out. "The redskins could've killed him."

Fairfax snorted contemptuously. "I'll believe *that* when I see it."

"Maybe the red devils wiped out the whole settlement."

"Then what's that smoke?" Fairfax asked, pointing to several columns of gray smoke spiraling into the clear blue sky above the valley.

"Some of the cabins still burning?" Sherwood suggested.

"It wouldn't look like that," Fairfax said with a shake of his head. "That's chimney smoke. The settlement survived, no matter how much damage the Indians may have done. Now, we've wasted enough time . . ."

"I'm goin', I'm goin'," Sherwood said. He propped his flintlock on his shoulder and started off toward the settlement, taking long strides through the calf-high grass. He glanced back and saw Fairfax watching him depart on the mission.

Fairfax had been funny-looking enough in that beaver hat he always wore. He hadn't reclaimed it from Campbell when he rejoined Sherwood and the other men, but still sported the coonskin cap instead. Sherwood thought he really looked ludicrous in it.

Sherwood had learned, though, not to underestimate Colin Fairfax based on the man's looks. Back in St. Louis, Shad Beaumont had told Sherwood about the hellish trek Fairfax had made back to civilization from the frontier. The man wouldn't have survived that ordeal unless he was tough.

And Fairfax was a cold-blooded killer as well. Sherwood had no doubts about that. Anyone who considered Fairfax not to be a threat because he was an odd-looking little man might find himself with a foot of cold steel in his gut or his brains blown out from a pistol shot to the head.

Sherwood didn't intend to let that happen to him.

A short time later, he came in sight of the settlement. Black smudges in the grass and piles of charred rubble marked where several of the cabins had been. The Indians must have torched them.

Most of the cabins were still standing, though, and so was the stockade. The trading post and the other buildings inside the log walls appeared to be intact. Sherwood could see them through the open gates.

As Sherwood approached, he noticed several guards posted on the parapet inside the wall. One of them turned and appeared to call down into the stockade. Warning those inside that somebody was coming, Sherwood thought. After the Indian attack the night before, those folks had to be pretty nervous.

Sure enough, a few minutes later a party of half a

dozen grim-faced men walked out through the gates to meet him. All of them carried rifles and watched him closely, even though he was obviously a white man, not a redskin.

Sherwood put a friendly smile on his face and raised a hand in greeting. "Howdy," he called. "Looks like you folks had some trouble here."

A well-built, dark-haired man wearing store-bought clothes nodded. "The Blackfeet paid us a visit last night," he said.

"I'm sorry to hear that," Sherwood said as he put a sympathetic look on his face. "I reckon I'm just lucky I didn't get here a day earlier, eh?"

The spokesman for the "welcoming" committee shrugged. "I guess you could look at it that way. What are you doing here today?"

"Why, I come to try my luck at fur trapping here in the mountains. Anything wrong with that?"

The dark-haired man seemed to relax a little. "No, of course not," he said. "When you get right down to it, the fur trade is why all of us are here, I suppose." He lowered his rifle. "I'm Corliss Hart. My cousin and I own the trading post."

So this fella was Corliss Hart, Sherwood thought. He'd heard plenty about the Hart cousins from Colin Fairfax. Corliss was the one who had the pretty wife.

Sherwood hoped that he got a look at the woman while he was here at the settlement. It had been too damned long since he'd laid eyes on a white woman.

"I'm glad to meet you, Mr. Hart. Sherwood's my name." He didn't see any harm in using his real name. Nobody here knew him.

A suspicious glint reappeared in Corliss Hart's

eyes. "If you're a fur trapper," he said, "where's your outfit? Don't you even have a pack horse?"

With the skill born of a long time spent as a criminal, Sherwood kept the friendly grin on his face even as he was cursing inside. Neither he nor Fairfax had even thought about that when Fairfax sent him here to the settlement.

He had to think quickly now, and luckily he was able to do so. Pointing over his shoulder with the thumb of his free hand, he said, "Back yonder a couple of miles. I'm just out scoutin' for a bigger bunch."

"How big?" Corliss asked.

"Oh, there's seven or eight of us," Sherwood lied easily. He wanted a number large enough to sound reasonable, but not so intimidating that these men might regard them as a threat of some sort.

Corliss appeared to relax again. "We'll be glad to see you," he said. "The settlement lost some men during the fight last night, and some others have gone off chasing the redskins who raided us."

"Really? Seems to me like you'd want to stay as far away from those savages as possible."

"They took some prisoners," Corliss answered with a solemn expression on his face. "Our men went to try to get them back."

"Captives, eh? That's a damned shame." Sherwood wanted to ask if Preacher had accompanied the rescue party. That sure seemed like something the mountain man would do.

But he didn't want to appear too curious, so instead he asked, "Reckon I could get a drink before I head back to my bunch and bring 'em on in?"

Corliss nodded and motioned for Sherwood to

follow him and his companions into the stockade. "Sure. We've got plenty of whiskey."

Sherwood licked his lips in anticipation, and there was nothing phony about that gesture.

He trooped inside with the others, who were friendly and welcoming now that they thought he would be bringing more fighting men to the settlement. They were clearly shaken by the Indian raid and the toll it had taken.

Corliss Hart took Sherwood to the trading post and led him inside the cavernous building. The sun had grown a little warm as it reached its zenith, so Sherwood was glad to step into the cooler interior.

He was even happier a moment later when he saw the woman standing behind the counter at the back of the room. Dark-haired like her husband and with a beautiful smile on her face, Deborah Hart was a welcome sight.

Sherwood could tell by the slightly swollen belly that the woman was with child. That condition affected her breasts as well, making them big enough so that Sherwood had a hard time not staring at them in open lust. He forced himself to look away.

Corliss pointed to a table in the corner and said, "Sit down. I'll bring you a jug."

"Much obliged."

Sherwood took a seat on a barrel chair and propped his rifle in the corner beside him. Corliss fetched a jug from behind the counter and brought it over to him.

"If you're hungry, there's food. It's just salt jowl and beans and biscuits, but it's filling."

"Sounds mighty good to me," Sherwood said. "Again, I'm obliged."

"There'll be a pot of stew for supper if you're still here."

Sherwood thought about having a big bowl of savory stew served to him by a pretty, big-titted pregnant woman. It was all he could do not to lick his lips and moan in delightful anticipation.

But then he thought about Colin Fairfax, and knew that his pretty dream would remain just that, a dream. Fairfax was waiting to find out where Preacher was, and he wouldn't be happy if Sherwood wasted a lot of time shoveling grub into his mouth and lusting after Deborah Hart.

Sherwood took a couple of swigs from the jug. A thin, fox-faced gent brought a plate of food and set it down on the table in front of him.

"I'm Jerome Hart," the man introduced himself as Sherwood began to eat. "My cousin and I run this trading post."

"Mighty glad to meet you, Mr. Hart," Sherwood said around a mouthful of salt jowl and beans. "Name's Sherwood."

Jerome pulled up a chair and sat down without being asked, which was his right, of course, seeing as how he was one of the proprietors of this business.

It played right into Sherwood's hands, though, that he was also talkative.

"I suppose my cousin Corliss told you about the trouble we had last night."

Sherwood nodded. "He mentioned it. Looks like you lost some cabins. I hope not too many folks were hurt."

"Unfortunately, we had numerous casualties,"

Jerome said. "And at least two people were taken prisoner by the savages."

"But some of the men went after them, right? I think that's what your cousin said."

Jerome nodded. "Indeed they did."

"You reckon they'll get the captives back?"

Jerome sighed and said, "I don't know. But at least they'll have a good chance. Preacher is leading the rescue party."

"Preacher," Sherwood repeated as if he'd never heard the name before. "You folks have got a minister here?"

"No, that's what the man is called. Preacher. His real name is Arthur, but no one calls him that."

"Who is he?" Sherwood asked, still playing ignorant.

"One of the fur trappers. He's been out here in the mountains longer than almost anyone else. He certainly knows his way around as well or better than anyone, including the Indians. Most of them are afraid of him. I've heard that some of them consider him an evil spirit rather than a flesh-and-blood man."

Sherwood understood that feeling. Fairfax acted like he was starting to feel the same way about Preacher.

"Sounds to me like he's the right man for the job."

Jerome Hart nodded. "There's no one better at following a trail, and no one more dangerous in a fight. Unfortunately, Preacher's not at the top of his strength right now."

"He's not?" Sherwood asked, making it sound like he was just idly gossiping as he continued to eat.

"No, he was injured in the fighting last night. He

has a broken arm, not to mention numerous other injuries that are less serious."

Sherwood raised his eyebrows. "A broken arm? How can a man chase down a bunch o' savages with a busted wing?"

"That's Preacher for you," Jerome said. "He doesn't let anything stop him."

"Well, it's too bad my friends and I didn't get here sooner. We could've gone along with the rescue party." Sherwood used a piece of biscuit to mop up some beans. "Which way did they go anyway?"

Jerome Hart didn't seem to find the question odd. "I believe they were headed northeast when they left the settlement. But of course, there's no way of knowing where the trail led from there."

Northeast, Sherwood thought. That meant the pursuit had led fairly close to where Fairfax was waiting with the rest of the men.

Of course, that would have been earlier in the day, before Fairfax's party got that close to the settlement. It was funny, Sherwood thought, with all these vast reaches of wilderness on the frontier, how often folks almost tripped over each other as they went about their business.

"Well, I wish 'em luck," Sherwood said. "I hope they bring back the folks you lost safe and sound."

"With Preacher on the trail, I think there's a good chance of it."

Problem was, Sherwood thought, Preacher wasn't the only one who was going to be on the trail. As soon as he could get back and report to Fairfax, they would join the pursuit as well.

Only they wouldn't be following the Blackfeet and their prisoners.

Their quarry would be the man called Preacher. With a bunch of savages in front of him, Preacher would never dream that death was closing in on him from behind . . .

Chapter 23

Ezra Flagg was a closemouthed man. Clyde Mallory had tried several times during the day to engage him in conversation, but most of Flagg's answers had been curt. Sometimes, he just grunted in response to Mallory's questions.

Laura was bored, and she regarded Flagg's attitude as something of a challenge.

She was riding one of the Blackfoot ponies, rather than riding double with her brother. Earlier, she had asked for a mount of her own, and Flagg had arranged it with Chief Walks Like a Bear.

Laura didn't know if the Indians would allow her to keep the pony and take it all the way back to St. Louis with her, but for the moment, she was rather enjoying it.

She had pulled her skirt up, tucked the excess material back between her legs, and now rode astride the pony's blanket-draped back. As she brought her mount alongside Flagg's, she saw him glance over at her bare calves and knees.

Laura was accustomed to men looking at her with avid interest in their eyes. She had been receiving attention like that ever since she was barely in her teens. Sometimes, the glances were veiled and discreet, and other times, they were openly lecherous.

Laura didn't care either way. All the looks represented the power she possessed over the men she encountered.

"I'm glad you're going to St. Louis with us, Mr. Flagg," she said. "How long has it been since you last visited civilization?"

"Not long enough," Flagg said.

Laura frowned, perplexed. "You don't care for cities?"

"I don't care for the folks who live there, and they don't care for me."

Laura sensed that there was something behind the bitter edge in Flagg's voice as he made that comment, and she was curious about what it was.

"I take it your last trip east was unpleasant?"

"You could call it that." He looked over at her. "No offense, ma'am, but what business is it of yours?"

"None at all," she said without hesitation. "Women are like cats, though. We're curious about things."

She didn't add the rest of the old saying about what curiosity did to cats.

Flagg didn't say anything for a moment. The two of them rode side by side in silence. Then he said, "I went back a few years ago. All the way back to Ohio, to the farm where I was raised."

"Wasn't your family glad to see you?"

"They were, I reckon. But there was a gal . . ."

"Ah," Laura said. "Let me guess. She promised to wait for you, but she didn't remain faithful."

"No, that ain't it. She waited for me, all right. I figured we'd get hitched and that I'd see her whenever I came back home, when I wasn't trappin'. Then she asked . . . if I'd been faithful to her."

Laura turned her head to look briefly at the squaw who rode about ten feet behind them. The woman's round face was as impassive as ever.

"Surely, you didn't tell her about . . . what is her name, Willow?"

Flagg nodded. "Weepin' Willow. And yeah, I told that gal back home. I've never been one for lyin'. Tell folks the truth, straight out, that's me. I said, sure, I've been faithful if you don't count Injun gals, which I didn't."

"But your sweetheart didn't see things that way."

"Nope." Flagg's voice was flat, devoid of emotion. "She got all upset. Told me to get the hell out and never come back. Called me a filthy squaw man. I don't know where she heard that term, but she'd picked it up somewhere."

He shrugged as if what he was telling her didn't really mean anything, but Laura had a feeling that wasn't the way he truly felt.

"So I figured I'd come back here to the mountains where folks don't get so upset about things that don't matter. Only, that gal's brother caught up to me before I rode out. Said he was gonna give me a thrashin' for hurtin' his sister."

Flagg's voice had a rusty rasp to it now, as if he weren't accustomed to speaking this much.

Laura watched him raptly, eager to know what had happened next.

"So there was a fight?"

"You couldn't hardly call it that. He hit me and I hit him back and he went over backwards and hit his head on a log."

"He was badly hurt?"

"Stove his skull right in. I didn't mean to kill him, but he wasn't any less dead 'cause o' that. I lit out for the tall and uncut." He waved a hand to indicate the wilderness surrounding them. "I reckon I'm wanted for murder back in Ohio. Not that I give a damn. I don't figure on ever goin' back."

The story didn't surprise Laura all that much. She had known from her first look at Flagg that he was a cold, dangerous man. She had seen death in his eyes.

"That sweetheart of yours was a simpering fool," she said. "I'll tell you something else, Mr. Flagg. She was probably no more faithful to you while you were gone than you were to her."

Flagg frowned. "But she said—"

"She lied to you. I don't know that for certain, of course, but I feel sure of it. The self-righteous, those who are so quick to judge others, are usually the wickedest of all."

Flagg appeared to be thinking it over for a long moment, and then he nodded. "Could be that you're right," he said. "It don't matter now, though. Ain't no goin' back."

Laura thought about her own life and said, "There never is."

* * *

Chief Walks Like a Bear and the surviving members of the war party were still with Laura, Mallory, Flagg, and Weeping Willow when they made camp that evening.

Laura was grateful for the presence of the Indians since they provided protection from wild animals and other savages, but at the same time they made her nervous.

She felt them looking at her, and while she was accustomed to such scrutiny from white men, it was different somehow when the men looking at her were red. They weren't bound by the rules—written *and* unwritten—of a civilized society.

There was no way of knowing what they might do. That very unpredictability was what worried Laura. She knew that she could nearly always get a white man to do whatever she wanted, simply because she was beautiful.

The Blackfeet kept their distance, though. Evidently, they were going to honor whatever arrangement thcy had made with Flagg.

The Indians built a small fire and heated some food, but they didn't offer to share it with the whites. They left Flagg to make another fire, and then Willow fried some bacon from a slab of it she took out of her saddlebags. She made some sort of flat, fried bread to go with the bacon.

She walked over to where Laura sat on a log and offered her several strips of bacon piled on a piece of the bread. Laura smiled, reached up, and took the food.

"Thank you, Willow," she said to the Indian woman.

Willow's face never changed expression and she made no reply.

"You're wastin' your time."

Laura looked over at Flagg, who sat cross-legged on the other side of the fire, smoking a pipe.

"What did you say, Mr. Flagg?"

He puffed on the pipe again and then took it out of his mouth. "Said you're wastin' your time talkin' to Willow. She won't talk to you."

Clyde Mallory asked, "Does she not speak English?"

"Don't know," Flagg said. "I never asked her."

"Perhaps something is wrong with her hearing," Laura suggested. "She might be deaf."

Flagg shook his head. "She ain't deaf. I tell her to do somethin', she does it. I know she hears me. But she never talks to me either. Ain't said a single word since she's been with me."

Laura could hardly fathom such a thing. "But that's . . . terrible!"

Flagg shrugged. "It has its benefits. I don't have to put up with a lot o' useless jabberin'."

Clyde rubbed his jaw and frowned in thought. "Perhaps she has some sort of physical disability that prevents her from talking."

Flagg had his pipe in his mouth again now. With his teeth clamped on the stem, he said around it, "Maybe so. I never took the time to check."

Laura rolled her eyes and shook her head. She had felt a few pangs of sympathy for Flagg that afternoon when he'd told her what happened to him the last time he returned to his home, but she put those feelings aside now.

He didn't deserve her pity. He was a heartless man, concerned only with money. Some people might think that she and Clyde were terrible because of some of the things they'd done, but at least they had done those things because they loved England . . . and hated the bloody Americans.

She didn't attempt to talk to Willow anymore, and she ignored Flagg. The food was greasy and not very good, but it filled the gnawing ache in Laura's belly, and after a while, she rolled up her blankets beside the log and went to sleep.

She was not the pampered beauty she appeared to be. This was not the first time in her life she had slept on the ground. This grassy hillside, for all its primitiveness, was better than a squalid London alley.

Laura slept fairly soundly, confident that if any trouble tried to creep up on them during the night, the Indians would be aware of it and would take steps to deal with it.

When trouble came, though, it was from within, not without. Laura woke up with someone's hot breath in her face and a hand groping roughly at her breast.

She tried to jerk away, but the weight of a man's body pinned her to the ground. She opened her mouth to scream. The hand that had been pawing at her clamped over her mouth instead, silencing her.

"Just be quiet, ma'am," Ezra Flagg whispered to her, his breath sour with pipe tobacco and whiskey. He reached down with his other hand and started fumbling with her skirt, trying to pull it up. "You just lie still and there won't be no trouble." He chuckled. "You might even enjoy it."

Despite the warning he had just given her, she began to struggle, twisting her head back and forth and pushing at him. He made a growling sound in his throat, and the fingers of the hand over her mouth pressed harder and more painfully into her cheeks.

"Damn it, woman! You want that brother o' yours to die? The chief and his men will do whatever I tell 'em, and if you give me trouble I'll tell 'em to kill Clyde. Then you'll be mine from now on."

That made Laura's struggles cease, at least momentarily. She didn't doubt that Flagg meant exactly what he said, but he hadn't thought it through.

If Clyde was dead, Flagg would never get the rest of the money that had been promised to him. She had to make him understand that, but she couldn't do it with his filthy hand pressed over her mouth.

She nodded, hoping he would think she was agreeing with what he wanted.

He put his mouth close to her ear. "You ain't gonna fight?"

Laura shook her head.

"Now you're showin' some sense. And it ain't gonna be too bad for you. I promise." He started to take his hand away, then paused while it was still on her mouth. "Don't you scream now."

She shook her head again.

He lifted his hand.

Immediately, she whispered, "Please don't do this, Mr. Flagg. It's not right. You have a woman—"

"A squaw," Flagg said. "A filthy, stinkin' squaw. You know how long it's been since I been with a white woman?"

Laura didn't know and didn't care. All she wanted was to talk Flagg out of what he intended to do.

"You may think that Weeping Willow has no feelings because she doesn't talk, but I assure you she does—"

"Hush up now. I don't want a lot of jabber from you, either. Just move your legs a mite . . ."

He was trying to get her skirt up again. Laura saw that he wasn't going to be persuaded to leave her alone. She had no choice now.

She let him feel the point of the knife she had gone to sleep clutching in her hand. She let him feel it at his most sensitive spot, too, pressing the blade to the front of his buckskin trousers.

Flagg stiffened. In the faint light of the fire, which had burned down quite a bit while she was asleep, she saw his eyes widen in surprise. She couldn't see his face very well because of the curtain of his long dark hair that hung down on each side of it, but she knew he was shocked.

"This knife is sharp enough to go through buckskin, Mr. Flagg," Laura told him. "And it will go right through what's underneath the buckskin, too."

"You bitch!" he snarled. "I'll break your neck—"

"And I'll be dead, but you'll never be a man again. Think about it, Mr. Flagg. Is it truly worth the cost?"

After a moment of silence, he asked, "What do you want? You want me to leave you alone?"

"Exactly. Go back to your own blankets and we won't speak of this again."

"You won't tell your brother?"

"I can take care of myself." Her tone was crisp

and cool. "I don't always need Clyde to save me, you know."

"You're makin' a mistake."

"I'm confident that I'm not." She increased the pressure on the knife slightly and said, "Well?"

"All right, all right, damn it!"

"Get off me. Now."

He pushed himself up and rolled off of her at the same time. As she sat up and pulled down her skirt, he grumbled, "You don't have to be so blasted persnickety. I wasn't gonna hurt you. Just wanted to have a little fun."

"I choose when and where I have my 'fun,' Mr. Flagg," she said. "You'd do well to remember that."

"I reckon I will." Flagg sat a couple of feet away and shook his head. "Where'd you get that knife? What do you do, sleep with it in your hand?"

"That's exactly what I do. You should remember that, too."

Flagg grunted. He stood up and moved around to the other side of the embers that remained from the campfire. He glanced back at her once and shook his head again, as if he couldn't believe that he had underestimated her so badly.

He wouldn't make that mistake again, Laura told herself. She didn't trust Flagg. Didn't believe that he wouldn't try something again if he thought he could get away with it.

But he would find that taking her by surprise was going to be difficult.

She hadn't survived those back alleys in London by being careless. Clyde hadn't always been there to look out for her. She had gone through some bad experiences, but she had learned from them. Painful lessons, but valuable ones.

Like the fact that having several inches of sharp, cold steel pressed to his balls would make just about any man back off, Laura thought to herself with a smile as she lay back down and drifted off to sleep again.

Chapter 24

The puzzled concern that plagued Preacher grew stronger during the afternoon when he found the spot where the tracks of seven or eight horses with unshod hooves crossed those of the other two horses.

"Lookee there," Uncle Dan said as he pointed to the tracks. Despite his age, he had the second-sharpest pair of eyes in the group, right behind Preacher. "'Twas Injun ponies left that sign."

Preacher agreed. "I reckon those must've been the survivors from the war party."

"And now they're trailin' that Englisher and his sister."

So Clyde and Laura Mallory were in danger from the Blackfeet yet again, Preacher thought.

Pete Sanderson brought his horse up alongside those of Preacher and his uncle. "How do we know these Injuns are from the same bunch that raided the settlement?" he asked.

"We don't," Preacher admitted, "but havin' a Blackfoot war party o' the size that one was roamin' around would make all the other Indians in the area lay low for a while."

He recalled the survivor of the Crow hunting party he had encountered. Even though those Crows had been wiped out, Preacher was confident that the word still would have gotten around about a Blackfoot war party moving down the valley.

"I think this is the same bunch," he went on, "but we won't know for sure until we catch up to 'em."

Something else occurred to him as he and his companions took up the trail. He frowned as he considered the droppings left behind by the horses they were following. To his experienced eye, all the piles appeared to have been there about the same amount of time.

He couldn't stand being curious, so finally in the late afternoon he reined Horse to a halt.

"What's wrong?" Uncle Dan asked.

"Somethin' ain't right," Preacher said. He swung down from the saddle, moving a little more awkwardly than usual because his splinted left arm was strapped to his side. He hunkered on his heels to study several deposits of horse droppings.

"You seem mighty interested considerin' that's horseshit you're lookin' at, Preacher," Sanderson commented.

Preacher ignored the man. He scooped up some of the brown stuff from one pile and rubbed it between his fingers, testing its consistency. Then, he lifted his fingers to his nose and took a good whiff.

Sanderson made a face and said, "You gone loco, Preacher?"

Still ignoring him, Preacher wiped his hand on

the grass and performed the same tests on several other piles. Then, he cleaned his hand again and straightened.

"I see what you're gettin' at," Uncle Dan said. "They was all left at the same time, right?"

"Near enough," Preacher said. He pointed to the tracks and went on, "All the horses stopped here to rest, both the shod horses and the Indian ponies. That means we're chasin' one bunch again, not followin' the Blackfeet whilst they follow Clyde Mallory and Miss Laura."

Sanderson nodded in understanding. "So you're sayin' the Injuns already caught up to those folks and took 'em prisoner again."

"That's the way it looks to me," Preacher agreed, a grim expression on his rugged face.

Sanderson shrugged and said, "So things are right back to the way we thought they were when we left the settlement. It don't change nothin'. We're still gonna track down those Blackfeet and kill 'em, ain't we?"

Preacher nodded. "That's the plan."

He still had a hunch that things weren't as simple as they seemed . . . but until they caught up to their quarry, all they could do was keep following the trail.

Colin Fairfax paced back and forth anxiously as he waited for Sherwood to return from the settlement. Fairfax's second in command had been gone longer than he had expected.

Finally, though, one of the men called, "Here he comes!" Fairfax swung around to see Sherwood striding across the grassy floor of the valley toward them.

"What took you so damned long?" he demanded as Sherwood came up to him a few minutes later.

Sherwood frowned at the sharply voiced question. "I didn't want to make anybody suspicious," he said. "How would it have looked if I'd gone in there, asked where Preacher was, and then rushed off again?"

Fairfax waved a hand impatiently. "Never mind that. Just tell me what you found out. Is he still there?"

Sherwood shook his head and said, "Nope. He and a group of men rode out earlier today on the trail of the Blackfeet who survived the battle. The Injuns took a couple o' prisoners with them, and Preacher wants to rescue them."

"He would," Fairfax said with a contemptuous snort. "Do you know who the prisoners were?"

"An Englishman and his sister. Mallory, I think their names were."

That meant nothing to Fairfax. He wasn't surprised that an Englishman would be out here on the American frontier. That was common enough. The prisoners were important only because they had caused Preacher to give chase to their red-skinned captors.

"That ain't all," Sherwood went on. "I spent some time with Jerome Hart. He's a talkative bastard."

"What did he tell you?" Fairfax asked, forcing himself to suppress the impatience he felt at the way Sherwood was dragging this out.

"Preacher's hurt. His left arm is busted, he's got a bum knee, and he was slashed all over with knives durin' the fightin'. Got barked on the head with a rifle ball, too."

"But he went after the Blackfeet anyway, even with all those injuries?" Fairfax asked.

"Damn right. From the way Hart was talkin', wild horses couldn't have held Preacher back from chasin' those Injuns."

That was just like him, Fairfax thought. Preacher always had to be the hero. Some might think he was simply displaying courage and determination, but Fairfax figured that the mountain man was simply a glory hound.

"Which way did the rescue party go?"

Sherwood waved a hand. "Off toward the northeast. They picked up the trail at one of the burned-out cabins on the edge of the settlement. I know where it started and which direction it was going, so we should be able to find it, too. And as long as we stay on it, we ought to be on Preacher's trail, too."

Fairfax nodded. Sherwood really had done a good job, but Fairfax wasn't going to tell him that. He still didn't fully trust the man, even now.

He knew that Sherwood's first loyalty lay with Shad Beaumont. If Beaumont hadn't wanted Preacher dead, too, he never would have sent these men with Fairfax.

And for all Fairfax knew, Sherwood had secret orders from Beaumont. As long as those orders didn't conflict with what Fairfax wanted, then Fairfax didn't care.

But if it ever came down to a decision, he knew that Sherwood would do what Beaumont wanted. That could cause problems.

Fairfax shoved those thoughts out of his head, telling himself that he was just borrowing trouble where there might not really be any. He would wait and see and not place too much trust in Sherwood or anyone else.

Once Preacher was dead, then there would be time to sort out everything else.

And with that in mind, Fairfax didn't spare even a single thought for the fate of the prisoners who found themselves in the savage hands of the Blackfeet.

By the time night fell, the group Preacher and his companions were following had moved through the pass that led out of the long, lush valley and into more rugged territory beyond.

A few days earlier, Preacher had followed the survivors from that bunch of would-be killers through that same pass. He still wondered who they had been and why they had tried so hard to kill him, but he didn't figure the answers to those questions would be forthcoming any time soon. Those varmints were probably a hundred miles away by now.

The bunch that the rescue party was following didn't have *that* big of a lead, but they were still well ahead of the pursuit. Knowing that he and the others from the settlement couldn't take a chance on losing the trail in the darkness, Preacher reluctantly called a halt and told the men to make camp.

As Preacher dismounted, Dog looked up at him and whined.

"I know," Preacher said. "You think you could follow that bunch just with your nose, and I reckon there's a good chance you're right. We can't afford to run the risk o' losin' a day or two, though."

Pete Sanderson laughed and said, "You're talkin' to that dog like he can understand what you're sayin."

Preacher regarded him gravely. "I think critters understand a lot more'n we give 'em credit for. I know damn well that Dog and Horse understand what I'm sayin' part o' the time. They've done what I said and saved my bacon too many times for me to think different."

"I didn't mean any offense, Preacher," Sanderson said hastily. It was obvious that he didn't want any more trouble with Preacher, even if the mountain man did have a broken arm.

Uncle Dan laughed. "You listen to Preacher, boy," he told his nephew. "Pay attention and learn ever'thing you can from him, and you might just live a while."

"It ain't like I'm a babe in the woods or somethin'," Sanderson said with a frown.

"Pete . . . compared to Preacher, *ever'body* this side o' John Colter is a babe in the woods."

Sanderson shut up after that.

It was a cold camp, the men eating jerky and biscuits that they had brought with them from the settlement. Preacher set up a schedule for guard duty, then said, "Dog and me are gonna do some scoutin'. We'll be back after a while, so don't shoot us by accident when we come in."

"You want some comp'ny?" Uncle Dan asked.

Preacher shook his head. "I'd rather you stay here and keep an eye on things."

The old-timer nodded in understanding. Next to Preacher, he was the most experienced man in the group.

"Come on, Dog," Preacher said to the big cur.

They set out on their scouting mission, vanishing into the shadows around the camp as if they had never even been there.

Preacher's arm hurt like a son of a bitch, but he could tell that it was just sore. The long day's ride hadn't done any more damage to it.

And being out in the night like this, just him and Dog flitting through the darkness like phantoms, revitalized him and made him feel better. With eyes like a cat's, he had always been at home in the dark. The chances of anybody spotting him before he spotted them were very small.

"Trail, Dog."

The low-voiced command sent the big cur leaping ahead, nose held close to the ground. With his keen sense of smell, the scents of the people and horses they had been following all day were as distinctive as giant painted signs would have been to humans.

Preacher loped after him, confident that Dog would not lose the trail. The jarring of his footsteps made his left arm ache a little more, but he easily ignored the pain.

For the next hour, Dog kept moving steadily eastward. Preacher could tell the direction by the position of the stars that floated overhead in the ebony sky.

Then their path began to curve in a more southeasterly direction. When Preacher noticed that he said, "Hold on there, Dog."

The big cur came to a halt, but he seemed to strain forward against an invisible leash. After having been on the scent for so long, he didn't want to stop now. His low growl told Preacher that he wanted to continue following the trail.

"Hang on a minute and let me think."

As long as the Blackfeet had been heading in a generally northward direction, they had been moving back toward their usual hunting grounds. Preacher wasn't even surprised by the drift to the east they'd been making.

But for them to turn south struck Preacher as odd. If they continued in that direction for very many days, they would be getting into country that was controlled primarily by the Cheyenne and the Pawnee.

The savage Blackfeet weren't scared of the other tribes. Preacher knew that.

But at the same time, it didn't seem likely to him that they would venture into the territory of their enemies without a good reason.

The war party had failed to wipe out the settlement, and most of the warriors had been lost in the battle. The survivors had a couple of white prisoners. They should have been heading home to lick their wounds and start healing their injured pride by torturing those captives.

Instead, they were headed in the other direction.

"What'n blazes are you varmints up to?" Preacher muttered aloud.

Dog had no answer except an eager whine.

"Go," Preacher told him, and once again the big cur took off, hot on the scent.

Chapter 25

Time meant little or nothing to Preacher in a situation such as this. He had the scent just like Dog, at least figuratively speaking, and he didn't want to give it up.

For the next hour, man and dog moved steadily through the rugged terrain. Over rocky ridges, down long valleys, across shallow, fast-flowing creeks.

The streams were the biggest challenge. Every time they came to one, Dog had to cast back and forth along the opposite bank until he picked up the scent again.

He never failed to do so, though, and usually fairly quickly because their quarry moved straight across the creeks and didn't try to conceal their trail.

With their usual arrogance, the Blackfeet weren't worried about anybody following them. Even though their raid had been a failure, and the war party was only a shadow of what it had been when it started out, they still had absolute confidence in their own fierce fighting skills.

Preacher wasn't sure what time it was, but he knew he and Dog had been gone longer than he'd intended to be when he left the others in camp. He was about to tell Dog to stop so they could turn around and go back when an almost imperceptible pinpoint of light in the distance caught his attention.

"Hold it, Dog," he said.

He stood there concentrating. The light winked out, then on again, and Preacher knew that it wasn't actually going out. Things were moving between him and it . . . people or horses or tree branches blowing in the wind . . . maybe all three.

But it was a campfire, he was sure of that, located about three miles away across a valley, just this side of a range of low hills.

Preacher's instincts told him that Laura Mallory was over there, along with her brother Clyde.

It was all he could do not to head for the distant camp then and there. He considered it briefly, thinking that he could slip in and free Laura and Clyde and get them out of there before their Indian captors even knew what was going on.

But the more pragmatic side of Preacher's brain told him that the likelihood of such an attempt being successful was dangerously slim.

These weren't white men he was dealing with after all. They were seasoned Blackfoot warriors. If he'd just been on a killing mission, he might have been able to pull that off because he wouldn't have to worry about anyone except himself.

He couldn't count on the Mallorys to be stealthy enough in their getaway, though. The slightest sound would be enough to alert the Blackfeet to the fact that something was wrong.

Then Preacher would have to fight his way out with the two prisoners, and the odds were that all three of them would die.

So, difficult though it was, he told himself to wait. He would have a better chance to free Laura and Clyde later, when the men from the settlement were with him.

He just hoped that nothing terrible happened to the captives between now and then.

"Come on, Dog."

Another whine of complaint from the big cur.

"I know. I feel the same way myself, damn it. But we got to use our brains and be smart about this. We'll catch up to 'em tomorrow or the next day, and then I expect you'll have your fill o' fightin'."

Reluctantly, Dog followed as Preacher headed back to the spot where he had left the others. The mountain man had been over this ground once before tonight, and even though it had been dark then, he had no trouble retracing his steps now. That sort of thing was natural with him, as easy and automatic as breathing.

He paid more attention to how much distance he was covering, and by the time he neared the camp, he estimated that he had come about two miles.

That meant the Blackfeet and their captives were between four and five miles ahead. Not an insurmountable lead, but Preacher and his companions couldn't afford to take it easy. They had to push ahead hard the next day.

In fact, they weren't going to wait that long, Preacher decided. He called softly, "Hello, the camp!"

"Preacher?" The sentry gulped after asking the question, revealing his nervousness. "Is that you?"

"It's me," Preacher said dryly, not adding that it was a good thing he wasn't a Blackfoot, else he likely would've been able to sneak up on the youngster and cut his throat. "I'm comin' in."

Uncle Dan greeted him when he came into camp with Dog trailing at his heels. "Find anythin' interestin'?" the old-timer asked.

"I saw a light at the edge of some hills about five miles southeast of here."

"Campfire o' the folks we're lookin' for?"

"That's what I figure."

Uncle Dan scratched at his beard. "Southeast o' here, you say?"

"That's right."

"Sort of odd, ain't it? That ain't the way I'd expect a bunch o' Blackfeet to be headin' with some prisoners."

"The same thought occurred to me," Preacher admitted.

Pete Sanderson had come up to listen to the conversation. "What's odd about it?" he asked.

"It appears those Injuns ain't headin' home after all," his uncle replied. "If they keep goin' that way, they'll leave their stompin' grounds behind and risk runnin' into some Cheyenne or Pawnee."

"We need to catch up to them before that can happen," Preacher said.

It was bad enough that they had to try to rescue Laura Mallory and her brother from the Blackfeet. He didn't want to throw the Cheyenne into the mix, too. They might not be quite as bloodthirsty as the Blackfeet, but they were still plenty dangerous.

"I hope you fellas got rested up whilst I was gone," he went on. "Get ready to move out."

"You mean we're goin' after them tonight?" Sanderson asked. "I thought you didn't want to risk losin' the trail in the dark."

"I don't, but there's not much chance of that now. Dog never lost the scent, and I saw where that campfire is. I reckon we can make up half the distance by mornin', so we'll have an honest chance o' catchin' 'em tomorrow."

Sanderson rubbed his heavy jaw and frowned. After a moment, he said, "Yeah, but . . . what if that fire you saw *ain't* the Blackfoot camp? What if you wind up leadin' us in the wrong direction?"

"Damn it, boy—" Uncle Dan began.

Preacher stopped him with an uplifted hand. "No, Pete's not askin' anything I ain't already asked myself. All I can say is that I'd stake my life I'm right. Problem is, it ain't just my life I'm bettin'. It's Laura Mallory's, and her brother's life." He looked straight at Sanderson. "And if I'm wrong, they'll likely die. Knowin' that, is there anybody who doesn't want to come with me?"

None of the men spoke up for a long moment, until Sanderson finally said, "I reckon if you're backin' the bet, Preacher, then we'll take it, too."

"Good enough," Preacher said with a nod. "Everybody get your gear together. We got some ground to cover before mornin'."

* * *

Ezra Flagg didn't make any reference the next morning to what had happened the night before. In fact, he didn't even look at her, Laura Mallory noted, which was fine with her.

They still needed Flagg to deal with the Blackfeet. Laura suspected that if not for Flagg's presence, Chief Walks Like a Bear and the other warriors might just kill her and Clyde and be done with it.

So for that reason, she was glad Flagg had backed off and evidently didn't intend to make an issue of her rejection. If Clyde found out what Flagg had tried to do, he might try to kill Flagg himself. That could lead to all sorts of problems.

Better to pretend that it hadn't happened. She was willing to do that, just as long as Flagg was.

Flagg went over to Clyde and said, "We'll be gettin' to the edge o' Blackfoot territory today. The chief and his men will want to turn back."

Clyde nodded. "You warned us about that. Will the tribes that we encounter farther east be hostile to a small group? None of them bothered us while the wagon train was on its way out here."

"Yeah, they'll leave a big, well-armed bunch alone for the most part," Flagg agreed. "The Cheyenne and the Pawnee don't like whites any more than the Blackfeet do. We'll have to keep our eyes open."

Laura felt a shiver of nervousness go through her. It was a long way to St. Louis. A great deal could happen between here and there . . . most of it bad.

"Our best bet," Flagg went on, "is to try to catch up with those wagons of yours that are on their way back. If we can join up with them, we shouldn't have much trouble."

"That's a splendid idea. We'll be able to travel considerably faster than the wagons, so it shouldn't take too long."

Once they had eaten breakfast, the group mounted up and headed into a range of low hills that ran north and south. Flagg seemed to know the country, and led them along a trail that twisted back and forth through the valleys.

It was pretty country, Laura thought. Not as spectacular as the mountains surrounding the valley where the settlement was located, but quite nice. The scenery, in fact, reminded her of parts of the English countryside.

That thought made a pang of longing go through her. "Do you think we'll ever go home, Clyde?" she asked her brother as she rode alongside him.

"Our home was lost to us a long time ago, darling."

"No, I didn't mean the place where we grew up," she explained. "I was talking about England in general."

He shrugged. "I suppose we'll probably return there at some point. If the savages had managed to wipe out those Americans, I thought we might make our home there, once an English settlement was established. That may still come about." His voice hardened. "It will if I have anything to say about it. We'll simply have to come up with another plan to drive them out. Perhaps our ally in St. Louis will have some suggestions along those lines."

This was not the first time Laura had heard her brother mention some mysterious ally in St. Louis. She knew that someone in the city had helped him put his hands on the guns that ultimately had gone to Chief Walks Like a Bear and the other Blackfoot warriors.

Most of those guns were now lost, along with the warriors themselves, she thought bitterly. A wasted effort all around. They had done some damage to the Americans, but not nearly enough.

Clyde was right, though. They couldn't give up just because of this one setback, terrible though it was.

They would devise some other plan to drive the Americans out of the western half of the continent, and once that had been accomplished, the British could sweep down from Canada. Gradually, the Americans would be pushed back and their expansionist dreams stymied.

The time would come, sooner or later, when the so-called United States would once again be part of the British Empire, just as God had intended all along. Laura was sure of it.

As they topped a rise around the middle of the day, Laura peered over several more ridges and saw the end of the hills and the beginning of the vast expanse of prairie in the distance to the east. The Great American Desert, some people called it.

Other than linking the words "great" and "American" in any respect, Laura agreed with that description. She remembered the seemingly endless days it had taken the wagon train to cross the plains.

She had been excited when she first saw the mountains looming in snowcapped majesty to the west. That sight surely meant that the journey was nearly over, she had thought.

But the days had continued stretching out into

weeks, and it seemed that the mountains retreated before them since every morning the peaks appeared to be as far away as they had been on the previous morning.

Finally, of course, they had reached the foothills—these same foothills, she thought now, although somewhat to the south of here, she guessed—and then the mountains themselves, and eventually the lush valley where the Americans had founded their settlement.

Up to that point, everything had gone according to the plan laid out by Lord Aspermont.

Then Preacher had shown up.

And ruined everything.

She ought to hate him, Laura thought. She wanted to since he was an American.

But she had seen the way he rushed to her defense a couple of nights earlier, when one of the Blackfeet caught up in the heat of battle had tried to kill her. She had regretted it when she thought he was dead, and when Walks Like a Bear had said that Preacher was still alive, an unaccountable feeling of relief had gone through her.

She couldn't help it. She wished him well.

Unless he interfered with their plans again.

Then she would kill him if she had to. She had no doubts about that.

"There are the plains," Clyde said as the group came to a halt atop the rise. "We should be able to catch up to the wagons in a day or two."

"If we don't run into any trouble," Flagg warned. "The chief and his boys'll be turnin' back when we get to the edge o' these hills. We'll be on our own then."

A shiver went through Laura at those words. Once

it was just her and Clyde and Flagg out there on those endless plains, what would Flagg do then? If anything happened to Clyde, she would be at his mercy . . .

And she didn't think he would make the same mistake of underestimating her as he had before. He knew now that she was armed and dangerous . . . which made him even more dangerous.

She would be awfully glad to see those wagons again, she thought as the group began the descent toward the prairie. That sight couldn't come soon enough to suit her.

Chapter 26

Preacher saw the sun glint off something in the distance, maybe a mile ahead of him and his companions.

Uncle Dan saw it, too. "Reckon that'd be them," the old-timer said.

"More than likely," Preacher agreed. "Probably the sun shinin' on the fittin's of one of those new rifles."

Uncle Dan scratched at his beard and asked, "Where do you reckon the Injuns got all them new rifles? It ain't like redskins to be so well armed."

"That's one thing I intend on tryin' to find out when I get the chance," Preacher said. "Right now, it's more important to rescue those prisoners, though."

"Oh, I ain't arguin' that. But it's right worrisome to think about somebody supplyin' the Injuns with new rifles. It'd sure make things a heap riskier out here if all the savages got their hands on spankin'-new flintlocks like that."

The same thought had crossed Preacher's mind. Even though more and more whites were venturing out to these mountains, they were still outnumbered by the Indians, and likely would be for quite a while to come.

The only thing that kept the trappers and the settlers from being overwhelmed was the fact that they were better armed than the Indians. At longer ranges, bows and arrows were no match for flintlock rifles.

Preacher couldn't think of any reason why a white man would want to arm the Indians, but that was obviously what had happened. Those Blackfeet hadn't gone to St. Louis and bought those rifles themselves.

And if it could happen once, it could happen again. That's why this problem had to be dealt with.

But not now. It would have to wait until Laura Mallory and her brother were safe.

Knowing that he and the others had cut the lead down to only a mile by traveling the rest of the night and then pushing on hard today, Preacher kept the pace up. The men were starting to look haggard with weariness, but they didn't complain.

How could they when Preacher was in the lead despite his injuries? His stony face betrayed no sign of the pain he must be feeling from his broken arm and assorted other injuries.

They forged ahead through the hills. Preacher led the way, and used all the skills at his command to keep them from being spotted while at the same time not losing sight of their quarry. That was a tricky task, but Preacher was up to it.

"They'll reach the prairie by early this afternoon," Uncle Dan predicted. "If they get there before we catch up to 'em, ain't no way in hell we'll able to sneak up on 'em after that."

Preacher nodded. He knew the old-timer was right. Out on those grassy plains, men on horseback could be seen from miles away.

"We'll just have to catch 'em before they get there," he said.

The sun rose higher and heated the air. Preacher's broken arm throbbed, and so did his head. He was capable of pushing himself to great lengths, but even he had his limits.

He couldn't give in to the pain, he told himself. Not while Laura was being held prisoner.

Assuming, of course, that she was even still alive. He didn't know that for sure. But they hadn't come across her body, and he was confident they were still on the right trail. The way Dog kept going without hesitation told him that.

If they were successful in rescuing the prisoners from the Blackfeet, the big cur would deserve a lot of the credit, Preacher thought. Without Dog's talented nose, they would have been forced to go slower in order not to lose the trail.

Preacher was careful not to let them be skylighted on hilltops, but even so, they were high enough from time to time for him to be able to see the plains in the distance.

He loved the prairie. Not as much as the high mountain country, which he had always felt was his true home, but there was something about the vast sweep of the plains that was awe-inspiring.

It made a man feel good to know that there were so many different things to see in his native country. Preacher had been from the Canadian border clear down to Texas, from the Father of Waters, the

Mississippi River, to the towering forests of the Oregon country.

One of these days, he thought, he'd see the ocean. Maybe take him a ride on a ship. He had been on keelboats and flatboats and rafts, but that was different. What would it be like to be out in the middle of the ocean, so far from shore that you couldn't see land anywhere you looked?

The idea made him a mite nervous, so he put it out of his head. He didn't need to be distracted right now anyway.

Within an hour or so, they would be closing in on their quarry, and then Preacher would have to decide just how he was going to get Laura and Mallory away from the Blackfeet without getting them killed in the process.

He should have insisted that Shad Beaumont find an experienced mountain man to come along with them, Colin Fairfax thought as he stood there studying the hoofprints that had been left in the sandy soil beside a stream.

Fairfax was almost certain that they were on the right trail, but the possibility that they had gone astray nagged at him. He should have had an actual tracker with him. When *he* was the most experienced frontiersman in the group, that was a definite problem!

"That's still them, right?" Sherwood asked. Like the other men, he was still mounted.

"Of course," Fairfax replied without hesitation. He didn't want Sherwood to see that he had any doubts.

"How far behind them are we?"

Who did Sherwood think he was, Daniel Boone? Just because he was still wearing that coonskin cap he had borrowed from Campbell, that didn't mean he could tell such things just by looking at some hoof-prints!

"We're closing in on them," Fairfax said. He put his foot in the stirrup and swung up into the saddle. "I expect we'll catch up to them either late this afternoon or sometime tomorrow morning."

That was just a guess, of course . . . but Sherwood and the others didn't have to know that. Fairfax sensed that as long as he continued to display an air of confidence, they would continuc to follow him.

But if they ever saw doubt or indecision coming from him, then he would lose them. He was sure of that. It wouldn't take much for them to bolt and actually head back to St. Louis, just as they had pretended to do several days earlier.

"What do we do after Preacher's dead?" Sherwood asked as their horses splashed across the shallow stream.

"Didn't Beaumont give you any orders?"

"Nope. Just said to do what you told us to do."

Fairfax didn't believe that for a second. But just in case Sherwood was telling the truth, he said, "I'd like to go back to the valley and burn that trading post to the ground."

Sherwood glanced over at him, evidently surprised. "Why? The Harts seemed like decent fellas, and that Deborah Hart . . . well, she's a mighty pretty woman."

"They ruined my plans just like Preacher did," Fairfax spat out. That wasn't strictly true; without

Preacher's help, the Hart cousins never would have reached the valley, let alone survived this long.

But he still bore a grudge against them. They had played a part in Schuyler Mims's death. During the long trek back to civilization the year before, Fairfax had devoted most of his thoughts to hating Preacher, but Corliss, Jerome, and Deborah Hart had come in for their share of hatred, too.

Sherwood rubbed his heavy jaw and then said, "I got to admit, it'd be mighty nice to spend some time with that woman away from her husband. Maybe we could kill Corliss and Jerome and burn the place down, then take her with us when we left."

Fairfax gave a noncommittal grunt. He didn't like the idea of taking the woman along. That would just cause jealousy among the men, which might lead to more problems.

But he was perfectly willing to dangle Deborah Hart in front of them as bait to get them to follow his orders. In fact, he would go one step farther than that.

"There are other women at the settlement, too," he said, "and some of them are probably attractive. We might be able to take several of them with us."

The men who were riding behind Fairfax and Sherwood heard the comment, and the word spread quickly throughout the group. Fairfax heard the excited muttering behind him and smiled to himself.

He knew he had just strengthened his grip on them. They would be anxious now to dispose of Preacher and then get back to the settlement. The prospects of rape and loot were powerful lures for men such as these.

Fairfax didn't care about either of those things.

He just wanted vengeance . . . on Preacher and on the Harts.

It took longer to reach the plains than Laura thought it would. By the middle of the afternoon, they were still winding through the foothills with their Blackfoot escort.

She still had mixed emotions about the situation. She didn't trust the Indians not to turn on them, but at the same time she didn't look forward to her and Clyde being alone with Flagg and his squaw.

Several times, Laura had noticed the Indian woman staring at her. The woman's round face was so impassive that it was impossible to tell what she was thinking. Looking at her wasn't any more rewarding than peering at a stone.

But Laura thought she caught hints of hatred glinting in the squaw's eyes. She remembered the things Flagg had said about kidnapping the Indian woman and forcing her to live as his wife. Perhaps Flagg had broken her spirit, but surely deep down, she hated him for what he had done.

What if she didn't, though? What if she had grown to care for the renegade American? If she knew that Flagg had tried to rape Laura, would she be angry at Flagg . . . or would she blame Laura for tempting her man?

Laura didn't know the answers to those questions, but she was beginning to wonder if she might not be in danger from Flagg's woman as well as from Flagg himself.

Finally, as they rode toward a notch in a long,

rocky ridge, Flagg said, "It won't be much longer now. The trail drops down to the prairie just on the other side of that gap."

Chief Walks Like a Bear spoke up, offering some long comment in his native tongue. When he was finished, Mallory asked, "What did he say?"

Flagg smiled faintly. "That he'll be glad to be shed of all of us. Says he was a fool for trustin' white men and that he'll never do it again."

"He's not going to double-cross us here at the last minute, is he?" Mallory asked with a worried frown.

Flagg shook his head. "I don't think so. If ol' Bear's got one failin', it's that he's a man of his word." Flagg's voice hardened as he added, "But if you ever run into him after we part company with him today, you better kill him and kill him quick, because he'll be doin' his damnedest to kill you."

"I'll keep that in mind," Mallory said.

The group continued riding toward the notch in the ridge, which flattened out on top and was littered with boulders. Laura winced at the pain in her thighs, which came from sore muscles unaccustomed to long hours spent riding as well as from chafed skin. Even though riding in a wagon hadn't been all that pleasant, she was looking forward to it now.

She was thinking about that as the group started up the slope toward the notch, so she didn't realize right away that something was wrong.

But then she heard her brother's startled exclamation, and Flagg burst out, "What the hell!" Excited muttering came from the Indians, too.

Laura lifted her eyes and saw that a man had

stepped out into the gap at the top of the slope, now no more than twenty feet from them. She recognized him instantly, even though he wasn't wearing his usual buckskins.

Preacher.

Chapter 27

It seemed clear to Preacher that the best way to get the prisoners away from the Blackfeet was to take them by surprise.

And nothing would be quite as surprising to the Indians as to find their pursuers in front of them instead of behind.

Uncle Dan agreed when Preacher laid out the plan during another brief halt to rest the horses. The wily old-timer had a word of caution, though.

"If they was white men and we had the drop on 'em, they'd do what you told 'em to keep from gettin' killed. You can't count on Injuns bein' that reasonable, though. They're liable to put up a fight no matter what the odds are agin 'em."

"I know," Preacher said. "If they make a move to kill the prisoners, we'll just have to shoot fast and straight."

Uncle Dan nodded. "Let's do 'er."

The rescue party pushed on shortly after that, urging their mounts on to greater speed as they circled to the north.

Preacher had been through this part of the country numerous time before, and figured that the Blackfeet and their captives were heading for Rutherford's Notch. That was the easiest way out of these rugged foothills. The trail led straight from there out onto the plains.

Horses and men responded gamely. They were all worn out from the long chase, but now, with the end in sight, they found fresh bursts of strength and energy.

By the middle of the afternoon, Preacher was confident that he and his companions had gotten ahead of the Blackfeet. They cut sharply to the south and reached the ridge that divided the foothills from the prairie.

As they reached the notch, they angled down the eastern slope and dismounted. The ridge itself would keep the Indians from being able to see their horses. One man was left behind to hold the mounts, while the others spread out on both sides of the gap and found hiding places among the rocks.

Preacher chose a spot very near the notch for himself. Dog sat beside him, panting in the warm afternoon sun. Preacher sleeved sweat from his forehead with his good arm.

Quiet lay over the landscape, so Preacher was able to hear the riders coming for quite a ways before they reached the gap in the ridge. The big cur at his feet heard the hoofbeats, too, and started to growl, but Preacher silenced him with a soft, "Hush, Dog."

Judging distance by the sounds of the horses' hooves, Preacher waited with the patience of a born frontiersman. He knew that his men would stay concealed behind the rocks until they heard his voice.

This had to be timed carefully. Since he couldn't handle a rifle, he wanted the lead riders to be within range of his pistol when he finally stepped out into the open and challenged them.

At last, they were close enough, he figured. He took a deep breath, looped his thumb over the hammer of the flintlock pistol, and took a long step into the middle of the gap, lifting the pistol and turning to face the oncoming riders as he did so.

He heard the startled reactions, then silenced them by calling in his deep, powerful voice, "Hold it!"

His keen eyes swept over the scene, taking in the tiniest detail since this was the first close look he had gotten at the group he and his companions had been pursuing.

Nine Blackfoot warriors glared at him, including one barrel-chested fella whose war paint and regalia marked him as a chief. Each of the Indians had one of those new rifles.

Laura Mallory and her brother Clyde rode in the forefront of the group, along with another white man in a beaded buckskin jacket and a flat-crowned hat. Preacher had never seen him before.

He was glad to have it confirmed that he hadn't been imagining things when he thought he saw Clyde Mallory with Laura while the settlement was under attack. He didn't know why Mallory was here instead of with the wagons on their way back to St. Louis, but at the moment, that didn't really matter.

There was one other person in the bunch, a round-faced Indian woman who brought up the rear, trailing a packhorse with her. Preacher didn't know her either, but his mind leaped to the assumption that she was with the white man he didn't know.

He felt a wave of relief go through him as he saw that Laura appeared to be all right. She was riding one of the Indian ponies, riding astride like a man with her skirt pulled up and her bare calves showing. She wore a look of utter amazement at the sight of Preacher.

But then a smile broke out on her face, and she cried, "Preacher! Oh, thank God you found us!"

He kept the Indians covered with the pistol, and knew that Uncle Dan and the rest of the men hidden in the rocks had their rifles trained on the Blackfeet as well. The members of the rescue party had been told to show themselves just enough so that the Indians would know they were there.

"Laura, you and Clyde come on over here," Preacher said.

Mallory's face was flushed with surprise. Laura turned to him and said, "I told you Preacher would come to rescue us, Clyde."

"Yes," Mallory said through gritted teeth. "Yes, you did."

What was wrong with the man? Preacher wondered. He didn't look all that happy to see them.

But maybe he was hurt. He acted sort of like he was in pain.

Laura dug her heels into her pony's flanks and rode forward. Mallory followed her. Preacher stepped aside so that they could move past him through the gap.

"Keep goin' when you get to the other side," he told them as they went by. "Who's that other fella?"

"That's Mr. Flagg," Laura said. "He helped us. He's a prisoner, too. You have to save him."

"Sure," Preacher nodded. "Flagg, get away from those redskins."

Flagg started his horse forward, but at that moment Preacher noticed something he should have seen earlier. He *would* have seen it earlier, he thought suddenly, if he hadn't been so relieved to see that Laura wasn't hurt.

That stranger called Flagg was armed. He had a pistol behind his belt and a rifle in a beaded sling on his horse. And he wasn't the only one . . .

Clyde Mallory had a pistol, too, and Preacher heard the metallic sound of it being cocked.

"Don't move, Preacher," Mallory said. "I don't want to kill you, old boy, but I will if I have to."

"Son of a *bitch*!" Preacher breathed as everything became clear to him.

Well, almost everything, he realized.

He didn't know *why* Clyde Mallory had turned out to be a double-crossing bastard.

"Preacher," Uncle Dan called from the rocks up above, "what the hell's goin' on here? You want us to open up on them Injuns?"

"Hold your fire," Preacher responded. He had no doubt that his men could bring down some of the war party survivors, but those Blackfeet wouldn't just sit there. They would fight back, and if enough lead started flying around Laura might be hit.

Besides, he didn't know yet if she was aware of her brother's treachery or if she was just as surprised as he was. It was important to him that he find out.

That question was answered for him as she said,

"I'm sorry, Preacher. When I heard about how badly you were hurt, I never dreamed that you would come after us."

"You're part of it," he said in a flat, hard voice. "You knew about those rifles your brother brought out and sold to the Indians."

"Figured that out, did you?" Mallory asked with a chuckle. "Well, you've got part of it wrong. We didn't *sell* the rifles to Chief Walks Like a Bear and his men. We *gave* the weapons to them."

Preacher couldn't help but turn his head to look at the Englishman. "Why the hell would you—" he began.

"Because this country shouldn't belong to you!" Mallory broke in, spitting the words out venomously. "England colonized America, and when we tried to take it back, you filthy barbarians killed our father! Tell him, Laura!"

"It's true, Preacher," she said with a regretful expression on her face. "Our father was a soldier. He was killed at the Battle of New Orleans."

A cold shiver went down Preacher's spine at those words. *He* had been at the Battle of New Orleans. He had taken part in the fighting, despite being little more than a boy at the time. Even though it was mighty far-fetched to think about it, he couldn't rule out the possibility that it had been a ball from *his* rifle that had ended the life of Clyde and Laura's father.

He didn't figure it would be a good idea to bring that up right now, though. Not with the look of murderous hatred that was already etched on Clyde Mallory's face.

Instead, he took a deep breath and said, "So. What are we gonna do about this?"

"What do you think we're going to do?" Mallory asked coldly. "Your men are going to let us go, and you're coming with us as a hostage to insure our safe passage back to the wagon train. Meanwhile, the chief and his men will be allowed to leave in peace."

His voice was loud enough in the hot silence that hung over the landscape so that the men hidden in the rocks could hear everything he said. Uncle Dan called down, "Preacher, that ain't gonna work. Too many of our fellas lost loved ones back yonder at the settlement. They ain't lettin' those redskins ride away."

Preacher smiled humorlessly at Mallory. "You heard what the man said. Only one way this stand-off's gonna end, and that's with powder smoke in the air."

Mallory's mouth tightened so that the skin around it grew white. "Then I might as well go ahead and blow your brains out right now," he said.

"No!" Laura cried. "There must be some way we can work this out."

Her brother shook his head. "I fear that too much blood has been shed for that to happen, my dear."

"Hold on," the man called Flagg said. "My squaw and me don't have any part in this fight. Let us ride away from here and then you can all kill each other as far as I'm concerned."

Preacher grunted. "No part in it, eh?" With the revelation of Clyde Mallory's villainy, all the other pieces of the puzzle had fallen into place. "I reckon you'd be the one who put Mallory in touch with the

Blackfeet, mister. That's the only thing that makes sense. They wouldn't have those rifles if it wasn't for you."

Flagg's lip curled in an angry snarl. "I've heard a lot about you, Preacher," he said. "Nobody ever told me you were too damned smart for your own good."

A moment of strained silence went by. There was no way of knowing how long this impasse was going to last . . .

But then Chief Walks Like a Bear reached the end of his patience. With a guttural cry, he jerked his rifle up and fired at the man he blamed for the failure of the raid on the settlement.

Preacher.

All his life Preacher had heard the old saying about being stuck between a rock and a hard place. With Clyde Mallory pointing a gun at him from behind and the Blackfoot chief in front of him, he was sure enough in that spot.

But he had seen the flare of rage in Walks Like a Bear's eyes and knew that was where the immediate danger lay, so he moved as soon as the chief's rifle started to come up.

The ball whirred past Preacher's head and slammed into the chest of Clyde Mallory's horse. The animal let out a scream of pain and reared up on its hind legs just as Mallory pulled the trigger of his pistol. Smoke and flame erupted from the weapon's muzzle, but the shot went harmlessly into the air.

The men from the settlement opened fire a second after Walks Like a Bear kicked off the ruckus. A volley of shots ripped out from the rocks, and three of the Blackfeet were driven off their ponies by the impact of the rifle balls that struck them. Two more of the warriors were wounded but managed to stay mounted.

Shots roared out from the rifles wielded by the Indians, and Preacher heard cries of pain from at least two of his companions. He swung his pistol toward Walks Like a Bear but before he could pull the trigger, something crashed into his back and drove him off his feet.

As he slammed into the ground, an arm looped around his neck and clamped down on it like an iron bar. "You bastard!" Clyde Mallory grated in his ear.

Preacher knew that Mallory had leaped off his dying horse and tackled him. The double impact—first Mallory and then the hard, rocky ground—sent incredible pain shooting through Preacher's body from his broken arm. Stars exploded in his brain.

Mallory might have choked him to death if not for Dog. The Englishman howled in surprise and pain as the big cur's teeth closed on his leg. He let go of Preacher and twisted around to slash at Dog with the empty pistol he still held in his other hand.

Able to breathe again, Preacher heaved his body up from the ground and flung Mallory away from him. Still half-blinded with pain, he staggered to his feet.

With a screeching war cry, Walks Like a Bear loomed over him. The Blackfoot chief had sent his horse surging forward. He swung the empty rifle at Preacher's head.

Preacher ducked under the slashing blow, but couldn't avoid the horse's shoulder. It clipped him as

Walks Like a Bear charged past and started up into the notch, still shrilling the high-pitched war cry.

It was his death song, Preacher realized.

And Walks Like a Bear knew it, too.

A pair of shots blasted from the rocks. The chief was jolted by them, but stayed on his pony's back. He tossed the empty rifle aside, plucked his tomahawk from his belt, and sent his horse lunging up into the rocks. Walks Like a Bear leaped off and landed in the middle of the Van Goorts. He grappled with the two Dutchmen, and they all fell out of sight behind the boulder.

The other surviving Blackfeet had reached the slope, too, and were now struggling hand to hand with the men from the settlement, who didn't have time to reload their rifles anymore. The fighting was fierce, but the Indians were outnumbered.

When they died, though, they were going to take as many of the hated whites with them as they could. To them, there was no shame in death, only in dying without an enemy's blood on their hands.

Preacher shoved the terrible pain in his arm aside and looked for Laura Mallory. He couldn't find her in the confusion. Dust swirled up, making it harder to see.

The man called Flagg burst out of the chaos, still mounted, and kicked Preacher in the chest. Preacher went over backward, but he dropped his pistol and managed to snag Flagg's leg as the man went past. He heaved with all his strength, dislodging Flagg from the saddle. With a startled cry, the man toppled to the ground.

Preacher bent and snatched up his pistol again. He

pressed the barrel to Flagg's head and ordered, "Don't move, mister!"

Flagg was going to try to scramble to his feet, but he froze at the touch of Preacher's gun. Then a cold smile curved his lips as he said, "Don't think you got the upper hand just yet, Preacher."

Preacher didn't have to ask the renegade what he meant by that.

The unmistakable sensation of a razor-edged knife suddenly pressing against his throat told him this fight wasn't over yet. The blade penetrated his skin, and blood crawled warmly over his skin.

"Drop your pistol, Preacher," Laura said. "I don't want to cut your throat, but make no mistake . . . I will if I have to."

Chapter 28

Preacher didn't react for a couple of long seconds. Then he said, "You can't cut my throat fast enough to keep me from blowin' Flagg's brains out, Laura."

"Perhaps not, but you'll still be dead, won't you?" A tone of wistfulness touched her voice as she added, "I truly wish things hadn't turned out this way, you know."

Preacher didn't give a damn about what she wished or didn't wish anymore. His gaze darted around the slope, what he could see of it from where he was anyway.

He saw Clyde Mallory struggling to his feet, bleeding in several places from the gashes Dog's teeth had left in his flesh. Preacher's heart seemed to stop for a second when he saw the shaggy shape lying on the ground at Mallory's feet.

Dog wasn't moving, but his side rose and fell as Preacher watched, telling the mountain man that the big cur was still alive. Mallory had probably just knocked him senseless by clubbing him with the pistol.

Preacher saw Uncle Dan and Pete Sanderson farther

up the slope, both of them bloody as well from hand-to-hand struggles with the Blackfeet, but apparently not hurt too badly.

Walks Like a Bear and the two Van Goorts lay in a gory tangle among the boulders. The chief had buried his tomahawk in the skull of one of the Dutchmen, cleaving bone and brains. The other had a knife sunk in his chest, but he had died with his hands locked around Walks Like a Bear's throat and the chief stared sightlessly as well, the life choked out of him.

Three more of the men from the settlement were still alive, including Sanderson's friend Dennison. From what Preacher could see, none of the Blackfeet were.

There weren't any loaded guns among the survivors, though. They had expended their shots during the battle and hadn't had a chance to reload.

"You men stay back!" Laura called to them. "I'll kill Preacher if you come a step closer!"

"What do you want us to do, Preacher?" Uncle Dan asked. "That Englisher gal looks like she means what she says."

"I certainly do mean it," Laura said. "I've nothing left to lose."

"Well, I'm gettin' a mite tired o' bein' shaved like this," Preacher drawled. He took the pistol away from Flagg's head and turned the weapon so that he gripped it by the barrel.

With a snarl on his bearded face, Flagg reached up and snatched the pistol away from Preacher.

Laura kept the knife at Preacher's throat anyway as he straightened.

"I done what you wanted," Preacher told her.

"Yes, but I'm afraid I don't trust you, Preacher. You have a way of showing up where you're least expected and doing the most amazing things."

Clyde Mallory limped over to them, blood staining his trousers where Dog had gnawed on his leg. "Go ahead and cut his throat, Laura," he urged. "We can't leave him alive."

Flagg had gotten to his feet, still clutching Preacher's pistol. "If you don't want to kill him, Miss Mallory," he said, "just step away from him. I'll take care of it."

Preacher sensed that his life was hanging by a thread. He should have taken a chance on twisting away from the knife and disarming Laura, he thought.

But he couldn't have done that without taking the gun away from Flagg's head, and then the renegade would have jumped him . . .

As much as it went against Preacher's nature, there were occasions when it was best for a fella to just bide his time. He hoped this was one of them.

Uncle Dan spoke up, addressing his words to Flagg. "If you pull that trigger, mister, it's the only shot you'll get. There are five of us, not even countin' Preacher, and only three of you folks."

"All your redskin helpers are dead," Sanderson spat. "Might as well give up."

"Shut up, you bloody American!" Mallory snapped. "We still have the upper hand here."

Preacher felt a wave of dizziness go through him. His knees threatened to buckle, but they stiffened when he felt the knife blade bite deeper into his flesh.

"I don't feel like standin' around jawin' all day," he rasped. "I reckon the best thing is for you folks to go your way, and we'll go ours."

"Preacher, no!" Sanderson exclaimed. "We can't let 'em go! Not after what they did to the settlement!"

"The Blackfeet are all dead," Preacher pointed out. "We came after 'em in the first place to rescue Miss Mallory and her brother, and it's mighty clear now that they never needed rescuin'."

It was a rare thing for him to be the voice of reason, and Preacher didn't care for it. Anyway, he was just stalling for time, because he had heard something that evidently none of the others had because of all the palavering.

The clicking of shod hooves against stone.

Somebody else was riding up to the far side of the gap.

Preacher had no idea who it could be, but their arrival couldn't help but change things here. One way or another, the current standoff would be ended.

"I don't care what you say," Sanderson insisted. "We can't let 'em go, Preacher. Those Injuns never would've attacked the settlement if they hadn't been able to get guns from the Englishers. And that bastard Flagg helped set up the deal."

Flagg sneered and swung the pistol up, aiming at Sanderson now. "That's mighty big talk for a man whose rifle's empty."

"Damn it!" Preacher bellowed. "Everybody just settle down! There don't have to be any more killin'—"

A new voice interrupted him. "That's where you're wrong, Preacher. The killing's not over yet."

Despite the knife at his throat, Preacher tipped his head back and gazed up at the top of the ridge. Colin

Fairfax, a coonskin cap on his bald head, stood there pointing a rifle at him.

Behind Fairfax were at least half a dozen heavily armed men, and more were crowding into sight with each passing second.

"You still have to die, Preacher," Fairfax went on with an evil smile on his face as he peered over the barrel of the rifle.

Those men Preacher had heard coming had arrived and ended the standoff, just as he'd hoped.

Unfortunately, things had just gone from bad to worse . . .

After everything that had happened, Colin Fairfax could scarcely believe that his luck had finally changed. He and his followers had heard the shots and circled around the battle, not knowing what they would find.

Fairfax expected to discover that Preacher had somehow emerged triumphant from the fighting, as he always seemed to.

But that hadn't turned out to be the case, and now Fairfax once again had the drop on Preacher. This time, the hated mountain man was already badly injured.

Not only that, Preacher had a knife at his throat as well, and his friends obviously held empty guns or else this stalemate wouldn't have come about.

The pretty blonde holding the knife must be the woman Preacher had tried to rescue from the Blackfeet. Clearly, she hadn't needed rescuing at all.

Fairfax didn't understand all of that, but right now

he didn't care about it either. He went on. "Why don't you just step away from him, ma'am? My men and I will take care of this now."

One of the other men stepped forward. "Who are you, sir?" he demanded in an accent that matched the blonde's. Both of them were English. That would make this fella the woman's brother, according to what Sherwood had learned during his visit to the settlement.

Fairfax had no idea who the other man and the squaw were.

"My name is Colin Fairfax," he introduced himself. "I have a score to settle with Preacher here, as it appears that you and your companions do, too."

The man motioned to the blonde. "Step away from him, Laura. We don't have anything to worry about now."

Fairfax wasn't so sure about that. The blonde was mighty pretty, and he knew she would be a temptation to his men. He didn't give a damn what happened to her or her brother or the rest of them. All he cared about was Preacher.

Laura lowered the knife, leaving behind a tendril of blood that trickled down Preacher's neck like a crimson snake from the cut the blade had made. With a worried look on her face, she moved over to her brother's side.

"I don't like this, Clyde," she said in a low voice that still carried to Fairfax's ears. "We don't know these men. We don't know what they'll do."

"I don't think we have anything to worry about," he told her. He took the knife from her hand.

Sherwood stepped up beside Fairfax and asked, "Are you gonna go ahead and shoot Preacher?"

Fairfax knew that he should press the rifle's trigger and end Preacher's annoying existence at last. Every minute the mountain man remained alive was another minute that Preacher might somehow, miraculously, turn things to his advantage.

But for the life of him, Fairfax didn't see any way Preacher could get out of this predicament. For God's sake, the man was so battered and exhausted he could barely stand! Fairfax could tell just by looking at him that Preacher was on the verge of collapse.

"Not yet," he said. "Take them all prisoner. Tie them up."

Sherwood hesitated. "Are you sure, Boss? I really think you ought to go ahead and shoot him."

"Blast it, I gave you an order!" Fairfax said. "Now carry it out!"

With obvious reluctance, Sherwood nodded. "All right, boys, you heard the man. Let's take 'em."

The men from the settlement clearly wanted to fight back, but menaced by a dozen guns as they were, they would have been throwing away their lives. Fairfax's men moved in and lashed their hands behind their backs with rawhide thongs.

They left Preacher for last. Following Fairfax's instructions, three men in addition to himself kept their rifles trained on the mountain man. Then three more men moved in with a rope.

Since Preacher's broken left arm was already lashed to his side, Fairfax's men wrapped the rope around his torso and bound his right arm to his side as well. That was the easiest way to make sure he couldn't fight back. They took several turns with the rope and then tied it tightly.

Then and only then did Fairfax lower his rifle and signal to his men to do likewise.

"At last," he said as he came down the slope toward Preacher. "You'll never ruin my plans again, you bastard."

"Won't need to," Preacher drawled with maddening coolness. "I reckon you'll find a way to do that yourself, Fairfax."

Fairfax felt his face turn hot as angry blood flooded into it. Without thinking about what he was doing, he gave in to thc impulse that seized him and rammed the muzzle of his rifle into Preacher's belly as hard as he could.

That brought a startled cry from the blonde. She put her hand to her mouth as if in horror as Preacher turned gray and doubled over from the blow.

Fairfax grinned as he said to the woman, "You were ready to cut his throat, but you don't like it when somebody else hurts him?"

He saw cold dislike in her eyes as she said, "I was trying to save our lives. You're just being vicious."

"Believe me, he's got it coming," and with that Fairfax smashed his rifle's stock across Preacher's face and drove the mountain man to the ground. Angry growls came from some of the men who had been part of the rescue party along with Preacher, but there was nothing they could do.

Blood dripped from Preacher's mouth as he looked up at Fairfax and somehow managed to grin.

"You got the upper hand right now, mister," he said, "but it may not always be that way."

"Your threats don't worry me. Not anymore." Fairfax gestured to his men. "Put him with the others."

A couple of the men grabbed Preacher's arms and hauled him to his feet. The rough handling of his broken limb made him curse under his breath, but that was the only sign he exhibited of how much it must hurt to be manhandled like that.

Fairfax turned to the woman and the other two men. "Now," he said, "what are we going to do with you?"

He paid no attention to the squaw, figuring that she belonged to one of the men and was inconsequential.

"I can make it worth your while to escort us farther east and help us find a wagon train on its way back to St. Louis," the Englishman said.

"You can, can you?"

"That's right. My name is Clyde Mallory." He nodded toward the blonde. "My sister and I are agents of the British government."

"You're spies?" Fairfax couldn't keep the surprise out of his voice and off his face.

"Nothing quite so crass. We represent the interests of the British Empire."

Fairfax shook his head. "I don't give a damn about politics or empires. I just came out here to see to it that Preacher dies."

"And you can accomplish that goal whenever it suits your fancy. He and his friends are completely in your power. Once you've disposed of them, there'll be nothing stopping you from accepting my proposition."

What Mallory was saying made sense, Fairfax realized . . . except for the fact that by going along with the Englishman, he'd be helping enemies of the United States.

On the other hand, what did he owe the United States anyway? The country had never fed him when he was hungry or put a roof over his head when he was cold and wet and shivering. It didn't care when Schuyler died, and it sure hadn't given a damn when Fairfax was trudging back to civilization, half starved and in constant terror that wild animals or Indians would kill him.

"You know what, mister?" he said as he came to a decision. "I think we can come to an arrangement. But we can't settle anything until Preacher's dead."

Clyde Mallory nodded. "Indeed. And the sooner the better."

Fairfax shook his head and said, "No, not quite. What I've got in mind is going to take some time, but we have plenty of it." He looked at the mountain man and smiled. "Yes, we have plenty of time for Preacher to die."

Chapter 29

Being trussed up like a pig ready to be taken to market had grated on Preacher's nerves and put a bitter taste in his mouth. As the rope around his body was drawn tight, it had sent fresh throbs of pain through his injured arm. He fought off the dizziness that went with it.

Then Fairfax had punched him in the belly with that rifle barrel and knocked him to the ground, only to stand over him gloating.

The fella was toting up a nice big score to settle, Preacher thought as he lay there. He didn't pay any attention to Fairfax's blustering threats. The man could threaten all he wanted to as far as Preacher was concerned.

Because that meant Preacher was still alive, and as long as he was drawing breath, he wasn't going to give up.

He knew good and well that Fairfax intended to torture him before killing him. That suspicion was confirmed as the afternoon wore on and evening approached. Fairfax had declared that they would camp for the night on the eastern side of the notch, at the base of the trail leading down to the prairie, and he ordered that a fire be built there.

"A good, hot fire," he said with a vicious grin on his face.

The son of a bitch was going to burn him at the stake, Preacher thought.

That brought back a passel of memories, and not good ones either. Several years earlier, a band of Blackfeet had captured him and planned to burn him to death, thinking that was a suitable vengeance because he had killed several of their warriors.

However, an idea had occurred to Preacher—who was still known at that time as Art—and he had begun to spout Scripture just like a wild-eyed preacher he had seen once on the street back in St. Louis.

It was common knowledge that not even the most bloodthirsty Indians would harm a man they considered crazy, because they figured crazy men were protected by spirits and nobody wanted to get on the wrong side of any vengeful spirits.

Preacher had seen right away that the ploy had a chance of working. The Blackfeet had stared at him in amazement as the words continued to pour out of his mouth.

They were still staring more than twelve hours later. Preacher's voice was raspy as an old rusty file by then, but he didn't care. He would keep forcing the words out until the Blackfeet decided he was a lunatic and let him go.

Which, of course, they eventually did, and as a result the rest of the mountain men had taken to calling him Preacher as soon as the story got around at the next Rendezvous. The handle had stuck for years now, and Preacher figured it was permanent.

As permanent as anything could be, that is, now that he once again faced a fiery death at the stake.

The light of day began to fade from the sky as Fairfax's men brought firewood down from the hills and heaped it next to the ring of stones that had been arranged according to the bald man's order.

Preacher sat cross-legged on the ground with the other prisoners, and watched bands of purple and gold and orange and blue make their way across the sky. It was a beautiful sight, as most sunsets were out here on the frontier.

If this was the last sunset he ever saw, then so be it. He was going to appreciate it, whether he lived to see the sun come up the next morning or not.

Laura, her brother, and Flagg were sitting together on the other side of the camp, talking quietly. Several times, Preacher had seen Laura stealing furtive glances at him. Even though she had been prepared to kill him herself if she had to, he could tell that she wasn't happy about the way things had turned out since Fairfax's arrival.

As Fairfax's men heaped wood on the fire and the flames began to leap ever higher and brighter, Fairfax came across the camp to stand in front of Preacher with an ugly grin on his face.

"You're blockin' the view," Preacher said. "I was lookin' at the sunset."

"It's the last one you'll ever see," Fairfax said, unwittingly echoing the possibility Preacher had been thinking about just a moment earlier. "Do you know what's going to happen to you?"

"To tell you the truth, I don't much give a damn," Preacher lied. He wasn't going to give Fairfax the satisfaction of seeing that he was worried.

"What *do* you give a damn about?"

"Well . . . I'm a mite curious."

Fairfax looked like that surprised him. "Curious?" he repeated. "About what?"

"For a while there, folks kept tryin' to kill me. Two men bushwhacked me whilst I was workin' my trap lines, and a couple o' days later three more varmints tried to crush me in a rock slide they started. Were those fellas workin' for you?"

For a moment, Preacher thought Fairfax wasn't going to answer, but then the man shrugged and said, "I don't see what harm it could do to tell you. Yes, they worked for me. For what it's worth, though, they weren't supposed to kill you. They were scouts. They were just supposed to locate you and then send word back to me and the rest of the men."

"Reckon they must've got carried away. Maybe they figured they'd earn a bonus if they killed me for you."

The heavy-jawed man who seemed to be Fairfax's second in command had walked up in time to hear Preacher's speculation. He said, "There's a bonus, all right. Five hundred dollars for the man who kills you, accordin' to our boss back in St. Louis."

Fairfax looked annoyed at that. Preacher found it interesting. He grinned at Fairfax and said, "I thought you was the boss. Reckon I was wrong."

"I'm in charge of this group," Fairfax snapped. "What I say goes." He looked challengingly at the other man, whose name was Sherwood.

"Well, sure," Sherwood said. "I didn't mean anything else."

Preacher wasn't so sure, though. He sensed a certain tension between the two men. Maybe he could exploit that and take advantage of it . . . if he could manage to live long enough.

He was mighty curious, too, about that boss back in St. Louis Sherwood had mentioned. Was there more to all this than Preacher knew about?

Again, maybe he could find out if he survived what Fairfax had planned for him.

If not . . . well, then, it wouldn't matter a whole hell of a lot, would it?

Fairfax glared at him and asked, "Have I indulged your curiosity enough?"

"Not quite," Preacher said. "You were tryin' to trick me when you and the rest of your bunch left the valley where the settlement's located, weren't you? You doubled back after a couple o' days, after you made me think you were gone."

Fairfax sneered. "I didn't just *try* to trick you, Preacher. I *did* trick you. I never left the valley."

"Then the fella I saw in the beaver hat . . . ?"

"Wasn't me. I traded hats with one of my men. They lured you away, and I went to the settlement."

Preacher frowned. "Didn't Corliss or Jerome recognize you from that dustup last year?"

"I was careful not to let either of them see me," Fairfax explained. "I planned to kidnap Deborah Hart and use her as bait to lure you into a trap."

Preacher felt a surge of hot rage inside him. "You'd do that?"

"Of course I would, if it helped me get what I want."

"You're lower'n a snake's belly, Fairfax."

The man laughed. "Your insults mean nothing to me." He went on. "My plan would have worked, too, if not for that Indian attack. That almost ruined everything."

"You didn't have anything to do with it?"

"Of course not." Fairfax waved a hand toward the trio huddled on the other side of the fire. "That was their doing, those two British spies and their henchman. All I wanted to do was kill you, not destroy the trading post and the settlement." He stroked his chin. "Although now that I've thought about it, that's not a bad idea. A certain someone in St. Louis would be quite happy to see the Harts put out of business."

There it was again, a mention of some mysterious person in St. Louis who seemed to be pulling the strings on Fairfax's vengeance quest. Preacher wondered if the same fella had been responsible for Fairfax and his partner trying to stop Corliss and Jerome from ever establishing the trading post in the first place.

It sure seemed possible, Preacher decided. Fairfax was a vicious little worm, but he didn't strike Preacher as any sort of mastermind.

"You attack that settlement, you'll be sorry," Preacher said. "Those folks there are plenty tough. They've proved it more'n once."

"Yes, but they won't be expecting trouble. Sherwood's been there, too. In fact, the Harts are expecting him to return with a large group of trappers." Fairfax laughed. "As long as I'm not with them, my men will be welcomed with open arms. And then, once they're inside, they'll strike and take the stockade. They'll control the food, and they'll be able to starve out any of the settlers who are too stubborn to leave. Once they're finally all gone, we'll burn the trading post to the ground, and everything else in the settlement, too!"

Clyde Mallory had been watching Fairfax intently from the other side of the fire. Now he stood up, circled the blaze, and came toward him.

"Do you mean that about destroying the settlement, Mr. Fairfax?" the Englishman asked.

"You're damned right I do," Fairfax snapped. "I've got a score to settle with Corliss and Jerome Hart, too. Maybe not as big as the one I have against Preacher, but I want those bastards to pay for the part they played in killing my friend Schuyler and ruining all our plans."

"Very well then," Mallory said crisply. "You can forget about taking us to the wagon train. We'll return to the settlement with you. Its destruction was our goal all along."

"Will that king of yours be willing to pay for that, too?"

"I'll see to it that you're properly compensated," Mallory promised.

Fairfax nodded. "We've got a deal then." He jerked a thumb at Preacher. "But he dies first."

"Of course."

Fairfax leered at Preacher again. "All this talk got me distracted. I came over here to ask you if you know what's going to happen to you, mountain man."

"I got a pretty good idea what you *think* you're gonna do," Preacher said. "You plan on burnin' me at the stake."

"Not exactly, although it's true that I want to hear you beg for your life as your skin blackens and cracks and curls away from your body. I want to hear you scream as the flesh melts right off your bones."

"Don't hold your breath waitin'. That ain't gonna happen."

"Don't be so sure. They say that fire does terrible things to a man."

Preacher just looked up at him stonily. He wasn't going to give Fairfax the satisfaction of showing any reaction, now or later, no matter what happened.

Fairfax turned away and ordered, "More wood on the fire! Build it up!" He looked over his shoulder at Preacher. "I'm not going to burn you at the stake. When that fire's big enough I'm going to have my men throw you in it like a piece of garbage!"

Fairfax stalked away. Uncle Dan, tied hand and foot like the others, was sitting fairly close to Preacher. He leaned closer still and said, "That fella's plumb loco."

"Yeah," Preacher agreed. "Hate'll do that to a man."

Fairfax was so consumed with the hatred he felt for Preacher that he couldn't think about anything else. Wiping out the settlement was just one more element to his revenge. He never would have thought of it if he hadn't set out to hurt Preacher.

Full night had fallen by now. Utter darkness surrounded the area lit up by the fire. If not for the blaze, Preacher knew he would have been able to see millions of stars floating in the prairie sky.

Laura Mallory stood up. As she started around the fire, her brother caught hold of her wrist and asked, "Where are you going?"

"I want to talk to Preacher."

Mallory frowned. "I'm not sure that's a good idea."

"Really, Clyde, what can he do? He's tied up, he's badly hurt, it's probably all he can manage to stay conscious. I really don't think he's much of a threat anymore."

Mallory thought it over for a second, and then shrugged as he let go of his sister's wrist. "All right. Just be careful. Hurt or not, I still don't trust him."

Laura came over and knelt in front of Preacher. She gave Uncle Dan a meaningful look, and the old-timer began to scoot away, giving the two of them a little privacy. Of course, he couldn't go very far, but Preacher supposed it was the thought that counted.

"I'm sorry things have turned out this way," Laura began.

"Wasn't long ago you were holdin' a knife to my throat," Preacher reminded her.

She made a face. "Yes, I know. And I would have done what I threatened to do. That was in the heat of battle, and what we are—*who* we are—makes us enemies, Preacher." A little shudder ran through her. "But that doesn't mean I want to see that . . . that horrible little man take his revenge on you."

"He *is* a horrible little man," Preacher said. "I reckon we agree on that much anyway."

Laura lowered her voice a little more. "I'd like to think that . . . if things had been different . . . then you and I . . . well, what was between us might have been different, too."

Preacher smiled faintly. "Ain't it pretty to think so?"

"But that can never be." She moved closer, reached

down, and rested her hand on the ground beside his leg for a moment to maintain her balance. "You're like a knight from England's olden days," she said. "A true warrior. A man like you should die in battle. Not being burned alive to satisfy the sadistic whim of a madman."

"I couldn't agree with you more," Preacher said.

"Laura!" Mallory called from the other side of the fire. "For God's sake, don't get so close to him! I told you we can't trust him."

Laura sighed in exasperation and stood up, turning to glare at her brother. "For God's sake yourself, Clyde. Can't you see that Preacher's no threat to anyone so long as he's trussed up like that?" She shook her head and then added, "I'm sorry, Preacher. Good-bye."

"So long, ma'am," he told her.

She crossed her arms over her chest and stalked away. "I can't watch this," she said to no one in particular. Mallory got up and followed her to the edge of the circle of light cast by the fire.

Preacher was glad that she had come over to bid farewell to him. Like she said, if things had been different . . .

But they weren't and never would be. There could never be anything between them.

Except for the gratitude that Preacher felt toward her at this moment.

Gratitude for the knife she had slipped under his thigh when she put her hand on the ground, the knife that was now within reach of his bound right hand. He got his fingers on the hilt, worked the blade around so that it was behind his arm where no one could see it, and started sawing at the rope that was wrapped around him.

If he had just a few minutes, he thought, a few minutes to cut through those ropes so that when Fairfax's men came to get him and toss him in the fire, he would have a surprise waiting for them.

And maybe like one of those knights of old she had talked about, he would die with cold steel in his hand.

Chapter 30

Uncle Dan was an observant old rascal. From the corner of his mouth, he said, "The gal gave you a knife, didn't she? I can tell you're cuttin' that rope."

"I plan on givin' 'em a tussle before I cross the divide," Preacher said. "If I just got time to saw through here . . ."

"If you get loose, you reckon you could maybe flip that knife over here without anybody noticin'?" Uncle Dan licked his lips in anticipation at the prospect of putting up a fight, even though the odds made it clear that the prisoners didn't have any real chance.

Preacher tried not to grin at the old-timer. "I'll sure give it a try," he promised.

Meanwhile, he kept sawing at the rope, feeling the strands part one by one. He thought that if he gave a good heave on it, he might be able to break the rope already.

And it looked like things might come to that . . . like Uncle Dan wasn't going to have a chance to free himself after all . . . because Fairfax was coming toward them again, and from the look of gleeful, evil anticipation on the man's ugly face, the time had come.

Fairfax even rubbed his hands together and chuckled. "I think the fire is big enough and hot enough now," he said.

It was true. The flames leaped high in the air, and the heat coming off the blaze slapped across the faces of Preacher and the other prisoners.

"Once your friends have watched you die, Preacher, we'll dispose of them as well," Fairfax went on. "I'm not without mercy, though. They'll be shot, so they'll die quickly. Unlike you."

Preacher shifted his grip slightly on the knife's handle. With his left arm hurt the way it was, he didn't know if he could break the rope or not, even partially cut through the way it was, but he sure as hell intended to try.

If he could, then he was going to lunge to his feet and plunge that knife into Fairfax's chest before anybody could stop him. Likely enough, the others would shoot him down quick after that, but Preacher didn't much care.

He would die fast, and Fairfax would be cheated of his revenge. Those were the only things Preacher cared about at this moment.

But then Sherwood, Fairfax's second in command, stepped up behind the man and said, "Hold on just a minute."

Fairfax looked back over his shoulder with an annoyed frown. "What the hell do you want, Sherwood? It's time at last for Preacher to die."

"Yeah, that's true," Sherwood said, "but before he does, I reckon you ought to die first, Boss."

Even as Fairfax's eyes began to widen in surprise, Sherwood moved, the muscles in his shoulders bunching as he put all his strength into the blow that he struck. The long blade of the knife he held went all the way into Fairfax's back. It went all the way to the hilt, skewering Fairfax like a bug.

Fairfax's mouth fell open as his eyes bugged out in agony. No sound came from his throat except a whine. His knees buckled, and he would have fallen if Sherwood hadn't been still gripping the knife tightly, holding him up by it.

Finally, Fairfax was able to gasp, "Why . . . why?"

"You don't think Shad ever trusted a fool like you to get anything done, do you? He let you think you were in charge, but told me to get rid of you when I thought the time was right." Sherwood twisted the blade inside Fairfax's body. "Well, the time's right, you stupid bastard. We don't need you anymore. Matter of fact, I don't reckon we ever really did."

He tore the blood-dripping knife free from Fairfax's back. Fairfax stumbled forward a step and then fell to his knees. He caught himself there, swaying back and forth for a moment as his agonized eyes stared into Preacher's eyes.

"Say howdy to the Devil for me when you get to Hell," Preacher told him.

Fairfax's eyes rolled up in their sockets and he pitched forward onto his face. He didn't move again as the dark stain spread on the back of his coat.

"Sorry, Preacher," Sherwood said as he bent to wipe off the blade on Fairfax's sleeve. "I know you would've liked to kill him yourself, but I didn't see any way to work that without lettin' you loose." He laughed. "And I'm not that big of a fool. You'll still die, just not in the fire."

Clyde Mallory was on his feet. Beside him, Laura still sat on the ground, a horrified expression on her face as she looked at Fairfax's body.

"What do you think you're doing, Sherwood?" Mallory demanded. "I made an arrangement with Fairfax—"

"Now you've got the same deal with me," Sherwood said as he swung around to grin at the Englishman. "Only better, because Fairfax would've found some way to ruin everything. I don't reckon he ever carried out a plan in his life without messin' it up somehow."

That was probably true, Preacher thought as he shifted the knife again. He didn't care what sort of deal Sherwood and Mallory made. The important thing was that their conversation gave him a few more minutes to cut that rope . . .

Mallory strode around the fire to confront Sherwood. "I heard you mention someone named Shad," he snapped. "Were you talking about Shadrach Beaumont?"

"Shadrach?" Sherwood repeated. "Hell, I never knew what his real name is. I just knew him as Shad. But yeah, Beaumont's the one I'm talkin' about. It was at his house in St. Louis a couple o' months ago that I saw you, mister. I was discussin' some other business with him when you got there. Shad told me to step out of the room while he talked to you, but I heard the whole thing. I heard you and him settin' up the deal for those rifles."

Rifles! Preacher thought. What Sherwood had just said explained a lot. This fella Shad Beaumont was some sort of criminal who lived in St. Louis, and he had helped Mallory get his hands on those rifles for the Blackfeet. Ever since Preacher had found out what Mallory was up to, he had suspected that the Englishman had somebody else working with him.

Mallory's face was stony as he began, "I'm not going to confirm or deny anything—"

"You don't have to. I *saw* you, Mallory. I got a good look at you." Sherwood smiled at Laura. "And I saw that sister o' yours, too, waitin' in the buggy outside. I ain't likely to forget a lady as pretty as her."

"Leave my sister out of this," Mallory snapped.

"Why? She's workin' for that king o' yours, too, ain't she? You're both part of the deal you set up with Shad. I'm not sure why he's workin' with a couple of Englishers, but that's his business, not mine. All I want to know is if you'll pay me to see to it that the Harts' tradin' post and settlement is wiped out, just like you were gonna pay Fairfax."

Mallory glanced at Fairfax's corpse, frowned for a long moment, and then finally shrugged.

"Why not?" he said. "You're right. Fairfax was positively obsessed with Preacher. The man was insane. Utterly undependable."

Sherwood nodded. "Now you're catchin' on. You'll be a heap better off workin' with me." He turned toward Preacher and reached for the pistol stuck behind his belt.

"Hold on," Preacher said. He sensed that only a

couple of strands of rope held together now, so he stopped sawing. "I don't understand. Why did this fella Beaumont send Fairfax out here to kill me? I never even met Beaumont."

"What does it matter now?" Sherwood demanded. "You're about to die."

"Ain't that a good reason to tell me?"

Sherwood sighed. "Oh, all right." He took his hand away from his gun. "The way I understand it, Shad wanted to establish a trading post out here himself, so he sent Fairfax and a man named Mims to try to stop them from even getting where they were going. But that didn't work out and Mims died."

Preacher nodded and said, "I knew about that. I figured Fairfax was dead, too."

"No, he made it back to St. Louis somehow on his own." Sherwood grunted and shook his head. "I'm surprised he made it. By all rights, he should have been killed in the first mile or two."

Preacher couldn't dispute that. Fairfax had had a mighty powerful hate to draw strength from as he kept going.

"So it was too late for Shad to stop the Harts from startin' their tradin' post, but he could still take over the fur trade out here by gettin' rid of them. Shad knew you'd be a thorn in his side, Preacher, so he sent us to help Fairfax kill you, which is what Fairfax wanted in the first place. At the same time Shad made the deal with Mr. Mallory here to wipe out the settlement. I guess he figured that once it was gone, he could send his own men in to run the fur operation."

"That fur business is going to be British," Mallory put in.

Sherwood's heavy shoulders rose and fell in a shrug as he turned toward the Englishman. "I reckon that would've had to be hashed out later . . . but I wouldn't be so sure about that, mister."

Laura spoke up, saying sharply, "What you mean is that your Mr. Beaumont would have betrayed us."

Sherwood shrugged again. "You said that, lady, not me. I don't know what would have happened. But I do know Shad Beaumont is a man who gets what he wants."

"So why should we trust you now?" Mallory demanded.

"What other choice do you have? You can go off on your own and try to find those wagons of yours before the Cheyenne find you, I reckon." Sherwood grinned. "You might wish you hadn't, though. The Cheyenne may not hate white men as much as the Blackfeet do, but they'll still—"

A choked cry cut off whatever else he was about to say. He staggered backward, pawing at the shaft of the arrow that had come out of the darkness surrounding the fire and lodged in his throat.

Preacher had taken advantage of the tense confrontation between Sherwood and Mallory to flip the knife behind Uncle Dan, using only his fingers to do so. Watching from the corner of his eye, he had seen the old-timer stretch his bound arms, and hoped that Uncle Dan had been able to get his hands on the knife.

As soon as he saw the arrow strike Sherwood, Preacher flexed his right arm and shoulder and pulled on the rope as hard as he could. He felt it snap, and as it fell away, suddenly he was free.

He rolled over to get some momentum going, put his right hand on the ground, and powered up onto his feet. He heard Flagg yell, "Look out! Preacher's loose!"

The hired killers who had been with Fairfax and Sherwood had other things to worry about besides Preacher, though. More arrows came whistling in from the darkness. Several men cried out, staggered, and then fell as the feathered shafts buried themselves in their bodies.

Men jerked up rifles and pistols and began shooting, but they were firing blind. The glare from the huge fire had ruined any night vision they might have had. Preacher had kept his eyes slitted as much as possible, so he could still see some. He hoped that Uncle Dan, Sanderson, and the other three men from the settlement had done likewise.

"Cut the others loose and get out of here!" Preacher called to Uncle Dan as he lunged around the blaze toward the suddenly terrified Laura Mallory.

She lurched to her feet as she saw him coming. Her hand plucked a small pistol from somewhere in the folds of her skirt. Clearly uncertain what to do, she didn't raise the gun.

Preacher grabbed her arm and told her, "Come on! We got to get out of the light!"

Escaping into the darkness was their only hope. He didn't know how many Cheyenne warriors were out there. Could be only half a dozen or so, or there might be a large war party. But he knew they were Cheyenne because he'd recognized the markings and the fletching on the arrow that killed Sherwood.

The other thing he knew for sure was that the fire

had drawn them. Just one more instance of Fairfax letting his hatred blind him to the fact that he was a damned fool.

The blaze must have been visible for miles and miles across the prairie, and of course some curious Cheyenne had come to investigate it. Preacher had thought all along that something like that might happen.

The Indians had slipped up close to the camp, seen white men walking around making perfect targets of themselves in the firelight, and naturally they hadn't been able to resist the temptation.

Their timing had been good, too. That arrow couldn't have picked a more fitting moment to strike Sherwood in the throat.

Preacher tugged Laura along with him as they ran crouching toward the shadows at the edge of the light. More arrows whipped through the air around them. Laura stumbled, and for a second Preacher thought she'd been hit, but as he slowed, she cried, "I'm fine! Keep going!"

Preacher long-legged it into the darkness. He didn't know where Clyde Mallory and Flagg were, and he didn't particularly care what happened to them.

He wanted to see about Uncle Dan and the others, though, so when he reached some good-sized rocks, he drew Laura behind one of them and told her, "Stay here."

She clutched at his arm. "Preacher, you . . . you can't leave me here!" Fear had made her breathless.

"I'll be right back," he promised. "Keep down. The Cheyenne won't find you."

He wished he could be sure of that, but he didn't intend to be gone for long. As much as he wanted to keep Laura safe, he couldn't turn his back on his friends.

As he ran back toward the fire, he saw that the combat had become hand-to-hand. Uncle Dan had succeeded in freeing himself and his nephew, and he and Pete Sanderson were struggling against the Indians along with the members of Fairfax's party who were still alive.

Preacher reached down and snatched a rifle from the ground as he ran into the camp. The hammer was down on the lock, and he assumed it had already been fired. Even if it hadn't, he couldn't cock it with one hand, so he swung it like a club and crashed the barrel against the head of a Cheyenne warrior. The Indian's skull shattered under the impact.

Preacher slashed sideways with the rifle and smashed it across the face of another warrior. The Cheyenne went down with blood spouting from his broken nose. Preacher tossed the rifle up, grabbed the barrel, and brought the stock down in the Indian's face, finishing him off.

He dropped the rifle and grabbed a knife that was sheathed at the Cheyenne's waist. He had just spotted a warrior about to send an arrow into the body of the helpless Dennison, who was still tied near the fire.

Preacher flung the knife with all his strength. The blade buried itself hilt-deep in the Indian's back. The Cheyenne pitched forward, releasing the drawn-back arrow anyway, but it went harmlessly into the ground.

Preacher raced over, yanked the knife out of the

Cheyenne's back, and knelt beside Dennison. It took a minute to cut through the tough ropes, but then Dennison was free and Preacher pressed the knife into his hands.

"Cut the others loose!" he told the man. Then he turned back to the fight.

Bodies lay scattered around the fire, white men with arrows sticking out of their bodies or heads cleft by tomahawks, red men with holes blown in them by rifles and pistols. Only three of the Cheyenne were still on their feet, struggling with Uncle Dan, Sanderson, and one of Fairfax's men.

Preacher didn't see Mallory, Flagg, or Flagg's squaw.

The last remaining member of Fairfax's party went down with a Cheyenne knife in his chest. As the warrior who had struck him down howled in triumph, Dennison lunged past Preacher swinging a burning brand from the fire. He smashed the flaming club across the Indian's back and knocked him to his knees. The thick piece of wood rose and fell repeatedly as Dennison smashed the Cheyenne's skull.

Preacher went to the aid of Uncle Dan, who'd been retreating before a fierce rush from one of the warriors. Preacher crashed into the Cheyenne's back. Both men sprawled to the ground. Preacher got his good hand on the back of the man's head and drove it down into the dirt.

The Cheyenne twisted and knocked Preacher off him. As Preacher fell to the side, Uncle Dan swooped in with a knife and drove it into the Indian's back. The Cheyenne thrashed for a second and then lay still.

That left Pete Sanderson. The burly mountain man

had his hands wrapped around the throat of the final Cheyenne warrior. "Stay back!" he growled at his friends as they rushed forward to help him. "I got this red-skinned son of a bitch right where I want him!"

The next second, though, the Indian brought a knife up from somewhere and drove the blade into Sanderson's belly. Sanderson screamed and heaved as the Cheyenne ripped the knife sideways, disemboweling him. At the same time, a sharp crack sounded, and Preacher knew it was the Indian's neck breaking. Both men collapsed in death.

"Oh, Lord, Pete!" Uncle Dan cried as he rushed to his nephew's side. Preacher looked on grimly as the old-timer cradled Sanderson's head on his lap and cried like a baby.

He left the old man to his grief and picked up a pistol as he turned away. A quick check told him it was still loaded. Dennison and the other two men from the settlement were the only ones left alive here other than the grief-stricken Uncle Dan. Preacher told him, "Gather up all the rifles you can and get 'em reloaded, just in case there're any more Indians out there."

Dennison nodded. Preacher thought it likely that the war party had numbered only a dozen or so, and all of them were dead. But he didn't want to bet anybody's life on that assumption.

He loped off toward the rocks where he had left Laura. He had already been gone longer than he'd intended.

Laura wasn't alone, though. Her brother and Flagg had found her. They stood over her as she sat with her back against one of the rocks, and as they heard Preacher come up, they turned to face him.

Each man held a rifle . . . and they brought the muzzles to bear on Preacher.

"I daresay you're the luckiest man alive, Preacher," Clyde Mallory said. "But it appears that your luck has finally run out."

Chapter 31

"Clyde, no!" Laura gasped. "There's no reason—"

"There's every reason in the world," Mallory said. "Do you think Preacher will let us go, knowing what he knows about us?"

"Not much chance o' that," Preacher said. "Lots o' good folks died back yonder at the settlement because o' you, Mallory. There's got to be justice for that."

"Justice? Justice?" Mallory laughed harshly. "You call it justice that you upstart Americans—you filthy *rabble!*—thumb your noses at the greatest empire in the history of the world? You call it justice when a good man . . . our father . . . dies trying to teach you a lesson?"

"I ain't here to argue about what happened all those years ago," Preacher said. "I'm just sayin' you got to answer for the harm you done."

"Go ahead and shoot him," Flagg urged. "Willow will be back with the horses any minute now. Don't give him a chance to call his friends."

"I think you're right," Mallory said. "We can't afford to waste any more time."

The rifle in his hands snapped up.

Laura lurched up off the ground and cried, "No!" as she grabbed the rifle barrel. The weapon exploded, but Laura had already forced the barrel down so that the ball went into the ground at her brother's feet.

Preacher was moving at the same time, darting to his right and raising the pistol. Flagg swung his rifle toward the mountain man and jerked the trigger. The rifle and Preacher's pistol roared at the same time.

The lack of a jarring impact told Preacher that Flagg's shot had missed. Flagg had stumbled back against the rock behind him, though, and the rifle slipped from his fingers as he tried to stay upright. He pressed a hand to his chest as he leaned to the side. Dark worms of blood crawled through his fingers.

He toppled onto his side and didn't move again.

With an incoherent cry of rage, Mallory knocked Laura aside and lunged at Preacher, swinging the now-empty rifle like a club. Preacher ducked under the sweeping blow and tackled Mallory. They went down as Preacher heard shouts from the other men, who must have been startled by the shots.

Mallory fought like a madman, slashing punches at Preacher as they rolled over and over. With only one good arm, Preacher couldn't fend them all off. The Englishman's fists crashed against his head, stunning him. That gave Mallory the chance to lock his hands around Preacher's throat.

Preacher grabbed Mallory by the hair and butted him in the face. That knocked Mallory's grip loose. Preacher slammed a knee into his belly and followed it with a jabbing punch to the face. Mallory's insane rage allowed him to ignore the pain of both blows and grab hold of Preacher's broken arm. Preacher howled in pain as Mallory twisted the busted wing.

They were in a fight to the finish. Preacher had no doubt of that. He didn't particularly want to kill Clyde Mallory, but the Englishman wouldn't stop as long as there was breath left in his body.

And the shape Preacher was in, he wasn't sure if he could stop Mallory either. Mallory bulled into him again, knocked him on his back. Panting, Mallory grabbed a rock as big as a man's hands clasped together and raised it into the air above his head. His eyes locked with Preacher's for an instant in the dim light.

That night in the trading post, they had fought side by side, shoulder to shoulder, back to back. Comrades in battle. Brothers in arms.

But that had all been a lie, Preacher knew now. Clyde Mallory was a murderous beast, and in another second that rock would come down and smash Preacher's brains out . . .

The crack of a pistol made Mallory jerk. His eyes opened wide. The rock slipped from his fingers and thudded to the ground next to Preacher's head. Mallory opened his mouth, but nothing came out except a tendril of blood.

Then he fell forward, collapsing on top of Preacher. Preacher rolled him aside, and knew from the dead weight of him that Mallory had been shot. He saw the bloodstain on the back of the Englishman's shirt.

Wearily, Preacher pushed himself up and looked

around, expecting to see Uncle Dan, Dennison, or one of the other men from the settlement.

Instead he saw Laura Mallory standing there with the still-smoking pistol in her hand and an agonized expression on her face.

"I couldn't," she said, "I couldn't let him . . ."

Her knees buckled, and as she fell Preacher saw the huge dark stain on her back, too. He scrambled to his feet and sprang to her side, not even feeling the pain from his broken arm or his other injuries anymore.

"Laura," he said as he dropped to his knees and pulled her into his lap. "What—"

Then his hand moved to her back and found the broken shaft of the arrow. She *had* been hit as they were fleeing after all. But she had told Preacher that she was all right, that he should keep going. And she hadn't said anything about it when he left her . . .

She opened her eyes and breathed, "There's been . . . enough killing . . . enough dying . . . Preacher . . ."

His name came from her lips in a long, quiet sigh, and then her head fell loosely against his shoulder. Preacher squeezed his eyes shut as he held her.

The men from the settlement found them there like that a few moments later. They didn't say anything, just stood there with rifles ready in their hands in case more hell broke loose.

But for once it didn't, and the night grew quiet save for the rasp of Preacher's breathing as he sat there on the ground holding the body of Laura Mallory.

* * *

"We're two of a kind, ain't we, old fella?" Preacher said to Dog. "Beat all the way to hell an' back, but still alive and kickin' somehow."

The big cur just licked his hand. Mallory hadn't killed Dog, just knocked him senseless for a while. Dog had recovered and come into camp while Uncle Dan was resetting and resplinting Preacher's broken arm.

"Try not to get it busted again 'fore it heals up this time," the old-timer had said.

"I'll try," Preacher had promised. "And Dan . . . I'm sorry about Pete."

"He was a good boy," Uncle Dan had said with a sigh. "A mite ornery at times . . . but hell, ain't we all?" A grimace twisted his bearded face. "I ain't lookin' forward to tellin' his ma."

It had taken all night to patch up everybody's wounds and tend to the burying. They didn't see Flagg's squaw until dawn, when she came riding in from wherever she'd been. Preacher went to meet her and pointed out the mound of freshly turned earth where Flagg's body lay.

She rode over to it, dismounted, looked at it for a moment . . .

Then spat on it, got back on the pony, and rode away. Nobody tried to stop her.

Now Preacher checked the cinches on Horse's saddle, since he hadn't fastened them himself. Dennison had done that. Preacher nodded in satisfaction and told the man, "Much obliged."

"You're welcome. You sure you ain't comin' back to the settlement with us?"

Preacher shook his head. "Nope, I'm headin' east. Got somethin' to do. You fellas tell Corliss and

Jerome and the rest of 'em what happened. Tell 'em I'll be back through those parts one o' these days, the Good Lord willin'."

"All right," Dennison said with a nod. "If you're sure."

"Never been more sure o' anything in my life." Preacher grasped the saddle, got a foot in the stirrup, and swung up awkwardly one-handed. He settled himself in the saddle and took hold of the reins.

"Hold on!" Uncle Dan called out as he rode up. "I'm goin' with you."

Preacher frowned. "I didn't ask for no comp'ny—"

"Hell, I know you didn't, but you can't even saddle a horse by yourself with that busted wing. Somebody's got to look after you till it heals up. I done elected myself to the job." He paused. "Anyway, I got to go back home and tell the folks there about what happened to Pete."

Preacher thought about arguing, but then he sighed and smiled faintly. "I reckon me and Dog and Horse can use the comp'ny after all."

The two men rode away a few minutes later, not looking back. Preacher had already said his farewells to Laura Mallory, and the same was true of Uncle Dan and Pete Sanderson. They headed east across the trackless prairie. There were no trails and damned few landmarks, but that didn't really matter.

They were frontiersmen. They knew where they were going.

"St. Louis, eh?" Uncle Dan said after a while.

"How do you figure?"

"That's where we'll find that varmint Beaumont,

ain't it? None o' this mess would'a happened if he hadn't made a devil's bargain with them Englishers."

"Yeah, that's right," Preacher agreed. "I thought it might be a good idea to look him up and have a word or two with him."

Uncle Dan grunted. "Yeah. A word or two. I figured to say a few things to the gent myself, since I got a score o' my own to settle."

Preacher nodded. He couldn't deny Uncle Dan the chance for vengeance, any more than he could deny it to himself.

With almost her last breath, Laura Mallory had said there had been enough killing.

But that wasn't true, Preacher thought as he and Uncle Dan urged their horses into a gallop toward civilization and Dog bounded along behind.

There *hadn't* been enough killing. Not yet.

Not as long as Shad Beaumont was alive.